THE RETURN OF GEORGE WASHINGTON

THE RETURN OF GEORGE WASHINGTON

GEORGE F. WORTS

ILLUSTRATED BY
ROGER B. MORRISON

COVER BY
EDGAR FRANKLIN WITTMACK

POPULAR PUBLICATIONS · 2022

TABLE OF CONTENTS

THE RETURN OF GEORGE WASHINGTON

THE WOMAN OF THE STORM 3

THE QUICK AND THE DEAD 9

GRAVE FOOD 21

THROUGH THE NIGHT TO DAWN 31

THE DORMANT CRUSADER 42

"SCIENTISTS ARE QUEER" 56

RENASCENCE! 67

"SO MUCH DYNAMITE". 76

MOB PSYCHOLOGY 82

THE ETERNAL GALAHAD 91

FLAT! 98

THIS PERILOUS ATMOSPHERE 105

LIFE RESTORING, A CORPORATION 113

FROM THE FRYING PAN INTO THE FIRE 127

BITTER FRUITS OF TRIUMPH 142

THE BUSIEST MAN IN NEW YORK 151

FAME HAS ITS PRICE 167

WHEN THE WORLD GOES MAD 180

DISTURBED IN HIS LAST SLEEP 193

"BRADDOCK! WHERE ARE YOU?" 204

THE FIRST AMERICAN 217

THERE IS NO DEATH! 224

A TALK TO MILLIONS 232

THE OLD STORY 244

A HUMAN BEING 254

THE INTERESTS OF MR. WASHINGTON 269

WHEN WOMEN FIGURE IN 280

CITY OF HEROES 287

THE GILT ON THE IDOL 298

COULD THERE BE A LINK MISSING? 308

WASHINGTON'S CONGRESSIONAL ADDRESS 320

A HOUSE OF CARDS 325

HIMSELF, TO THE END 337

"YOU'RE A FAKE, TOO" 339

EPILOGUE 341

THE RETURN OF GEORGE WASHINGTON

"If George Washington could only see America as it is to-day!"—Plaint often voiced by our elder statesmen, leading editors, and average citizens.

1

THE WOMAN OF THE STORM

RAIN DRIVEN BY a mad northeast wind lashed the walls of the cabin, crackled on the window panes, drummed on the roof. The wind whistled through cracks, howled in the pines, roared in the open. Beyond the cabin, Black Bay hissed under the downpour. Angry lightnings flashed. Thunder added its deep grumbling to the crackling, the drumming, the howling, the whistling.

The man seated by the fire, pipe in teeth, was absolutely contented. A snug cabin shielded him from the buffets of the storm. Let the wind shout! Let the rain roar!

Lawrence Galloway stretched out his hands to the twisting red flames and placidly puffed at his pipe. He took a boyish delight in the raw, wet, wild night on that side of the walls; the warmth, comfort, snugness on this.

Now and again he glanced at the thick green book open on his knees and, now and again, stroked his beard, four days' growth of it, a tough, reddish-brown stubble.

Lawrence Galloway would have been contented if the gale hung on for a week. It wouldn't, of course. It would blow itself out by morning or noon at the latest. But it gave him a feeling of primitive pleasure to know that his larder was full, that the shelves in the little kitchen were sagging with provisions; with flour, with canned stuff, with bacon and ham and vegetables and eggs. And that the built-in shelves by the fireplace were loaded with enough books for a month of delightful evenings.

Nothing light or frivolous about those books. History, biography, philosophy, the sciences. For one month in every year he was a studious young man, a Thoreau and a Voltaire; a philosopher wresting the truth from Nature, a questioner asking riddles of Life.

The rest of the year he was the earnest managing editor of *The Daily It,* which was a tabloid newspaper.

In this month he indulged in a veritable orgy of contrasts: the simplicity of log cabin existence against the complexity of his office routine; deep, rich minds embalmed in books against the irritating contact with shallow people, with blundering reporters, with self-seeking actresses, with greedy politicians, with sports, crooks, cranks, liars; the lonely majesty of the pines, of Black Bay, of the primitive wilderness against the round of compulsory social activities.

Here, he would be granted a clear mind with which to think certain problems out. Should he fire Morrisy? Should he promote Doyle to the city desk? Should he yield to Benjamin Sturm, his owner, on that Sunday supplement matter?

A month of luxurious simplicity, of echoing solitude, in which to think; a month of not shaving unless he felt like shaving; a month of woollen shirts, of corduroy breeches, and moccasins, of rod, gun, and compass!

A gust of wind crashed against the cabin.

Larry Galloway placidly puffed his pipe. There was peace in the very bellowing of the wind, the savage clatter of the

rain. Back home, the presses were just warming up, running off the early mail edition.

Let 'em run! Thank the Lord he wasn't there! Thank the Lord for a month of freedom! A lazy month of reading and fishing and roaming through the woods and just stewing. Black Bay was boiling with fish. A girlless month! Long ambles through the woods with pine needles underfoot and breath of pine in his nostrils.

His smile saddened. The picture would be complete if Paddy were only here. Dear old Paddy! Paddy, his Airedale, had died at the ripe old age of eleven. Two years ago he had dug a grave for Paddy at the edge of the woods behind the cabin.

To Paddy the doubtful compliment could be paid that he had been almost human. He had had some amusing habits. He had had a trick of muttering to himself, of pacing to and fro in this room, with a wrinkling nose, muttering just as do some men who are trying to think out a tough problem. And he had "talked back" to Larry.

Larry would talk to him, making comments on this and that as he walked through the woods or prepared a meal, and Paddy at his side would watch him with sharp golden eyes, sometimes concerned, sometimes amused, but always alert and affectionate—and make sympathetic mutterings or utter low barks or whines in answer.

Paddy would seem to frown, to ponder what his master was saying. More than once, Galloway had burst out laughing when Paddy had whined, with an air of wonderment, as if he were exclaiming, "Is that so? Well, well! I would not have believed it if you had not told me so!"

The Airedale's going had left an emptiness in Larry's life, had taught him never again to "give his heart to a dog to tear."

The storm sounds were rising again. They would seem to rise and rise to a howling crescendo and then fall away again.

A black mass of wind hurled its weight against the north wall. A puff of smoke floated from the fireplace into the room and drifted off into the rafters. Rain came down with a crash. The back door rattled as if some one were shaking it.

Larry Galloway found himself growing tense. His nerves, he decided, were in pretty bad shape. He had been overworking; he was jumpy.

Rain spat against the north windows with the force of small shot. Beyond them existed black nothingness. Queer shadows danced on the panes and mingled with the rivulets flowing down. With the creakings and groanings about the cabin you expected, almost, to see some ghostly countenance pressed against a window.

The persistence of the storm noises created a fantastic state of mind, as if you were being prepared for a crisis unreal and startling. Once, many years ago, the young man reflected, Indians crept to isolated cabins and scalped their occupants.

The drumming of rain on roof became a sullen roar.

Crash! That was lightning, not far away. Perhaps a tree had gone down. The windows simultaneously blazed with a pale-green. A queer smell, identified with electrical discharges, came drifting in.

Yes—the night was growing a little spooky.

Larry Galloway threw another log on the fire and wondered at a whine that rose above the wind. It was like the wind, but different from the wind. An uneasy whine.

Now the wind was moaning in the chimney.

Then the door resounded, sharply, to three quick knocks.

Larry sat up, startled, almost alarmed. The book on his knees slid to the floor with a thump. It had come so neatly timed, that knocking. The devil himself might have been at the door.

He found that his throat was thick, in need of clearing; that his heart was beating rapidly.

A loaded Winchester rifle stood in a rack beside the bookshelves. His hand reached out for it as he sprang up, then fell at his side. Indians! He'd been day dreaming of Indians who slid through the grass on their bellies and slaughtered lonely people and sliced and tore strips of hair from their heads!

His reason argued: Some wayfarer—a fisherman washed ashore from a wreck outside—some one lost—a camper or hunter—some poor devil caught out in this storm.

Yet his imagination clung to an Indian with a tomahawk in one hand and a scalp knife in the other.

He lifted the doorlatch. Pressure of wind flung it aside

and carried a shower of raindrops into his face. Spinning leaves and a flying branch followed. Last of all came a slender girl in a shiny blue raincoat, who was fairly catapulted into the middle of the room. She wore rubber boots and a boy's rubber hat. Her brown eyes sparkled with excitement.

She was an attractive girl: young and radiantly good looking. Her smile was art exclamation of apology for her intrusion.

Larry Galloway, prepared for Indians, fisherman, campers, hunters, the devil himself, was not only disappointed but indignant. A beautiful missing girl on his hands on a night like this!

"I beg your pardon," she said, breathlessly. "But aren't you Lawrence Galloway?" And flames danced in her eyes.

"I am," he sternly acknowledged. "Are you lost?"

"I? Lost?" she cried. "I've driven ninety miles through this storm to find you!"

He turned as she hastened to the door. Then was explained the queer whining he had heard. Twenty feet away, through the slanting rain, the lights of an automobile whitely glittered and shone.

"Come on in!" she yelled. "This is it! I've found him!"

2

THE QUICK AND THE DEAD

THERE WAS NO answer from the car. Larry, staring, saw the silhouette of some one descending from what appeared to be a coupé. This one was trying to raise an umbrella. He came running—a tall, alarming man who strode in behind a ballooning umbrella.

The force of the wind in the umbrella dragged him into the center of the room. He wrestled with it savagely, as if it were some beast to be conquered. The girl in the blue raincoat gave frivolous advice:

"Hit it on the head with a club, Jason. The bite of one of those things is deadly."

The man at length found the catch to press, which permitted the ribs to be folded down. He went about all this grimly; you at once knew that here was a man who did not take life lightly.

Larry was conscious of harsh energy. The man's eyes were alarming: dark almost to blackness and possessed of a strange burning quality, perhaps because they were set in cavernous sockets. He was tall, almost cadaverous; his mouth was like a slash across his long, pale face. His chin was powerful and cobalt with unborn beard. He must have been about thirty-eight or forty.

Larry remembered having seen this man before—but he met so many people. The unknown wore a small black felt hat and a black raincoat. He stood the conquered umbrella in the corner near the door with a gesture of triumph and his voice seemed to crackle:

"You're Lawrence Galloway, are you?"

"I am."

"Well—I'm Jason Ortola."

His manner was that of a man making an important announcement.

"Are you?" said Larry. The name was familiar but the associations with it were vague. Presumably, Jason Ortola was some one of consequence—probably he called half the head waiters in New York by their first name. Presumably, he was running away with this pretty, impudent girl. Larry was accustomed to thinking in headlines.

"I hope we're not interrupting your work."

"I'm not working," Larry said, none too graciously. "You'd better take those wet things off and pull up chairs by the fire."

The girl promptly stripped off her raincoat and tossed it on a chair with her hat. She then ran long white fingers up into her hair, which was of the darkest known shade of red, and fluffed it out.

"My name is Polly Morgan," she said demurely. "I knew you wouldn't be glad to see us. You're up here taking a month's vacation, far from the madding crowd, and you want to forget the world and be by the world forgot, or however it goes. We're sorry, but it's terribly important."

With her sparkling eyes, her flushed cheeks, her air of

wanting not to be disliked, she was appealing; but Larry did not smile.

He waited. Jason Ortola unbuttoned his raincoat and plunged his hand inside. It returned with a beautifully mated pair of smooth, blond cigars. The tabloid editor accepted one, but did not light it. Mr. Ortola chewed the end off the other, lighted it above a kerosene lamp and puffed voluptuously while he gazed about the cabin, at the fire, the shelves of books, the built-in bunk. He now fixed his dark, burning eyes on his host.

Something like a smile curved his razor-thin lips. He was, Larry sensed, going to try to be charming.

"You seem to be pretty well fixed here."

"I think it's adorable," said the girl. "Where do you keep your cigarettes?"

"In that green jar." He resented her and he resented Jason Ortola, but the amenities called for a little civility. She was already reaching for the lid of the jar, when he attempted to anticipate her. Their hands met awkwardly. Their shoulders bumped. Rather, her shoulder collided with his arm above the elbow, because she was perhaps six inches shorter than he.

Miss Morgan looked up at him through a thick lace-work of lashes. He backed away instantly, angry because he disliked girls who acted this way. Flirting at the sound of the gun! He'd come hundreds of miles to his cabin in the wilderness largely to escape the girls who looked up at him that way—all trying to exploit him for one reason or another.

"You can give me a light," she said.

Larry, with an utterly blank expression, struck a match

and held it steadily to the end of the cigarette protruding from her red lips. She didn't look at the flame, but into his eyes. He turned away from her, when her cigarette glowed, with actual distaste.

What did they want, and how in the devil was he going to get rid of them? But he saw, from the corner of his eyes, white smoke spilling in little streams from her nostrils.

"Thanks," she said huskily.

She was conscious of herself, and he was extraordinarily conscious of her. Some girls affected you that way. She was, so far as he knew, the only woman who had ever been in this cabin. Thank God, it looked like a pigsty!

He found himself frowning into the bleak, hard, dark face of Jason Ortola.

"Mr. Galloway, we are very sorry to intrude, but I'm sure that after we've told you why we came you'll agree that it is quite as excusable as our making this difficult and dangerous drive to see you. The reason we are here to-night, Mr. Galloway, is because we bring you"—his voice sank and he paused, as if for dramatic emphasis—"the greatest news story in the history of the world."

Larry smiled faintly and glanced at the girl. She was holding the cigarette to her mouth and staring at him broodingly. How many times had he heard that before? His curiosity over Jason Ortola had already faded. Undoubtedly, Jason Ortola was a man of some consequence. He had that manner.

But he had as well the air of a crank; in the course of his day's work Larry encountered his kind frequently. That type seemed perpetually to be rushing about the world with ideas for the annoyance of hardworking managing editors.

Sometimes they were accompanied by charming girls and sometimes they were not. His chief objection to them was that their importance made it impossible for you to have them thrown out of your office as you did with the unimportant cranks.

He said dryly:

"Mr. Ortola, before you tell me about it, let me warn you that if Calvin Coolidge and the Prince of Wales were to engage in a fist fight; if John D. Rockefeller were to elope with Peggy Hopkins Joyce; if Henry Ford were to found a synagogue and then bequeath his plant and good-will to Wall Street, and then commit suicide by letting a flivver run over him; if Lindbergh were to fly around the world from New York to New York on a non-stop flight; if England, France, Italy, and Russia were to declare war on the United States—and if all of these things had happened simultaneously this afternoon—I would still stay where I am until this month is over."

"You haven't heard our story yet," said Miss Morgan. "When a fisherman bites a shark, *that's* news."

But there was no reflected humor in Jason Ortola's smoldering black eyes. A flush crept into his cheeks. He darted a reproving glance at the girl. Jason Ortola was preparing to be indignant.

"I did not come here to-night. Mr. Galloway," he said, in his discordant voice, "for the purpose of exchanging pleasantries with you. We have driven ninety miles through this storm because, as I have said, we have the biggest piece of news that the world has ever known. Perhaps you don't know who I am."

Larry did not smile at that. He leaned against the wall and waited. He had learned not to smile when these fierce gentlemen made that inevitable statement of hurt pride: "Perhaps you don't know who I am."

"Mr. Ortola is the president and the chairman of the board of directors," put in the girl in her sweet, husky voice, "of the Ortola Chemical Industries."

"I see." He knew of the Ortola Chemical Industries— knew them to constitute dozens of factories for the production of drugs and chemicals consumed medically and industrially the world over. Another man might have been impressed, humbled.

But Lawrence Galloway was not impressed. Millionaires, movie queens, and sports all had the same motive where he was concerned—to exploit him and *The Daily It.*

"I've heard of you," he said.

Mr. Ortola glared at him. He seemed undecided whether to be perplexed or angry.

"The news I've gone to the bother to bring to you to-night is more important, more sweeping than any of the hypothetical cases you mentioned, Mr. Galloway."

He was obviously trying to arouse Larry's curiosity. But Larry's curiosity had long ago been subjected to a case-hardening treatment; his attitude remained that of a man who has been everywhere, seen everything, and met everybody.

"If you have a big piece of news," he answered, "you should put it on the wire or telephone it to some newspaper—any newspaper. Eleven months in the year I am a hard-working editor. The twelfth month I haven't the slightest interest in newspapers or news."

The girl came over and stood beside him, to look up wonderingly into his composed face.

"Aren't you the least little bit curious?"

"I'm sorry," he said, "but a piece of news to me is just about as thrilling as—well, let's say, a pound of salt would be to Mr. Ortola. News—news—news—news! I'm fed up with news. I'm sorry, but I am, Miss Morgan. Holdups, robberies, murders, murder trials, divorces, elopements—"

"Pathetic," she murmured. "Especially the elopements. As if anybody cared!"

Mr. Ortola, it appeared, was the possessor of a one-track mind.

"Mr. Galloway, when a woman brings a child into the world, it is seldom news, is it?"

"If we are having an amiable philosophical argument," answered Larry, "I'll be glad to discuss that point. When a woman brings a child into the world, it is seldom news, unless the child chances to be a prince or the richest baby in the world."

"Or one of quadruplets," added Miss Morgan.

Jason Ortola darted a disapproving glance at her and went on.

"If I were to tell you that a certain famous scientist has worked out in his laboratory a method of restoring the dead to life—would that be news?"

Lawrence Galloway sighed. It was much worse than he had been expecting. Jason Ortola was a nut—nothing but a nut. This girl and he were a pair of nuts.

"It would be news for certain papers," he agreed. "I take

some pride in being able to say that *The Daily It* is not that kind of a paper. There are newspapers which would fall with glee upon that statement, coming as it does from your lips, Mr. Ortola. I have had a long, hard fight keeping *The Daily It* honest. I have tried, against the greatest opposition within and without, to deal only in facts."

Jason Ortola's long, dark countenance was now evenly crimson. Even his nose and the tips of his faunlike ears were crimson.

"I am a chemist, Mr. Galloway. I likewise deal only in facts—facts which must be proved again and again and again under the strictest conditions. I leave *nothing* to chance. When I make a laboratory experiment, I check it forward and back and forward again. I would not be here to-night if I were not confident that it is facts and nothing but facts that I am discussing. Let me ask you if you have, by chance, ever heard of Professor J. Hendricks Morgan?"

His intention was broadly sarcastic. Who had not heard of J. Hendricks Morgan? It was like asking an intelligent man if he had ever heard of Thomas Edison or Charles Proteus Steinmetz or Senator Marconi.

Lawrence Galloway gravely nodded. "I have, indeed." He glanced sharply at the girl. "Are you Professor Morgan's daughter?"

"I am," she said soberly.

"You will agree with me," Mr. Ortola went on, "that Professor Morgan is one of the world's leading scientists?"

"I will, of course."

A malicious smile played about the chemist's thin lips.

"Then I will say what I would have said earlier if it had not been for your cynical attitude. We have come here with an invitation from Professor Morgan for you to visit his summer laboratory on Lake Grallon. To-night."

"To get the story that he has discovered a method of restoring dead matter to life?"

"He discovered it, if you wish to put it that way, about five years ago. Recently he has perfected the technic. No, Mr. Galloway, if I had simply wished to spread this news about the world, I could have telephoned to some news agency. What Professor Morgan and I most want is to enlist your expert knowledge. It is not a simple problem."

Larry glanced speculatively at Miss Morgan. She gave an impatient shrug.

"I'm nothing but the chauffeur."

Larry said carefully:

"Mr. Ortola, the world is full of newspaper men as good or better than I am. I don't see why you went out of your way so far to pick me. If what you really want is a press agent, go down to Park Row any morning and let your wants be known, and a dozen good—"

"I'll explain myself further," Mr. Ortola took him up. "Professor Morgan and I selected you by a process of careful elimination. Don't think for a moment that we selected you at random. We have had you very thoroughly investigated.

"We know that you will be satisfied with nothing short of the truth. In placing the information that we have to place before the world, we want nothing garbled; we want no one to gain false impressions. We believe that you, more than any newspaper man available, can insure us against that.

"I said I believed that we have the greatest news story

the world has ever known. We must go deeper than that. We want the world to get the facts straight, and we want the facts to be kept straight. We believe that this news will fall upon the world as a bombshell.

"We want, if you will permit me to mix my metaphors, a steady, sure, expert hand at the helm during the thick of the excitement.

"Your ambition, naturally, is to increase the circulation of your paper by honest methods. That is why I think our proposition should interest you. The service you can render us is worth a great deal of money.

"I am prepared to pay any price you ask, but from what I have learned about you, I don't believe that that kind of proposition will interest you. My present proposition is to let you have this story for your paper as it develops—exclusively—in return for the expert and honest way we are sure you will handle it."

Lawrence Galloway looked thoughtfully at Professor Morgan's daughter. She was perched on the edge of the table beside the kerosene lamp. She was gazing at him solemnly, her chin supported by a white fist. By accident or design, her dark dress had slipped up to reveal slim perfect knees. Between the hem of the dress and the tops of the rubber boots extended eight or ten inches of slim perfect legs in translucent rose-taupe.

All this was, he supposed, part of the stage setting.

"Let me have some details," he said. "Just what has Professor Morgan actually done? Please sit down, Mr. Ortola."

Jason Ortola lowered himself to the arm of a chair and lighted a fresh cigar.

"My first contact with Professor Morgan in this matter occurred about three years ago, when he came to me for certain unusual chemicals. As a matter of fact, he brought us chemical formulas which he wished us to try to compound. Some of these compounds, as far as we could learn, had never been attempted in any laboratory; My head chemists believed that they could be produced, but that the cost would be prohibitive, particularly because Professor Morgan wanted them in such large quantities.

"To go over that period very briefly: Professor Morgan was bitterly disappointed when I told him what these compounds would cost. He confessed to me that the cost would prevent him from going ahead with certain vital experiments. He ended by taking me into his confidence."

Again that strange grimace, passing for a smile, twisted Jason Ortola's thin lips.

"I was, naturally, very much flattered. I told him I wanted to help, and since then I have been actively helping. By 'actively,' I mean to the extent of upward of two million dollars, Mr. Galloway. I was carried away. I intended to spend, perhaps, a quarter of a million.

"This money, used chiefly to defray the cost of the chemicals employed, came out of my own pocket. Don't think that I begrudge it. I am mentioning it now because I want you to bear it in mind.

"I won't mention the failures and disappointments we have had. When I tell you that I have seen fifty thousand dollars' worth of chemicals used without result—thrown out on an ash heap—at the end of *one hour's experiments,* you may understand how great the strain has been.

"Professor Morgan has worked himself into a state of

exhaustion, but this afternoon, the years he has spent and the two millions I have spent, were paid back in the fullest measure. To a scientific mind, this afternoon's success was epochal.

"This afternoon, Mr. Galloway, I saw, in his laboratory, a guinea pig restored to life that had been dead ten months!"

3

GRAVE FOOD

LAWRENCE GALLOWAY'S EYES had a trick of turning dark when he was greatly interested. They were dark now, almost inky.

"The experiment," Mr. Ortola went on, "was made, not with an animal that has been in alcohol or a formaldehyde solution, but with the bones and dried skin and hair of a guinea pig!"

"He brought that guinea pig actually to life?"

Jason Ortola's eyes were glittering with excitement.

"Yes, Mr. Galloway!"

"Is it living now?"

"It is as alive now, after ten months of death, as it ever was! It is eating. It is hopping about its cage. We were afraid of creating some horrible kind of monster—a Frankenstein's monster. We examined that guinea pig for two solid hours. As far as we can see, it is perfectly normal. It has simply taken up life where it left it off ten months ago!"

Larry glanced quickly at Polly Morgan; not for corroboration, because he didn't believe a word that Jason Ortola was telling him, but because he was curious about her.

"I saw it," she affirmed in her sweet, husky voice. "I'm

not an authority on guinea pigs or chemistry. In fact, I'm pretty dumb. But it did happen and the guinea pig is alive."

"Did you see it happen, Miss Morgan?"

She nodded. "It was very exciting and awfully confusing. I was afraid we were all going to be blown to kingdom come."

"You cannot harness a million volts to five pages of chemical formula for twelve minutes," the chemist interjected, "without getting a pretty violent reaction. But there is actually no danger of an explosion."

"Twelve minutes?" Larry repeated.

"It took twelve minutes; yes."

"To restore dead bones and skin and hair to life?"

"We are working with certain unknowns," the chemist elucidated. "The chemicals we were sure of, but how they would combine and recombine we could not be sure of. It was the electrical voltage that puzzled us most. Now that that is known, there is absolutely no question in our minds that any animal—any creature that once lived and breathed—can be restored to life."

"A man?" Larry murmured.

"Why not? In nature, life is life; size is of no account. It would simply be a matter of more materials—greater expense."

"How much?"

"I have estimated the cost of the chemicals for a man of average weight at seven hundred thousand dollars."

Larry remained grave.

"But would it be the same man?"

"We believe so."

"But his personality—his self—his soul—"

"We can't reckon with souls," said Mr. Ortola. "We have given life a chemical formula that fills five solid pages of foolscap. The soul may be tangled up in there somewhere."

"But if you use the same chemicals, wouldn't you be giving the same soul to every man?"

"I can't argue that point," said Mr. Ortola, irritably. "No one knows what the soul—the self—the personality—is. Your character, or your soul, or your personality, for example, is totally different from mine. This difference extends into every part of us—literally into our very bones. Perhaps it lingers in our bones after our death. Who knows? Who can say?"

"If a method is ever discovered," said Larry, "for recreating a man out of his dried-up skeleton, the world will be revolutionized."

"Time will cease to be of any importance," Mr. Ortola eagerly concurred. "We firmly believe that it will be possible to bring back to life a mummified Egyptian dead five thousand years."

"Why not recreate the animals of past eras?" suggested Larry. "I would walk a mile to see a saber-tooth tiger fighting a pterodactyl. What a boon to humanity a live dinosaur would be!"

"These things," Mr. Ortola muttered, "are interesting but unimportant. My object in coming to you was to get your advice on public opinion. First you must be convinced that I am telling the truth. You are laughing now, but, later, I think you won't."

"If this story gets into print," Larry took him up, "people will raise the very devil. Millions are going to resent a scientist bringing the Biblical day of resurrection."

"That is where your help will be invaluable," the chemist agreed. "We have no means of guessing how the world will receive this news. You have. Even you will have to guess, but your guess will be closer than ours."

"My offhand guess, for what it is worth," said Larry amiably, "is that you will be lynched."

"Professor Morgan and I are willing to risk that."

Jason Ortola tossed his half-consumed cigar into the fireplace and sprang up.

"Will you drive with us to the laboratory now?"

Larry glanced at Polly Morgan. She had slipped down from the table and was looking at him with narrowed eyes.

"You're awfully suspicious, aren't you?" she said.

"After all," he answered, "have you anything to show me but a guinea pig? Can that guinea pig tell me that he was dead for ten months, and is now delighted to be eating carrots again?"

"Won't you take my father's word?" she cried. "It seems to me you ought to be tickled simply pink. Here, Mr. Ortola is offering you an exclusive piece of news that will give your paper the biggest circulation in the world—"

"If it is true."

Polly Morgan nipped her full lower lip with impatience. She snatched up her hat and raincoat from the chair.

"You're wasting your time arguing, Jason. We've got a ninety-mile drive ahead of us—mostly over rotten roads. I missed a perfectly good night's sleep just for this! Let's go!"

"Will you come with us?" the chemist snapped.

Larry countered: "Will you show me a dead guinea pig or a rabbit or a cat in the process of being restored to life?"

"I'll do better than that," Ortola grimly answered. "I'll

prove before your very eyes that we can restore the dead to life! And I'll prove it in such a way that you'll be absolutely convinced. Let me have the dead body, the bones, of some pet animal you have owned and whose habits or tricks or traits you are thoroughly familiar with. I'll furnish the materials—a hundred thousand dollars' worth if necessary—and Professor Morgan will bring it to life!"

"Before my very eyes?" said Larry.

"Before your very eyes—as soon as we can reach the laboratory!"

"I hate to desecrate the grave of the best friend I ever had," Larry considered, "but I'll do it to call your bluff. I owned a dog that died two years ago. I buried him in an oak box near this cabin. There will be nothing in that box now but—bones. The flesh will be gone. Even the hair will probably be gone."

"All we want," insisted Ortola, "is the bones. What kind of dog was it?"

Larry smiled. "If it was a German police dog, is there a chance that it might be reborn an Irish wolfhound?"

"I assure you, Mr. Galloway," the chemist coldly replied, "I asked the question merely because Professor Morgan must know the animal's approximate weight."

"He weighed about sixty pounds. If the experiment fails, I want the bones back."

"You will have a live dog at your heels by morning, I'm sure, Mr. Galloway. The experiment, of course, might fail. We have had so many failures! But we believe that we have worked out the correct procedure at last. You have got to consider a certain element of chance."

Larry nodded. He slipped into a yellow slicker, clamped

a sou'wester on his head and went into the kitchen for a
spade, a burlap sack and a lantern. When he returned, Miss
Morgan was at the door, buttoning her blue raincoat.

"Will we be starting back right away?" she wanted to
know.

"Your father is expecting us," said the chemist.

"I'll be turning the car around while you play ghoul,"
she said to Larry.

They went out together. The gale promptly fell upon
them as if it would destroy them. Rain slashed into their
faces and hissed on the hot lantern chimney. Behind
them, Black Bay roared. A branch, flying down the wind,
narrowly missed them and crashed into the juicy mud.

They sloshed toward the car. The Airedale's grave was
beyond it.

Larry waited for the girl to speak. He was convinced that
that sinister man and this sophisticated girl were conspir-
ators, planning to weave him into some intrigue.

"It was bad coming up," she shouted above the wind,
"but it will be worse going back. A tree barely missed us.
I think we ought to wait till morning. I'm pretty nearly
all in."

"Whatever you say," Larry answered.

"Jason is champing at the bit. He wouldn't consider it.
There isn't any place to sleep, anyway, is there?"

"Nothing but my bunk and a hammock in the yard."

She made no answer, or if she did, the wind smothered
it. She was bending against the wind and suddenly she
missed her footing. She slipped and fell against Larry. At
least, that was how it seemed to happen. But he had had

experience with her kind before. There was nothing they wouldn't stoop to.

Having started slipping, to save herself from falling, she flung her arms about his shoulders. The impact of her body and the greasy yieldingness underfoot made it imperative for him to maintain the delicate balance of their swaying united bodies, to clasp her likewise.

The lantern hissed against her raincoat and a faint breath of scorched rubber was in the air, to be instantly blown away. Rain rattled on their rubber hats.

He was apprised, as they clung with their arms and with slipping feet tried to remain erect, of her slender softness. There was no doubt in his mind that this was all clever engineering. Part of whatever their scheme was, was for him to respond actively to her attractiveness. Probably she expected him to kiss her.

Larry found surer footing and let her go. But she held to his arm.

"You'd better help me into the car. My boots are all gummed up with this mud." Her voice was a stirring yell in his ear.

His heart was pounding unnecessarily. This girl—Polly Morgan or whoever she actually was—knew that she was provocative. He supposed she was as modern as airway passenger service. Probably she had learned a great deal about men in parked sedans.

He readily called up a picture of her in action—her full red lips unsatisfied with endless kisses. Not passionate, but greedy. Her beauty would ensnare almost any man. Gin drunk neat out of silver flasks. A face that had launched a thousand wild parties! Harder than nails; more brazen than brass. Blatantly aware of her physical perfection.

Her voice, a shout, seemed to pierce to the heart of his thoughts.

"You are the most suspicious man I ever knew in my life!"

"I have been lied to oftener than any man you ever knew!"

She had reached the car, was holding to the door handle. The light outlined her profile in silver.

"Even if it were all a put-up job, even if nothing came of it, wouldn't it still be a story? Dr. Carrol has kept a chicken's heart alive in a solution for fifteen years. That's news, isn't it? When Edison says he believes there is a hereafter— that's news, and he doesn't even have to prove it! I should think you'd get a thrill out of it, anyhow."

Larry went unerringly to the one phrase that concerned him.

"Is it a put-up job?"

"There you go again!" she wailed. "How do I know if it's a put-up job?"

"You're Professor Morgan's daughter, aren't you—or are you?"

She passed over the innuendo.

"What of it? I'm Professor Morgan's cook and bottle washer. I'm his errand boy and his chauffeur. When it isn't important, I'm his stenographer. You look as if I'd just murdered your mother. I don't get you at all, Mr. Galloway. You're riding for a fall!" she cried. "All I hoped for out of this devilish drive was to meet somebody who might be some fun. I thought all newspaper men were funny. You're grimmer than death. Go on and dig up the bones!"

Larry departed, wondering, dragging the spade through the mud, angrily swinging the lantern. He had been accused before of taking himself, his work, too seriously; it always irritated him. Perhaps Polly Morgan was only frivolous, but by the time he reached the two pines where Paddy's grave lay, he had returned to his older opinion of her. She was ultra-sophisticated and utterly without scruples.

He placed the lantern on a knoll and drove his spade into the porridge-like mud. The grisly character of his employment did not occur to him. He dug up and tossed aside clumps of dripping earth near the little oak marker he had whimsically put in place when Paddy died. He presently struck with a corner of the spade a wooden obstruction. That would be the oak box which had served as Paddy's casket.

It struck him, as he shoveled the dirt aside, that he was letting this girl make him ridiculous. Some rival newspaper was, perhaps, preparing an elaborate hoax to make his name a laughing stock. It then occurred to him that this theory was too far-fetched. Her scheme—her and Ortola's scheme, whatever it was, was of a more sinister nature than that.

Perhaps some enemy he had made—and how many enemies he had made with his ruthless championing of truth!—had hired this pretty girl and this coldly sinister man to lure him from his cabin for some purpose of vengeance.

That, too, he found too far-fetched, yet when one is engaged in digging up old bones in the midst of a roaring black gale, his thoughts are apt to be a little twisted.

The box, responding to his pull, released itself from the

hole with a soggy, suckling pop. The lid fell away from the rusty nails and the lantern light poured in on the coffin's distressing contents. Larry hastily decanted these into the burlap sack.

This he gingerly carried across the windswept clearing toward the white glitter of the coupé's lights. The cabin door swung in and Jason Ortola, long and thin, was an Ichabod Crane silhouetted against the lamplight.

The shiny black rubber hat of the girl protruded from the window.

"Got them?"

Larry, coming into the light from the cowl, nodded. "Where shall I put them?"

"Throw them in the back." She blew the horn. "Tell Jason we're ready, will you? It's chilly. Are they clean bones?"

"Very," growled Larry.

4

THROUGH THE NIGHT TO DAWN

THEY DROVE OFF, the three of them tightly packed on the driver's seat, Larry wedged between Miss Morgan and Jason Ortola. For the first mile or two the road was raw mud; black, greasy mud. Ruts frequently expanded into potholes, and the ruts were traversed at short intervals by thick roots. The coupé, in second gear, jerked and pitched and rocked. Occasionally it would execute a violent seesaw, the front and rear ends alternately leaping up and down, and at these times, something in the rear deck would make a thumping, rattling noise, which Larry supposed was the sack of bones tumbling about.

Little conversation was exchanged as the coupé, like a ship on a storm-tossed sea, floundered through the mud for the first mile. It emerged at length upon higher sandy ground, a lane running for five miles through thick pines, this lane, in turn, joining an improved state road of gravel.

Wedged between the girl and the man, Larry nursed his suspicions. They were probably laughing at the slight credulity which had permitted him to exhume Paddy's skeleton. Digging up those bones had been an unspoken confession of weakness.

Yet he saw no amusement in either face. Jason Ortola,

his skin an unpleasant pallid blue in the dim diffusion of the cowl light, stared with black glittering eyes at the uncompromising mud in the path of the headlights. Polly Morgan—or whoever she was—occupied herself with steering wheel and gear-shift lever.

In the dim light her face stood out against the black surface of her rubber hat as if it were set against a dark shield. All three relaxed perceptibly as the car climbed the slope that led to the lane through the pines.

"Thank the Lord, that's over," said the girl. "The rest of the way is a concrete boulevard by comparison. We made it in four and a half hours."

Jason Ortola celebrated his relief by lighting another cigar.

"Our next step," he said, speaking as if he were taking up a conversation dropped but a moment ago, "will be to restore to life some man, to prove to the public that Professor Morgan's process will work equally well with any variety of life, any species."

"And then—" Larry encouraged him.

Jason Ortola puffed his cigar and turned so that he could see his questioner.

"Mr. Galloway," he answered, in a low voice that was charged with importance, "I am, first of all, a business man. I am going to put all my cards on the table."

Larry waited.

"I will be perfectly frank," went on Ortola, "in telling you that this epochal discovery of Professor Morgan's is not to be presented with a beautiful gesture to the world."

"Isn't it?" said Larry.

"Absolutely not!" declared the chemist, vehemently.

"Long ago, some scientist—I wonder who he was!—set a precedent by giving some great discovery to the world—and was probably permitted to starve to death! Why should a scientist give away the fruits of his life's work? Does an inventor? Do corporations?"

He waved the cigar wildly.

"It is self evident that this process will not be available to any but the rich. How many people are there in the whole world who can afford to have, let us say, a dead ancestor restored when the cost will amount to three-quarters of a million? In time, these chemicals, in great quantities, can be manufactured more cheaply, but I doubt if the cost will ever be reduced to below half a million. Well, what's the answer?"

"It isn't as great a boon to suffering humanity as one might impulsively suppose," Larry promptly answered. His irony was lost on Jason Ortola.

"Looking at it in another way," that sinister man proceeded; "Professor Morgan's health is broken, perhaps permanently, as a result of these nerve-racking years of failure."

Larry listened to him with a begrudged admiration. To Jason Ortola, the strangeness of their situation did not seem to exist. He talked as if he were in his own private office, with a quality of concentration that Larry could not help marveling at.

"Certainly he is entitled to live luxuriously the rest of his life—if that is the thing that he wants. Whether or not he himself realizes it, I know that it is the thing he should have. His life has been one of martyrdom. All of his life he has spent with his nose in test-tubes, surrounded by retorts and Bunsen burners and high-voltage apparatus. He is tired. The time has come for him to enjoy what remains of life."

"It seems reasonable," Larry agreed.

"And here is Professor Morgan's daughter," Ortola exclaimed. "Why should she be denied the things that other girls of her age enjoy?"

"I won't be talked about that way," Polly Morgan spiritedly interrupted, without withdrawing her eyes from the road. "You can count me entirely out of this discussion. I hate it. Dad hates it. I haven't complained, have I, because I'm the chief cook and bottle washer, the errand boy and the chauffeur?"

"At least," said Larry, with a laugh, "you're a good chauffeur."

"It's nice to know there's something about me you don't disapprove of! When you taste my ham and eggs, as you'll be doing about five hours from now, you may even concede there are nicer things about me!"

Larry continued to laugh, but the girl's mouth was set in a hard line. She was really a superb driver; gauging curves and slopes nicely; using the brakes seldom; keeping instinctively to her side of the road. His experience with women drivers had convinced him that they were all bad, lacking judgment and that strange intimacy with space and speed without which no one can handle a car properly. But it amused him to think of this girl in a kitchen.

"To finish what I was saying," the harsh voice of Ortola took up again, "Professor Morgan and his daughter must profit by this success."

"You can believe me or not," said the girl with the glowing eyes, "I heartily disagree with Jason. His interest is selfish. I think all scientific discoveries should be given to the world for what they are worth."

"I insist," Ortola argued, "that my interest is purely businesslike. I have spent almost all of my personal fortune on these experiments."

"You aren't going to starve if you don't get a nickel back," cried the girl.

"I'll get every nickel back," said the chemist. "I was taking a gamble. It was a thousand-to-one shot. I was lucky enough to hit it, as the gamblers say, on the nose. Somehow, I'm going to collect my winnings. Galloway, don't you think I should?"

Larry said nothing. To him, this long discourse was ridiculous. Whatever Ortola's real object may have been, all this conversation was so much red herring; a clever attempt to cram his mind with all possible facts pertaining to something that had not happened and never would happen. He was simply waiting for a word to be carelessly dropped that would give him an inkling of their real purpose. When you taste my ham and eggs! In the privacy of his bosom, he continued to laugh.

"Galloway, the actual cost of the materials used in resurrecting that fifty-cent guinea pig was close to thirty thousand dollars!"

His tone had become more and more emphatic; his voice louder and louder, as a man's voice will when he is trying, with thin arguments, to compel approval.

"The actual cost, paid out of my own pocket, for the materials used in bringing this dog of yours back to life will be close to a hundred thousand! The cost of restoring a man to life—to prove to the world that it can be done—will be close to three-quarters of a million! Am I going to go on throwing my money away? Am I going to permit Professor Morgan to make the grand gesture?"

He puffed angrily at his cigar, giving a very fair, imitation, in Larry's opinion, of a man who thought he was being dealt with unfairly.

"Between you and me, Galloway," the chemist vigorously went on, "the world can go to the devil. We are undertaking the business of manufacturing *life,* and I, for one, am going to be properly compensated for it!"

Larry maintained a solemn silence, as if he were weighing all these things Mr. Ortola was so excited about.

The crackling voice startled him: "Well, what do you think about it, Galloway?"

"You've got the world by the tail, haven't you?" Larry answered jovially.

"You may disagree with me," the chemist continued. "I simply wanted to give you the complete picture. There are going to be so many things to talk over at the laboratory. I want your expert advice on such points, Galloway. The public is going to jump to the conclusion that, in a little time, you can put a bag of bones in one end of a machine and a silver half dollar in a slot—and a live man will come popping out. You've got to educate the public to the truth."

"Listen, Jason," the girl broke in; "don't you realize that Mr. Galloway doesn't believe a single word that you've said all evening, and that he's laughing at both of us, and that he's going to keep on laughing and keep on being suspicious of our real motives until you prove what you're saying?"

Larry was startled at the accuracy with which, not for the first time, she had penetrated his thoughts; but he could only consider what she had said as so much more red herring.

"Is that true?" Ortola snapped.

"I haven't said so, have I?" Larry answered.

"You don't have to say so," said the girl. "I can feel you bristling. You think we're a pair of liars. Maybe you're too polite to say so out loud, but that's what you're really thinking."

"I've learned, after years of bitter experience," said Larry coldly, "to consider everybody guilty until his innocence has been proved. I'm nothing but a burned child who dreads the flame."

"It must be awful," the girl feelingly took him up, "to go through life thinking that about people. Always suspicious!"

Jason Ortola had lighted still another cigar and relapsed into brittle silence.

The car plunged on through the night. The girl urged it along with perfect skill. Occasionally they came to a blubbering stop, and the two men would debouch into the teeming rain to drag a bough, gleaming like a boa constrictor through its foliage, from the road.

They sailed through a town in which not a light was burning in any window. It was like a deserted village which, Larry thought, was the most appropriate kind of village they could have selected to go through on this wild ride.

He settled back against the cushion and tried to doze. From time to time he opened his eyes to glance at the road and from the road to the white, set face of the driver. He offered to relieve at the wheel.

These offers, submitted four times, she spurned, but with gratitude and kindliness, as if she was not resentful of him except on those occasions when their wills clashed.

He found her shoulder to be warm and soft. It was his cheek which found this out when, opening his eyes, his bead was reclining there. He had been asleep. His head had fallen over on her shoulder, and she had permitted it to stay so. For a moment, before he fully awakened, he inhaled a sweet aroma which was given off by her hair; mingled with it was that of the warm rubber of her hat.

Larry straightened up. The sky was grayly aglow and his mind was, in the mist of withdrawing sleep, in that state when one beholds, for a precious little interval, things as they truly are or ought to be; when problems that were baffling the night before are neatly solved; when the tangle of one's life appears blessedly simple.

In this sweet if momentary interlude between the easy achievements of dreams and the cruel uncertainties of reality, he saw this girl who called herself Polly Morgan as a fragrant young person of charm and warmth; spunky and fine and valiant.

Then his eyes cleared upon the profile of a face that had launched a thousand wild parties. She was, he reflected, observing a tendril of hair that curled about one small pink ear, the most dangerous of all types of women, the salamander. Her air of young innocence unaffected by the harsh experiences she had gone through; her face betraying, by not so much as a line, the infamy of her nature.

Most men, he mused, fatuously thought that the look of

young innocence was inseparable from young innocence. What fools most men were! How quickly most men would have fallen for this innocent looking adventuress!

His ears were greeted by a sweetly husky voice that had ensnared countless weaklings and fools.

"Enjoy your nap?"

He rubbed his eyes with gritty knuckles.

"I didn't mean to fall asleep."

"Oh, I'm used to carrying the white man's burden on my shoulders, and you sounded as if you were enjoying your snooze. You have a very easy snore to get along with. It's almost musical, except when we go over bumps, then it sounds like a buzz saw striking knots. Jason is one of these people who strangle when they snore. I almost ran into a ditch once. We're nearly home. How would a nice big cup of hot coffee go?"

"Great," said Larry and lighted a cigarette. He considered her humorously. "Can you really cook?"

"I suppose I'm guilty until I prove I'm innocent," she answered, and laughed. "I'm a perfect whirlwind in the kitchen. You see, there are so few things I can do, that I've got to be proud of the ones I shine at."

"If you can cook as well as you can drive," Larry complimented her, still slightly under the spell of that misty awakening on her shoulder and that tendril of hair curling lovingly about her small pink ear; "the jury will let you off with recommendations for a gold medal."

"Coming from you—" she began, and switched off to: "The rain stopped an hour ago. It's going to be a swell day."

Larry glanced at the sky for confirmation. The windshield wiper was no longer flicking back and forth and only a few drops lingered on the glass's dusty surface. The clouds were rolling back from the deep purple of the night sky; a silvery glimmer on the horizon hinted at a fine sunny day.

Jason Ortola gurgled, lifted his head and automatically reached for a cigar.

"Where are we?" he wanted to know.

"Just coming into Brookhaven," the girl answered.

Ortola stretched himself and groaned. His appearance in the early morning was even less prepossessing than it had been the night before. In the few hours, his black beard had sprouted and his eyes had a lawless look.

The world was gray with dawn when they rushed through the sleeping town of Brookhaven. A mile beyond Brookhaven they left the macadam for a wet dirt road that forked off to the right near a lake which shimmered through slim young birches, its surface rippled by a faint dawn breeze. Clouds piled up in the east were blooming pink peonies. The air was fragrant of earth freshly washed and awakening to the promise of a clear summer day.

The lake was presently left behind and the road now went up and up, winding through a pine thicket.

The girl glanced at her wristwatch and solemnly said, as a large red barn hove in sight: "Four hours and forty-two minutes."

A small crystal stream flowed noisily past the barn and went tumultuously on down the valley. On a rise of ground, perhaps five hundred feet beyond, was perched a low white house of Colonial design with green shutters.

The girl stopped beside a heavy unpainted oak door in the barn and switched off the engine.

"This," she told Larry, "is my father's laboratory. It used

to be a flour mill, some time after the Revolutionary War. It was built around 1790. Of course, it's been rebuilt a lot of times since. Don't you think it's a lovely spot—or does it have to prove itself innocent first?"

Jason Ortola was crossing around in front of the car. He went to the heavy oak door and knocked. The girl's eyes were smiling into Larry's.

He was surprised at the accuracy with which she had once again pierced his thoughts. He had been thinking that the stage setting was most elaborate, and he was prepared for almost any dénouement. He had been giving free rein to his suspicions, basing them on his certainty that the girl who called herself Polly Morgan and the man who called himself Jason Ortola were impostors. He would not believe that, somewhere in this barn, was Professor J. Hendricks Morgan.

Glancing eagerly past her, he saw the heavy oak door swing open and a man step out. Nowhere in the world where newspapers and illustrated magazines circulated would that aristocratic head and that boyish smile have been mistaken.

5

THE DORMANT CRUSADER

IF HE HAD not been a successful scientist, he might have been one of the most popular actors on the American stage—or an adventurer. He had that air about him. He was one of the handsomest men Larry had ever seen: with smooth, silver-white hair, a broad, high forehead, the carriage of a military officer, and the rich tan of a man who has spent much of his time outdoors.

He wore a long white coat, the kind that laboratory workers put on over their clothes to protect them. It was stained with chemicals. The pockets bulged with accumulations. From one of them dangled a long red rubber tube.

"Dad," the girl introduced Larry to him, "this is Lawrence Galloway. He thinks Jason and I are a pair of liars. He's been making dirty cracks at us all night long."

Professor Morgan laughed. It was the vague, nervous laugh of a man of many preoccupations.

If Lawrence Galloway was surprised by this unexpected turn of events, he did not betray it. He was observing with shrewd eyes that Professor Morgan was more than merely exhausted—he was ever so slightly intoxicated.

His rich tan, his good looks, his proud carriage were those of a man who enjoyed life; who liked good food, good liquor, good times. His eyes sparkled with the same imp of deviltry that Larry had seen more than once in Polly Morgan's eyes. They were alike, these two; and Larry sensed that a strong romantic attachment existed between them.

The scientist was as businesslike as a city physician.

"Mr. Ortola tells me you have brought along the skeleton of a dog you owned. Is the skeleton in good condition?"

"I believe so," Larry answered.

Professor Morgan lifted out the burlap sack and folded it back about the mass of bones it contained. In the bright summer sunlight they were merely bones.

Professor Morgan pawed over the bones with long, stained fingers. It occurred to Larry, as he watched him, that he had never before met a man with such claims upon distinction. The glamour of greatness was definitely attached to this tall, handsome man.

His eyes, when they did not sparkle impishly, were the gray of clouds, seeming to glow with an inner light which, Larry skeptically thought, might have been produced by synthetic gin. They seemed to infold him, to be looking at all parts of him at once, as he glanced up from the dog's dismembered skeleton.

"How long has this dog been dead?" he crisply asked.

"About two years."

"What was his age at death?"

"About eleven."

"What was his weight?"

"Somewhere around sixty pounds."

"Muller!" the scientist called.

A thin, blond man appeared in the doorway. When he came into the sunlight, Larry saw that he was a cripple.

He laboriously dragged one leg behind him as he walked, and his square homely face had that blank look acquired by men who have long endured physical suffering. His smile was a fleet grimace.

"Mr. Galloway, my assistant, Mr. Muller."

A bony hand enveloped Larry's and squeezed it until Larry winced. Mr. Muller, releasing it, stooped down to examine the bones.

"Airedale," he announced.

"Mr. Muller is an osteologist," Professor Morgan explained, with his quick smile. "You can take it in and begin assembling it, Muller. I'll join you directly."

He beamed at Larry.

"So you're skeptical. Has Mr. Ortola told you about our guinea pig experiment?"

Larry nodded.

"And you weren't convinced?"

"Convinced!" echoed Polly Morgan. "He's been sneering at three-minute intervals ever since we opened the door of his cabin,"

Professor Morgan smiled anew.

"I think Mr. Galloway is taking the proper attitude," he said. "It is the scientific attitude: don't believe a thing until it is proved, demonstrated, before your very eyes."

"That was what I said," Larry murmured. "How soon can you make this experiment?"

"In about an hour," the scientist answered. "Perhaps you'd rather go up to the house with Polly, and wash up and have a bite of breakfast while we're getting things ready. The actual demonstration you'll find rather spectacular, but the preparations are dull.

"Besides"—and he again gave Larry his quick, youthful smile—"there are things I won't let Mr. Ortola see, there are other things I won't let even Muller see. I'd prefer not to let a sharp-eyed newspaper man see anything, but—you must be convinced. I want you to remain a skeptic to the very end."

"That won't be hard," said Polly Morgan. "Skepticism is the one thing he's got nothing else but."

They all laughed. Even Jason Ortola managed a twisted smile. The bright morning sun was scattering Larry's gloomy doubts. He was already casting aside the mental reservations be had made concerning Polly Morgan.

But, as regards the experiment, he would continue to be skeptical, as Professor Morgan had warmly urged him. Bright summer sunlight made the miracle of transforming dead bones into a living dog even more preposterous.

"You might send us down some coffee and sandwiches," said Professor Morgan, as Polly placed her foot on the electric starter.

"Is Mike around?" she asked.

"I'll send him up," said her father.

Larry climbed in beside her, and they drove on to the house. It was of the familiar New England colonial type, a "salt box," of clapboard, and painted white, addition having been added to addition until it now gave the effect of sprawling, the whole seeming to have settled until it had become one with the contours of the hill on which it sat behind a screen of old elms.

They went into a large, low living room, sparsely furnished with early colonial pine and maple. A curving

stairway ascended to upper regions. Larry followed her up
the stairs, and at the head of the stairs she paused and said:

"One of dad's hours can always be multiplied by at least
three. You'll have plenty of time to take a shower and shave
before breakfast is ready. You look pretty seedy. There's
your room, if you ever stay overnight, as you probably will.
There's a bathroom off it. The guest of honor always has it.
Steinmetz and Koch and Dakin have slept in that room.

"Simply yell if you need anything. You will find towels,
razors, and shaving soap in the bathroom. If you've never
been in a scientist's house before, I'd better warn you that
they're all run on a catch-as-catch-can basis. You'll find
I'm a pretty obliging servant girl, in spite of your marvelous judgment of people. Meet me in the kitchen when
you're ready."

Larry, betraying the first humanity he had shown this
girl since she had been catapulted into his life by that gust
of wind, said:

"Forget about me. You need sleep. You've driven two
hundred miles since last night, and you're all in."

"I'm not all in," she flatly contradicted him. "I'm used to
longer stints than that. I nursed Hutchinson, the English
paleontologist through three weeks of flu last fall, and kept
house for nine absent-minded scientists without any help,
at the same time."

She hesitated and gave him the intent personal look
through her long, dark lashes that had caused him to arrive
at such amazing conclusions. Then, brightly: "See you later,
old settler."

Larry reluctantly went into the room she had designated
and tried to marshal his thoughts; but they declined to be

marshaled. It was still hard for him to swallow, that Polly Morgan was what she appeared on the surface to be—a young person of great charm and beauty, spunky and amiable and valiant. Spunky, he reflected ruefully, no end!

The room he entered profoundly disturbed him. It was a large, airy bedroom with wide oak planks smoothed to a dull gloss by the passage of feet over a hundred and fifty years, brightened here and there by rag rugs. The room contained only a sleigh-back bed, three rush-bottom chairs, and a low chest of drawers with an oval mirror hung on the wall above it, a sampler dated 1821, and a Currier & Ives print of the Brooklyn Bridge. He wondered who had rubbed down the old pine furniture and who had made the yellow counterpane and the window curtains.

Larry went into the bathroom. Things here were as she had said they would be. It was a spacious white-enameled bathroom. Large, rough-looking Turkish towels with yellow borders hung on a rail. He found a safety razor, several kinds of shaving cream, an assortment of shaving brushes, and a packet of new blades on a glass shelf above the washbasin.

Certainly this was a man's household. You walked in, and you simply clicked. His editorial mind heartily approved the old Americanism of the Morgan house.

The brook he had admired below the laboratory splashed by under elm trees outside his window. Delightful spot! Larry shaved and bathed leisurely, then made his way downstairs.

He passed through a study that was large enough and filled with enough scientific works to be the reference room of a university library. The four walls were solid with books.

There were books in Greek, Latin, German, French, reaching from the floor to the ceiling.

He next found himself in a dining room facing a glorious green valley and pleasantly aglow with hand-rubbed pine and early American colored glass; through a long, fragrant pantry, and on into a kitchen that fairly glistened, so clean it was.

A slender, dark-haired girl in a brown homespun dress and a fresh white apron was standing with her back toward him at a gigantic coal range. The sizzling of ham and eggs intimately filled the silence and the air was redolent of coffee.

Polly Morgan turned about, flushed with the heat, and Larry Galloway was aware of a pleasurable glow throughout his being. A beautiful girl, radiant from the exertion of cooking a breakfast that you are about to devour, is always an ennobling spectacle.

He was only slightly let down when she corrected his impression.

"This is for the shock troops," she told him. "I hoped I'd have it out of the way before you were ready. You're next, Mr. Galloway."

Larry lounged against the wall and watched her. She went about her work with a minimum of exertion and a maximum of efficiency; quick, sure, and with an easy grace.

"Don't hurry on my account. I've been admiring your furniture."

"I'm interested in early American," she told him as she opened the oven door, peered in and closed it again. "I have combed the countryside for things to match this house."

"Who scrapes them off and rubs them down?"

"I do. I'm really not half bad at some things."

"Miss Morgan," he said impulsively, "I want to apologize for the way I've been acting."

"How can you help yourself?" she merrily responded. "It's your nature to be suspicious."

"It isn't my nature," he denied. "My work demands it."

"I've known newspaper men," said this frank young person, looking at him brightly, "who came for news and interviews, and weren't in the least suspicious."

"And look at the stuff they put over on the public!" Larry exclaimed. "Fake cancer cures! Fake tuberculosis cures! I am trying to give my readers the straight truth."

"So you said," she murmured.

"I've made *The Daily It* a success in the tabloid field by keeping it honest. My readers know they won't find unsubstantiated rumors in *The Daily It* when they buy it. Believe me, it hasn't been easy sailing."

A black, grinning face was pressed against the screen door.

"Come in, Mike," said Polly Morgan.

The possessor of the black face, a boy of twelve or thirteen, came wiggling in, displaying magnificent pearls of teeth.

"This is Mike, Mr. Galloway. His real name is Theodore Roosevelt Boggs. We call him Mike because he almost ruined us by broadcasting an experiment dad was doing, determining the length of a rabbit's life in an atmosphere of pure oxygen, around Brookhaven. Didn't you, Microphone? But he learned his lesson and you can't pry anything out of Mike now with a crowbar.

"Mike is dad's willingest assistant, Mr. Galloway. He

worships pure science and is absolutely fearless. Dad has been using him for blood transfusions in connection with some experiments he's been making with the cardiac rhythm of monkeys. I don't know what it's all about, but I do know that we'd all be tarred and feathered if the simple folks around here guessed half of what goes on. What are you doing now, Microphone?"

"Jus' restin'," responded the grinning colored boy.

"Been around the birch lab lately?" she asked.

"No, ma'am," Mike answered emphatically.

She laughed softly. "The birch lab is our chamber of horrors. It's about a mile back in the woods, in a grove of birches, hence the name," she explained to Larry. "You couldn't hire me to go near it. Mike is terrified of the place.

"Any scientist who wants to perform some experiments that would horrify the civilized world if it leaked out slinks off to the birch lab. I strongly suspect they're vivisecting cats up there now or doing some ghastly control experiments with rats or guinea pigs in the sacred name of behaviorism.

"And they're always so mysterious and so suspicious! There's a tall lanky one up there now who works at nights with Mr. Muller when dad isn't using him. I've never even seen him, but Mike caught a partial glimpse of him with the moon over his left shoulder one night. He said he was nine feet tall and had green electric lights for eyes. What did you do, Mike."

"Ah run," said Mike, with large round eyes.

"He sounds like a cat vivisector to me," went on Polly Morgan. "He won't come near the house and no one but Muller's been permitted near the birch lab for months.

A woman who is just twice as suspicious as you are does his cooking and cleaning. She may be his assistant, but I haven't been able to make her talk. I'd like you to see her. She wears a diamond on one finger as big as a Concord grape. She looks like just the kind of woman who would enjoy torturing a poor helpless cat. I detest vivisection.

"I suppose you know that scientists are more jealous than prima donnas. Two ornithologists got into a dreadful row one day near the birch lab and one of them went home with a beautiful shiner. Well, something is always going on in a scientific household. It isn't dull, anyway."

While she chattered to him, she moved swiftly, with a grace that Larry found delightful, about her appointed task. The skillet of ham and eggs she had pushed to the back of the stove with the coffee pot. There was a large black tin tray on the table near Larry. This she now rapidly filled; and Mike staggered away with the tray, picking his way carefully toward the laboratory.

"Now," said Polly Morgan; "it's our turn. I could eat a raw mule!"

"Have you always lived here?" Larry wanted to know.

She forked thin slices of bacon into the skillet.

"Since dad left his last university job about ten years ago, yes. I've been growing up, so to speak, with the establishment. Dad is a little friend to all the starving scientists in the world. There are at least half a dozen little laboratory buildings scattered through the woods where a man can work alone and uninterrupted.

"If a man has an idea, he can always get a hearing from dad. Dad's only handicap is money. If he had enough money, this whole farm—sixty-five acres of it—would be nothing but labs, where any man with an idea to work out could come and have his living and laboratory expenses free.

"Of course, a lot of them are nuts, and if they are, dad turns them over to me and I gently but firmly shoo them away. But we have had some pretty big men working here. Did you ever hear of Suzukawa, the Japanese biologist? He was here all last summer, catching fireflies and trying to reduce their twinkling to a mathematical equation.

"When there are eight or ten of them working here at once, the place is a madhouse. You never heard such arguments! My mother died of bewilderment a year after we came up here. She never understood the discussions, and she thought vivisection and all control experiments were cruel and useless. Can you imagine an anti-vivisectionist married to a biologist? How do you like your eggs—blind on both sides?"

Larry nodded vaguely. "But don't you ever get away from here?"

With a pancake turner in one hand, she gazed at him, puzzled.

"I mean," he explained, "you seem to be harnessed here."

"I am harnessed here. Who would look after things if I didn't?"

"You could hire a housekeeper."

"And dad would stay awake nights begrudging her wages and thinking of all the guinea pigs and test tubes he could be buying with the money!"

"He must be mighty selfish!" Larry exclaimed.

Polly Morgan laughed softly. "All scientists are selfish. They think they are selfless. In fact, most of them say so.

They will freely admit that they are sacrificing themselves for humanity or some other sacred cause. Anybody who thinks scientists are unselfish should see three of them at a table when there are only two pieces of cake!"

"It isn't fair," Larry declared warmly, "to make a prisoner of you as he's doing."

"Mr. Galloway," she said, "you have the burdens of the world on your shoulders already. Don't take on any more. Do you like your coffee strong or weak?"

"Strong," Larry answered. "What do you know about these—what do you call 'em—resurrection experiments your father has been making?"

"Not much more than you do. I suppose it's the triumph of his lifetime. For months and months he's practically forbidden anybody to come to the house, and the only men he'll permit near him are Muller and Jason. All the labs are empty except the birch lab, where the vivisectionist is working—and he's probably secretly working with dad, too.

"He hoped I'd grow up into a laboratory assistant, but I've been too busy running the house. I hardly ever go near the big lab, anyway. I think he's afraid I have inherited some of mother's aversion to vivisection. I only watch him on state occasions, when he must have an audience for his vanity's sake.

"He let me watch the guinea pig experiment yesterday, but, as I told you before, it meant nothing to me. I'm no scientist. I am a cook and a captain bold and the mate of the Nancy brig. I'm too busy feeding scientists to watch them.

"Most of them are so pathetic! They come up here so enthusiastic and a week or a month later they go away looking so dejected. Wouldn't you like to look at some pictures while I'm setting the table in the yard? Wouldn't you like to have breakfast under the apple tree?"

"I'd love to," said Larry.

She vanished with a twinkling of slim young ankles in the direction of the study and returned with a photograph album.

"A Professor Hornbrook," she said, placing the book on the table before him and opening it, "comes up to visit dad every spring and he's hypped on photographic chemistry. He's been snap-shotting me for years.

"Photography is his hobby. He's really pretty well known for his research work in bio-chemistry. He worked with dad for almost a year on sargolyn. That's the specific dad finally derived from atoxyl for curing beri-beri. You've probably heard of it."

Larry had never heard of it, and he promptly forgot sargolyn as he gazed at a brightly smiling child of twelve with pigtails descending her flat bosom to her waist.

He was fairly bursting with amazement at this girl who chattered so wisely of the sciences, who managed this difficult and complex household, and who could be naïve enough to bring him an album of photographs of herself. For two out of three of the snapshots were of Polly Morgan.

As he turned the pages of the thick book, he saw Polly Morgan growing up, the pigtails disappearing into a nest of curly hair, the skirts covering more and more of the long spindleshanks. Then fashion made its influence felt, and the skirts grew shorter and shorter while the legs they revealed ceased being spindleshanks and became slim and then slender and finally perfection itself.

The subject of these numerous photographic experiments frequently bent over his shoulder explaining this and that, but never halting in its forward march the breakfast she was preparing.

"That was my saddle horse, Bones. We never could make that horse put on weight! He was so spoiled! He used to try to follow me into the kitchen for sugar. Bones died of colic two years ago—and one of the greatest stomach specialists in the world was here at the time and couldn't save him. He had lots of fun afterward, though, carving into him and performing an autopsy. He proved beyond the slightest doubt that Bones had died of colic! Will you carry out this tray, Mr. Galloway?"

She had loaded another tray with bacon and eggs, hot rolls and coffee, butter and sugar and salt and pepper and silverware. She held open the screen door.

Larry put the album down and picked up the tray. His brows were drawn together in a pucker. He was thinking. The crusader in him—never far beneath the skin of any true newspaper man—was aroused.

Somehow, he was determined to free this beautiful, unselfish girl from this life of drudgery!

6

"SCIENTISTS ARE QUEER"

A LONG PINE table with benches on either side of it stood under an apple tree heavy with green fruit. Insects hummed in the thick foliage. Near-by the brook splashed and sparkled.

It was, Larry declared, a heavenly spot for breakfast. The apple tree grew upon a knoll which commanded a breathless view of a sun-filled valley. In the distance dark green hills rose and beyond them were other hills, range upon range, until the sky was met finally by a ridge all misty and purple.

Polly Morgan was busily setting the table for two and Larry, withdrawing his eyes from the valley, gravely watched her. It pained him to observe, that in the cruel brightness of outdoors, her hands were not white and smooth as they should have been, but rough and somewhat red. An indigestible lump settled in his chest as be pondered this girl, so bright, so tireless, so unfairly treated! Lavishing her youth on a tavern for selfish scientists! He repeated to himself, as she raised glowing questioning eyes from a coffee cup for his specification as to lumps of sugar, that something would have to be done about it.

He asked boldly: "Miss Morgan, how old are you?"

"Twenty," she answered. "You're twenty-seven, aren't you?"

"No, eight," he solemnly corrected her.

"You take life so seriously that anybody might think you were thirty-four or five."

"Do you blame me for taking you seriously?" he cried. "A girl as beautiful as you are, wasting your youth like this!"

The glance she gave him was kindly and sympathetic. "Your eggs are getting cold, Mr. Galloway."

"If my sister had lived," he harshly told her, still under the spell of his emotion, "she would have been about your age. Do you mind if I call you Polly?"

"Why not?" was her cheery answer. "Everybody else does. 'Polly, bring me another cup of coffee!' 'Polly, where is that quartz retort I ordered last week?'"

"It's monstrous!" he fairly shouted. "Wasting your life like this—hardly more than a servant!"

"A handmaiden to science," she disagreed. "I hardly consider my life wasted. Somebody has to wash the pots while genius performs the miracles. My father wouldn't have stumbled upon the secret of resurrection if I hadn't kept the home fires burning."

"You simply don't realize what you're missing," Larry muttered. "And you'll keep on being a—a handmaiden to science until, some day, you will realize. And it'll be too late then."

Her eyes over the rim of her coffee cup were provocative. "What am I missing?"

"Life!" he said sternly.

"Well, what's life?"

"For you," he said; "for a girl as good looking as you, a

girl with your—your million-dollar personality—it ought to be fun—dancing—parties—" He was glaring at her. In the intensity of his zeal, he was forgetting that, only a little while ago, he was thinking of her as a salamander, a girl who swigged gin neat from flasks, the owner of a face that had launched a thousand wild parties!

"I haven't the time," said Polly Morgan. "I've never had time even to learn to dance."

"You've never learned to dance?" he exclaimed.

She buttered the half of a roll and pushed it toward him.

"You're as bad as any scientist," she sighed. "Your coffee is getting cold. Your eggs *are* cold. You remind me of Dr. Corcoran and Professor Warburton. They utterly ignored a chicken I roasted especially for them—they were so lost in a passionate argument. Dr. Corcoran is an embryologist and Professor Warburton is an ichthyologist. The argument lasted three hours and was about pipe tobacco and pipes. Please drink your coffee, Mr. Galloway!"

Larry swallowed coffee and considered Polly. He put the cup down with an emphasis that almost cracked it.

"Look here, Polly," he said. "Have you ever been in love?"

"I haven't had time," she answered.

"Do you intend to marry one of these scientists?"

"No," she said gravely; "I don't. I intend to marry a man who plays a saxophone in a jazz orchestra."

"I thought so!" he said triumphantly, and again: "I *thought* so!" As if her answer had given him the key to the entire riddle. "You're fed up with this life and you know it! Where did you go to school—Polly?"

"I don't know much," was Polly's modest answer. "I never actually did go to school, except when I was little. I think

I attended school about two years altogether. But in my spare time I read a great deal and I've had tutors.

"The last tutor I had was studying biochemistry under dad and he tutored me in his spare time. He was awfully absent-minded and his heart really wasn't in tutoring. He wanted to hold my hand all the time!"

"He did?" Larry gasped.

Polly chuckled. "I'll never forget the day he tried to kiss me. We were down by the brook under that big elm. He was sitting on a stone beside the brook and I was sitting on a smaller stone beside him. He leaned down without any warning and tried to kiss me and I gave him a push—not a hard push. It was just a little push, but he was off balance, and the next I saw was his heels flying up as he went into the brook.

"He said he hurt his back when he fell in. He looked pretty sick for a day or two, anyhow, and he went away without even saying good-by. Oh, a lot of scientists have tried to kiss me, and they're so funny and absent-minded about it. Most of them act as if they didn't know what they were doing. But some of them are quite ferocious. Professor Warburton, the ichthyologist, was very ferocious."

"My God!" Larry hoarsely cried. "When I think of the life you've led here it makes me feel like committing murder!"

"Don't you think I should let scientists kiss me?"

"Certainly not!" he roared.

"But they's so funny!"

He only groaned.

Polly said in a low, thoughtful voice: "Jason Ortola feels exactly the way you do. He wants to marry me."

"No!" Larry moaned.

"Yes, he does. And he has all the arguments you've been using. He says it's a shame for me to waste my life up here mothering selfish scientists when I ought to be enjoying myself. He wants to give me all the things I've been missing. Well, you heard him last night."

Larry, with pursed lips and contracted brows, slowly nodded. His curly light brown hair was rumpled. Leaning toward her, with his fist under his chin, his elbow on his knee, he said:

"Well, why don't you? Why don't you marry Ortola? He is a millionaire a good many times over. Just because I don't like his looks isn't an argument."

"He's so old," said Polly. "He's eleven years older than you are. I don't want to marry a man thirty-nine years old. That's nineteen years difference. I've always thought that seven or eight years is plenty. You aren't married, are you?"

"No," said Larry, "and I've seen enough of it to sour me, too. Marriage for a man in my business is the bunk."

"Why—in your business?" Polly wanted to know.

"Because a man must be free to come and go in the newspaper business," he informed her. "One of my friends worked on a morning paper in Chicago and he often didn't get home until seven in the morning, usually all in. He came home one morning, and found his wife cleaning house. Poor old Bill! He slumped down on a piano stool and his wife came in with a broom. 'What are you doing?' Bill asked her. 'I'm cleaning house,' said his wife. 'And I'm going to sweep you out with the rest of the rubbish!'"

The laughter with which Larry concluded this anecdote was bitter and knowing.

"Any girl who marries you," said Polly, "would have loads of trouble. You'd be suspicious of every move she made. She wouldn't dare call her soul her own."

"No girl is going to have the chance to find it out," Larry laughingly assured her. "I seriously think you'd be wise in considering Ortola, Polly."

"But I hardly know anything about him," she protested, "except that he's a very successful, very rich manufacturing chemist. A girl wants to know more about a man she considers marrying than that."

"When I get back to town," said Larry, "I'll find out all about him and let you know. There isn't a man of any importance in this country that we haven't information about. I'll get the dossier on Ortola out of our files and I'll let you know whether or not he's the kind of man a girl of your inexperience ought to marry."

"I wish you would," said Polly.

"I will."

"Because he's very insistent. He wants to take me to Europe on our honeymoon. Of course, I'd love to go to Europe. I'd love to travel—anywhere! I want to go to Rome and Constantinople and Cairo and—Paris! Oh, Paris!" Her eyes glistened. They became softly unfocused in a mist of dreams at the other end of the sunny valley—and infinitely beyond the end of the valley.

"You're really awfully nice, Mr. Galloway," she said presently, as if she were discussing him with herself. "I didn't like you a bit at first, but I think I've changed my mind. You have a terribly suspicious and serious nature, but you're awfully kind. Have you ever been in Paris?"

He shook his head. "I've been too busy, too. I've been

working on newspapers ever since I was fifteen. I'm going to Paris some day, though. Yes, and Rome, too. I want to prowl around Rome in the moonlight. The Coliseum by moonlight!"

"Yes," she sighed. "Oh, yes! And that *piazza* in Florence where they mix every kind of cocktail in the world on little tea carts while a marvelous orchestra plays! Dad has told me about it so often. He went to Italy to consult with Stromboli, the Italian biologist, on the nervous system of frogs.

"Stromboli took dad to the *piazza* and got him tight. Dad is a rabid anti-prohibitionist. He has a still in a little room under the lab where he makes his own grain alcohol. He smelled as if he'd been making a fresh batch of it last night. You won't tell on him, will you?"

"Of course not!" Larry cried.

"Is *The Daily It* against prohibition?" Polly asked.

"Tooth, nail, and claw!" he declared.

"Dad is like a child about that still," she said dreamily. "He's so proud because it costs him only eleven cents a gallon to make pure grain alcohol and the bootleggers charge twelve dollars."

With a sudden lift of her shoulders, Polly Morgan straightened up. She whispered excitedly:

"Here comes Mrs. Gore!"

"Who," Larry asked, "is Mrs. Gore?"

"That's the woman I told you about—the wife or the assistant of the vivisectionist who's using the birch lab. There! That flash was the diamond!"

Larry turned so that he could look down the hill. He saw a thickly built woman of medium height in a gray dress and a gray sunbonnet. She was climbing the path which ran into the valley with a covered basket over her arm. She was in the shade now, walking under trees. She came trudging up the slope, holding the basket tight to her side and keeping her eyes fixed on the irregularities of the path.

He saw the diamond on her left hand before she looked up. It was one of the largest solitaires he had ever seen, a stone of fully ten carats. But once it blazed in the sunlight. Then her eyes were upon him: cold gray eyes set in a brown, leathery face. Her lips were tightly held together, as if she were angry or peevish.

She examined him keenly, thoroughly, taking him in bit by bit as she came toward them. There was something, he thought, malignant about her eyes, but perhaps his imagination supplied that. They were, in any event, hard, unfriendly eyes.

Polly caroled: "Good morning, Mrs. Gore!"

And the woman replied tonelessly: "Mawnin'."

She passed them and went up the kitchen steps and disappeared within the house.

"From the South," Larry murmured.

"I'm sure of that," Polly affirmed. "She is queer. Well, I don't blame any scientist's wife for being queer—let alone a vivisectionist's. Imagine cutting open live cats without using even local anæsthetics!"

"What makes you so sure they're using cats?" Larry, shivering slightly, wanted to know.

"Cat vivisectionists," Polly answered, "are the meanest. I think cats suffer more. At least, they yell loudest. Well, she looks like a cat vivisectionist. I may be way off, but I heard dad tell Muller one night at dinner that the biggest obstacle was the nervous system: it puzzled him most. Then they began discussing the reaction time of various animals under various stimuli and they agreed that cat animals reacted more quickly to a pain stimulus than pig animals.

"That meant," Polly went on, "that *somebody* was going to apply hot needles or electric shocks to the ganglia of cats. And I took one good look at Mrs. Gore and simply decided that she was the kind of woman who would love to torture a cat.

"Besides, both our barn cats have mysteriously disappeared. I'm making a case against her out of pure circumstantial evidence, but I saw her kick a neighbor's dog once—without any reason whatever. I knew then that she was a Sadist."

Larry's forehead was wrinkled. His hound's nose scented a story in Mrs. Gore—a true story that would thrill and horrify his readers. He was thinking that *The Daily It* might profitably embark on an anti-vivisection campaign. Vivisection had been let alone for more than a decade. With a villain as sinister as Mrs. Gore featured, the campaign would be a circulation getter.

Polly was pouring coffee into his emptied cup. Once again she demonstrated her shrewdness as a mind reader.

"We always tell newspaper men who drop in for stories, Mr. Galloway, that we hope they won't betray our confidence by publishing things that would get us into trouble. I hope you're not thinking of attacking Mrs. Gore." Larry chuckled.

"Where did she get that diamond?"

"I haven't dared ask."

"It's worth a fortune," said Larry. "Scientists' wives don't sport stones like that one."

Polly shrugged. "I don't know anything about her. I only see her when she comes up from the birch lab at about this time every morning for her 'rations,' as she calls 'em. She fills up the basket and goes away. If I'm working in the kitchen when she comes in, she takes what she wants out of the icebox and pantry and goes away again. If I say anything, she just grunts. If I ask a question, she pretends she's deaf. She's about as sociable as a porcupine. At that, she's no queerer than some of the other scientists' wives I've met."

It occurred to Larry's cynical mind that the simple explanation of the mystery was that the vivisectionist and Mrs. Gore were not man and wife. The birch lab was, in the frank, easy speech of the tabloids, a love nest. But Polly was prepared with a simpler.

"Some of them are so jealous—so afraid some one else may steal their ideas—that they slink around like burglars. She and her husband have probably worked out a terribly important link in dad's process of restoring the dead to life.

"I know that there have been mysterious goings-on and that she and Jason have had some terrific quarrels. He simply loathes her. It may be because of the Gores that Jason has to commercialize dad's discovery. The Gores may be holding out for a fat royalty.

"But one guess is as good as another. I've seen scientists almost ready to murder each other when an experiment is just on the verge of success. You have no idea what a nervous strain they're under—working twenty, thirty, forty hours at a stretch—and having things go wrong just at the last moment."

The screen door squeaked and Mrs. Gore came out and down the steps with the basket, now heavy, over her arm. She came striding down the path with her cold, gray eyes on Larry, seeming to challenge him.

Her eyes took on more and more of a squint as she neared him. Cold fires, it seemed to him, blazed in those brown slits. His muscles stiffened as repugnance went through him like an electrical wave. Her stare was positively malevolent.

Without a word she strode past, and once again the diamond flashed. The diamond puzzled him, irritated him, worried him. It simply didn't go with the rest of her; with her sunbonnet, her gray calico dress, her cheap, ill-fitting, scuffed shoes.

The enigma vanished into a thicket on the valley's slope. He pictured her hurrying back to the disreputable business of torturing cats; strapping them into their troughs; making slow, brutal incisions while the helpless cats screamed.

He jumped as a bell shrieked in the kitchen. Polly leaped up and went in. He heard her voice in brisk monosyllables. She returned presently, so pale that he was alarmed. Her eyes, their size emphasized by her pallor, were black with excitement.

"They want us to come down," she said. "Dad's ready for you. He was terribly excited. Please don't let him see how skeptical you are, Mr. Galloway."

7

RENASCENCE!

LAWRENCE GALLOWAY WAS surprised at his nervousness. He was in the act of lighting a cigarette when Polly came down the kitchen steps. His hand began to shake so that he could hardly hold the flame to the end of the cigarette. But he managed to control his voice:

"I'll try to conceal my skepticism."

"It requires the most delicate manipulation," she told him, her own voice thin and fluttering. "Dad really needs every bit of sympathy and encouragement we can give him. You can't realize what he's been through, Mr. Galloway. Yesterday's success with that guinea pig may have been pure accident. You heard Jason say last night that they have solved the last unknown, but I've heard that before.

"Scientists try harder than people in any other profession not to be overconfident. But you can hardly blame them now for letting their enthusiasm run away with them. They think every last detail is solved. I know that dad has checked the formula and the electrical factors backward and forward until he is absolutely confident he's working with all known quantities.

"He's absolutely sure of the purity of his materials, and he's just as sure of his reactions. They came out all right

with the guinea pig. I hope they'll come out all right with
your dog. But if they don't, you mustn't jeer."

"I'm prepared," the cynical young man assured her, "to
be the soul of sympathy and encouragement."

They were walking rapidly down the hill toward the big
red barn. Polly Morgan glanced at him furtively.

"I think you'd be skeptical of an earthquake until a building fell right down on top of you," she said. "I wish you
could see it our way—as something really experimental.
All you can see is tricks. If they can bring that dog of yours
back to life, it means that the greatest advance has been
made in science in the world's history. The work of Pasteur
and Curie and Lister and all the rest becomes utterly insig-
nificant in comparison. If the experiment fails, will you
promise not to laugh—or make sarcastic comments?"

"I'll promise that." Larry agreed, "but I can't promise
not to be skeptical to the bitter end. I mean, Polly—my
dog died two years ago. To ask me to believe that a mess
of chemicals and a shot or two of electricity will bring him
back— But I'll promise to be good."

"What was your dog's name?"

"Paddy."

"I'm going to watch you like a hawk," she warned him.

Jason Ortola unlocked and opened the heavy oak door of the converted barn. He was in shirt sleeves. His sunken black eyes were aflame and his face was bloodless. A smudge of black extended along one side of his nose and his hands were white with some powder.

The oak door gave upon a small room where coats hung and brooms and mops stood.

"Everything is ready," said the chemist in his dissonant voice.

He led them into a large whitewashed room in the north wall of which a studio window containing hundreds of square panes had been set. Stained benches ran along the walls and across the center of the room. All manner of chemical paraphernalia was littered along these without any apparent scheme or method, and in one corner loomed a high-voltage cabinet. It was hissing when Larry followed Polly and Ortola into the laboratory, and its hiss reminded him of a snake.

His nerves were on edge. His heart, in spite of his skepticism, was riding high in his chest and beating rapidly.

Professor Morgan and his assistant, Muller, were busily at work over a low bench which seemed, at first glance, to be the focal point of every piece of apparatus in the room. A cylinder padded with gypsum or some white caked substance lay upon the bench; it was perhaps three feet in diameter and ten feet in length.

Glass and rubber tubes ran down into it from copper and glass and silver retorts. Wires from the cabinet terminated in two plates which were lying on the floor, evidently not yet in their places. One of the terminals was of some red metal, the other of some white metal.

The air was sharp with acid fumes.

Professor Morgan, Larry saw, was adjusting wires to still another piece of apparatus—the largest vacuum tube he had ever seen. It was shaped after the conventional pattern of the X-Ray tube, but the bulge in the glass, or quartz, was at least fourteen inches in diameter and the whole tube was easily a yard long.

The famous biologist glanced up as Larry came forward. He smiled nervously. Like the others, he was pale and obviously excited.

"We're just ready to close up the cylinder," he said to Larry. "We want you to see what goes into it, so there won't be any question in your mind when a live dog comes out of it—if a live dog comes out of it. I suppose the process has been roughly explained to you."

"Not yet," said Larry, in a voice that sounded to him high and squeaky. "Rather," he corrected himself, "I've simply been told that chemistry and electricity are combined in some way."

Professor Morgan smiled at him.

"You will have to be kept in the dark, I'm afraid. Even if you understood chemistry, you would have a difficult time following me. I am working with at least five reactions that have never before been attempted in any laboratory. The process of synthesizing life from a vast assortment of chemicals would baffle the mind of any but the most modern of organic chemists.

"But I think I can satisfy your curiosity on two or three of the main points. This cylinder contains the bones of the subject to be treated, plus certain of the chemicals we employ. Others must be added to this chemical mixture in a nascent state, mostly in a gaseous form from these retorts you see scattered about. The mass in the cylinder is slowly being heated by a high voltage electrical current of such low amperage that it will not destroy life. There is an aperture on this side of the cylinder covered with a quartz lens through which the emanations of this tube penetrate. Just within the aperture, in this gelatinous substance, is the germ of life."

"The germ of life?" Larry repeated, having ceased to follow the explanation with anything but his emotions.

Professor Morgan laughed excitedly. "You don't suppose, do you, young man, that I would try to tell you that I or any other man could produce living matter from inorganic materials? I am not, thank you, a believer in the spontaneous germination theory.

"Life cannot arise where life is not, can it? In nature, we begin with the egg, and we end with the chicken or the man or the walrus. In this experiment we begin with a nucleus simply of life. I happen to be using an infusoria that is particularly immune to the high voltage current we must employ."

Jason Ortola coughed sharply. Professor Morgan chuckled.

"That is supposed to be one of our most vital secrets— the nucleus we use. But now that the cat is out of the bag, I might as well tell you the rest. We have tried hundreds of different kinds of nuclei, but yesterday—yesterday we hit upon this particular infusoria which has a high resistance to high electrical voltages.

"I will say briefly, Mr. Galloway, that from this spark of life the living organism will—or ought to—grow. Yesterday it worked with the guinea pig. To-day we hope to see it result in a dog—your dog. Next time, if to-day's results are fully satisfactory, we will attempt to recreate a man.

"If you will sit down over there, Mr. Galloway, you will be out of our way—and safe. There is only one point in the entire chain of reactions which will go forward when there is the slightest danger of—well, an explosion. But it lasts only a few seconds, and you won't know when it's taking place, anyway. Very well, Muller, you can light the burners in the A group."

Larry seated himself on a bench, and Polly Morgan dropped down beside him.

"You can smoke if you want to," she said.

Larry lighted a cigarette with hands that shook. His skepticism was forgotten in a rising excitement. Professor Morgan's nervousness was contagious. Larry could not remember when he had seen a man so excited, so eager.

Muller was striking matches and applying the flames to Bunsen burners which flared up blue and hot under bellying retorts of copper and glass and silver.

Ortola was at the cabinet, turning levers and watching dials, and the hissing changed to a deep and soul-disturbing hum, then to a menacing rumble until the laboratory floor commenced faintly to vibrate.

Larry addressed his attention to Professor Morgan; saw the last of the bones of Paddy lost in a grayish-blue powder; saw the cylinder closed and its halves bolted tight along the top seam; saw the huge vacuum tube swung into place beside the aperture.

"Does it all mean anything to you?" Polly asked.

"Not a thing," he answered.

"An electric power house doesn't, either, does it?" she exclaimed with a return of her old antagonism. "Yet you'll admit that a queer, invisible fluid without weight comes streaming out of it. I'm confident that some ancestor of yours stood on the bank of the Hudson River and hissed when Robert Fulton went by in the Claremont."

Larry, watching, said nothing. He was too busy receiving impressions to think.

Professor Morgan shouted: "All ready, Jason! All ready, Muller. Watch your time! We'll start at fifteen after."

Larry glanced at the electrical clock on the western wall. The hands pointed to ten fourteen. He watched the minute hand creep to fifteen after ten. The three men at once became tremendously busy, yet nothing, so far as he could see, happened.

Through the reverberations of the electrical machine in the corner he could hear the animated bubbling of retorts. Ortola was manipulating levers and watching the dials on the cabinet. Muller was limping about, turning valves here and there. Professor Morgan was spinning a steel wheel which evidently did something to the tube. But nothing spectacular happened.

Then one of the retorts, a great glass one, began to glow pinkly. This pinkness became a luminous effusion; it seemed to creep out and stain the atmosphere for yards around.

"Keep your eyes off the Z-ray tube," Polly Morgan warned the nervous young man, "or you'll have a splitting headache. If you caught the beam properly a foot away, you'd be paralyzed for life."

Vapors, all unpleasant to smell, began to creep about the room. They began to fill it with a fine, dry mist, pale-blue in color. The retort glowed a brighter pink, and Larry saw that the minute hand had slipped down to twenty-one.

The mist tickled his throat and burned his eyes. He darted a glance at Polly. Her eyes were swimming. She was holding a handkerchief to her nose.

The blue fog grew thicker. Professor Morgan and his helpers became gnomes laboring in a fantastic artificial atmosphere. In this vaporous, reverberating room a mystical presence was somehow felt.

Suddenly, on the lid of the cabinet, a white, fat spark leaped into being with savage snappings. The final stage of the procedure had evidently been reached. Through the pale-blue fog Larry saw the three men standing tense, all facing the cylinder. He became aware that Polly Morgan was clutching his arm and that his mouth was bitter with pulverized cigarette tobacco.

Ortola turned to the switchboard on the cabinet. Copper blades hissingly flamed orange and green. The rumbling abruptly ceased. Muller was limping about grotesquely, shutting off Bunsen burners.

The clock pointed to ten twenty-seven. "Twelve minutes!" said a voice in Larry's brain.

The blue vapor was strangling him. He was seized with a fit of coughing. When he could catch his breath, Professor Morgan was pulling with all his might at one end of the cylinder.

Larry sprang up. Through the faint bubbling of the cooling retorts, he heard a muffled scratching, followed by a whine. An almost uncontrollable impulse to laugh was accompanied by a definite lifting of the hairs on his nape: it was impossible for him to suppress his trembling.

With a loud clank the end of the cylinder fell to the floor. A furry thing came scrambling out.

A dog sneezed.

Larry heard a man laughing hysterically: himself.

He choked out: "Paddy!"

A dog with tough, curly hair was leaping up on him, licking his face, yelping excitedly. Against all intelligent reasoning, tears filled the young man's eyes and reduced the frantic dog to a brown blur.

Professor Morgan said, in his familiar, businesslike voice: "You'd better take the young man up to the house, Polly, and give him a stiff drink. As soon as we've cleaned up we'll follow you. That went off very nicely, Jason."

8

"SO MUCH DYNAMITE"

THE SKEPTICAL MANAGING editor of *The Daily It* found himself outside the barn, moving insecurely up the path toward the house with Polly Morgan beside him, her hand under his arm, her aspect that of a wise young woman who was prepared to act efficiently in case he fainted. The Airedale bounded along ahead of them, stopping to roll in the dirt, to push his muzzle through the grass, to come leaping back to his master in ecstasy.

Larry watched him with dazed wonder.

"You poor, poor thing," crooned the girl. "What a blow it must be!"

"You'll have to excuse me for acting like this," Larry said huskily. "I could sit down on that log and cry!"

"It might make you feel better."

"It—it's too much to grasp," he stammered. "That's my dog! It is! It's Paddy! Didn't I see him die two years ago? Didn't I bury him with my own hands?"

"You'll grow used to it, Mr. Galloway," she comforted him. "Imagine what it will be like when we take a living man out of that machine—a man who's been dead perhaps hundreds of years!"

"It's too much to grasp," he repeated. "Paddy! Come here!"

The Airedale came bounding to him, its golden eyes bright with alertness and affection. Larry seized the dog by the ears and stared into its face.

"Paddy!" he said softly.

A nervous whine came from the dog; the stump tail was wagging violently. With a bark, Paddy leaped up on him. A wet, warm tongue blinded the young man's left eye.

"Down, Paddy! Heel!"

The Airedale instantly quieted. With dignity it trotted to the rear.

"Two years since I told him to heel!" Larry marveled. "Polly, where has he been? Where has he come from? What's he been doing since I saw him last?" he excitedly demanded. "I mean, after all, does this mean a dog—a man—a living thing doesn't die? Does he keep on living? It's so damned bewildering! If they'd simply brought a dog to life—a dog that was a perfectly normal dog—it would be wonderful enough. But this is *my* dog. This is *Paddy!*"

Polly Morgan looked up at him with warm sympathy. "Mr. Galloway, don't you think you'd better lie down awhile? You missed your night's sleep and this has been quite an ordeal."

"Sleep!" he exclaimed. "As if I could sleep! Paddy, come here and let me look at you!"

Paddy, whining low in his throat as he had always done when Larry talked to him, gazed up at him expectantly.

"Charge!" snapped his master.

Paddy sank down, but did not remove his glowing,

golden eyes from Larry's face. Larry picked up a stick. He tossed it into the air.

"Catch it, Paddy!"

The dog leaped up and caught the stick neatly.

"It's a rat, Paddy!"

Paddy at once fell to growling. He growled ferociously and shook the stick.

"Drop it, Paddy!"

The Airedale dropped the stick.

"Heel, Paddy!"

Paddy again dropped back sedately to the rear.

"This story," announced Larry, "is going to set the world on fire. It's a bigger story than Lindbergh. It's a bigger story, Polly, than the World War!"

"And you were so skeptical, so suspicious!"

"I'm not skeptical any longer, Polly. I'll have a talk with your father, then I'll phone the office and, believe me, the fur is going to fly! But there's one thing I want to do soon. I want to take Paddy to the cabin—and watch him. I want to see how he'll act when he sees that cabin again. I used to keep him in town, in my apartment, and when we went up to the cabin you should have seen him. He almost went crazy."

"I'll drive you to the cabin after lunch," said Polly. "I think we both should take a nap first."

"You've done enough," Larry protested. "I'll rent a car in the village."

"No," she firmly denied him. "I'm going to drive you up. I'm as curious to see what he'll do when he sees the cabin as you are. I don't blame you for wanting to cry. I want to cry myself. You two must have been wonderful friends."

"Weren't we! Why, Polly! No one needs to be afraid of death any more! There won't be such a thing as death. When a man dies, his funeral will be nothing, but a trip to a laboratory! How old will he be? How old is this dog? Paddy!"

They had seated themselves on the kitchen steps and Paddy, with forepaws extended, lay in the gravel path, panting, tongue lolling. He sprang up and walked to Larry. Larry lifted his upper lip and laughed excitedly.

"Look here, Polly! He's got all his teeth! He can't be more than six years old. Somewhere along the way he's lost half his age."

He gazed dreamily down the slope toward the big red barn. The impact of the biggest news story in the history of journalism had dazed him; but now his editorial mind was beginning to function. The thing would have to be handled carefully; would have to be sprung just so.

Three figures were coming up the path from the barn, Ortola, Muller, and Professor Morgan. They were deep in a discussion and they advanced slowly. The chemist, with hands thrust into coat pockets, was sucking at a fresh cigar; the osteologist, limping along, was brandishing his fists; the great biologist was nodding slowly and smiling his childlike smile.

Larry pictured him a few weeks hence, riding through the streets of New York, Washington, Chicago; this handsome, white-haired man tumultuously acclaimed as the savior, the rejuvenator, of humanity!

A pucker appeared between the glistening eyes of the managing editor of *The Daily It*. His trained mind saw trouble also. It would not all be clear sailing.

"It would take my Newark plant three weeks to produce the materials," Ortola was saying as they came up. "Professor Morgan can't wait to try his luck with a man," he explained to Larry and Polly. "But I argue that we should proceed now with the utmost caution. Mr. Galloway, will you tell us candidly if you honestly think we have answered all your doubts?"

Larry, looking up at him, nodded.

"I won't apologize for my skeptical attitude," he answered, "because I honestly believe it was justified. You came to me with a story that was absolutely incredible— the most incredible story, I'm sure, a man ever listened to. You've proved your point. You've raised a thousand questions, but I'll pass them over for the time being."

"I suppose," said Professor Morgan, "you want to get this story into print without any delay."

But Larry shook his head. "I think we should proceed with the greatest caution, Professor Morgan. This story is so much dynamite. It must be handled carefully. The greatest danger now is going off half-cocked. There is no chance of this story leaking out, is there? Who knows about it aside from us?"

"No one," Ortola answered.

"How about the cat vivisectionists?" Polly asked.

Jason Ortola gazed at her blankly.

"The Gores," she added.

"They are perfectly safe," said Professor Morgan. "The story cannot leak out unless one of us talks. I think it is quite safe."

Muller was on his hands and knees examining Paddy. He was poking a long, exploratory forefinger here and there into the Airedale's anatomy, and Paddy was growling resentfully. He examined the dog's teeth.

"This dog," he burst out, excitedly, "has a biological age of less than five years, professor. You were right."

Professor Morgan smiled boyishly. "The most satisfying feature of our success," he said, "has been the way in which it has worked out according to every one of my pet contentions. My contention has been all along that any subject *must* come alive at the period of perfect maturity. The last doubt in my mind has been answered. I will undertake without the slightest hesitancy to bring back to life any man who ever lived. If you, Jason, will only provide me with the materials!"

"I am in favor," was the chemist's rather irritable reply, "of settling, before anything else is done, the questions in Mr. Galloway's mind. I don't think we can overestimate the importance of the public reaction to our announcement. It seems to me our next step should be guided by him. How is the public going to react? I would suggest that we go into the house and thresh it all out. I can put in a call for my Newark plant while we talk."

"And I'll be mixing grain alcohol highballs for four highly self-satisfied men," said Polly.

9

MOB PSYCHOLOGY

A LITTLE SQUARE mahogany clock with a sunset painted on its face busily ticked on a shelf in the kitchen as the four men passed through, and Larry was aware that it was measuring off perhaps the richest hour of his life. As he beheld it, there was nothing fortuitous in his hour of triumph, and he readily forgave himself the pride which glowed in his eyes and caused his lips to form a nervously eager smile.

How tirelessly he had worked for this unexpected reward! In the face of the most powerful, most insidious opposition within and without, he had made *The Daily It* an anomaly among tabloid newspapers—a tabloid founded upon honesty. Unfalteringly, he had borne, amid ridicule and menace, the standard of truth. Was his presence here fortuitous?

Had not his principles been vindicated by the very invitation which made him a cornerstone of this conference? Let those who wished jeer at his skepticism! Let those who would laugh at his suspicious nature! He had been selected from the entire field of journalism to sit on the right hand of J. Hendricks Morgan!

His vanity crowed: "I have been appointed, because of

my merits, to tell the unprepared world that death has ceased to be! I am passing along to humanity the boon of life everlasting!"

His dislike of Jason Ortola, he found, had vanished. The man was merely the possessor of an unfortunate personality.

The chemist, a telephone in his hands, was calling a Newark number. He replaced the receiver and set the instrument on the table before him.

"Don't you think," he said, "that the entire public will believe at first that we are perpetrating a hoax?"

"I do," Larry answered. "We can expect that, no matter how the story is handled. I am in favor of feeding the facts to them slowly. I naturally want to handle it in such a way that *The Daily It* will get the utmost benefit. I'd like to have the best people on my staff come up here, bring their typewriters and do the story under my direction.

"Then I'd like to release it piecemeal. I'd start with the guinea pig story. Next day I'd run a story on Paddy. I'd say nothing until the third day about the possibilities of bringing a man to life. While these stories are running, it would please me very much if all of you hid somewhere."

Larry grinned. "That's selfish, but if I can keep the story exclusive for the first three or four days, I'll have a running start on all the rest of them."

Professor Morgan looked mystified. Muller was staring at his stained hands.

"You may handle it any way you wish," was Jason Ortola's decision. "We want you to be our spokesman. Professor Morgan and Mr. Muller can't be hounded by reporters. They will need all their time and energy to prepare for the next experiment. I'd prefer to have all newspaper men sent to you."

Larry's grin broadened. "The newspaper men will hate that, but it suits me perfectly. I will have a photographer make dozens of pictures. I'll phone my office as soon as I've been to my cabin. I'm not doubtful now, but I want to watch this dog when he sees that cabin. It will, of course, be an important part of the story—how he reacts to that cabin in which he died two years ago."

"I speak for all of us," Ortola replied, "when I say that, for a reasonable time, we are absolutely at your command. If you want us to hide, we will hide. If you simply want us to keep our mouths shut, we will do that. Now I want to bring up the subject we discussed during the drive down from your cabin. You recall it, don't you?"

Larry nodded.

"Go ahead and talk about it."

Jason Ortola lighted another cigar.

"The public, as I see the thing, must be told fairly soon that Professor Morgan cannot be expected to make the customary beautiful gesture. We are too deeply involved. Some of the heavily endowed institutions would gladly take the whole thing out of our hands and supply all the funds necessary—for the glory that would go to them. But we are three selfish men."

Professor Morgan moved about uncomfortably in his chair.

"I don't like this phase of it at all," he said, brusquely. "I'm not worrying about the credit going where it belongs, and I'm not worrying about the financial end of it."

"I am," Ortola irritably took him up, "because, I *am* the

financial end of it. You must remember that I have put upward of two millions of my own money into these experiments. My only reward so far has been a thirty-thousand-dollar guinea pig that would bring fifty cents in the open market and a hundred-thousand-dollar dog that promptly is acquired by his old master."

"That was your ballyhoo," Larry put in amiably.

But the chemist did not smile. "My ballyhoo also involves seven hundred thousand dollars' worth of materials to create a man out of."

"You're forgetting another important item," said Larry. "Protection."

"Protection?"

"Part of the public, when the public really grasps that we are telling the truth, is going to want all of you lynched."

Muller gasped: "For bringing them the greatest blessing ever given to mankind?"

"Some of them won't look at it that way," Larry explained. "I don't know how you are planning to protect yourselves and the laboratory, but I do know the public well enough to warn you that you can expect trouble. You are trespassing on sacred territory. When a topic in any way religious pops up in the day's news, letters from religious cranks come into the office by the bag. A religious editorial will almost start a riot."

"I can't see the religious angle on this," growled Ortola.

"Religious fanatics," Larry told him, "will accuse you of monkeying with God's job. The Bible promises a day when the dead will rise again, and the fanatics will want God to attend to it personally. Scientists have always been accused of monkeying with God's job, anyway. You know what has happened to scientists who announced startling discoveries—since there have been scientists. Some have been burned at the stake, others have been stoned to death, and a few have merely been thrown into dungeons."

"It won't happen in this enlightened age," the chemist objected.

"You will find," Larry answered, "that you are dealing with the same human race that locked Gallileo into a cell for declaring that the earth is round."

"The human race," Professor Morgan concurred, "has not changed fundamentally since the days when it lived in treetops."

"I wouldn't let a line of this be published," Larry went on, "until the laboratory is protected by a riot-proof fence and an armed guard. The mass of intelligent people will hail Professor Morgan's discovery as the greatest scientific triumph in the world's history, but—how about the moron mob? Don't forget there are entire States in this country where evolution is looked on as a heretic theory."

"And all references to it expurgated from textbooks," put in Mr. Muller, sourly.

"You will also," Larry continued, "be dealing with a large mass of mentally twisted people who have recently been bereaved. You will be stormed by widows and widowers and orphans wanting their loved ones restored to life—who will be just as apt as not to kill you if you don't listen to them."

The ringing of the telephone bell interrupted him. Jason Ortola picked up the receiver. His eyes narrowed.

"Mr. Ortola is talking," he said harshly. "Connect me with Mr. Schlemmer." A pause. "Mr. Schlemmer? Mr.

Ortola. I am talking from Brookhaven. I want you to begin preparing at once one hundred pounds of Formula Eight Seven Six Four, one hundred pounds of Formula Eight Seven Seven Nine, and twenty-five-pound lots of Formulas Nine Four Three Three, Nine Five Four One, Nine Seven Two Eight, and Nine Six Two Three. Repeat that back to me."

A longer pause. Then: "Very well. I will see you later in the week."

He hung up the receiver and turned again to the three men with an ugly smile.

"That was pretty nearly a million-dollar order," he stated. "Very well, Mr. Galloway. You were saying—"

"I had practically finished," said Larry. "I simply want you to realize what a bombshell this is we are dropping on an unsuspecting world. The reaction will be terrific. We can have no idea how far it will go because the problem boils down to one of mob psychology and mobs are unpredictable. It does seem to me, though, that we are going to have difficulties enough without telling the public that a sort of corporation has grabbed off the discovery and plans to recreate life at a profit."

"If they are not told at first," said Ortola, "we won't dare tell them later. As I said before, they will leap at once to the conclusion that we have perfected a great complicated machine that manufactures a live man out of bones and chemicals and works when you drop a half dollar in a slot. The public consists chiefly of idiots and must be educated to what our purpose really is."

"All I can promise," Larry murmured, "is that I'll think it over and let you know later what course I think is best."

Polly Morgan entered the library with a tray sustaining four highball glasses filled with an amber liquid and ice.

She asked cheerily as she presented the first glass to her father:

"Is everything settled?"

"As clearly as I can see it," Professor Morgan wearily answered her, "we are entering upon an era of horrible confusion. Religious fanatics will destroy our peace and trample down every growing thing on the farm. Hoodlums will shy bricks at us. Morons and maniacs will come out with shotguns and declare an open season on scientists. I am thinking of pitching a tent on Pike's Peak."

Polly turned bright questioning eyes on Larry.

"What are your plans, Mr. Galloway?"

"He is our mouthpiece," said her father. "From now on, this young man has us at his mercy, representing as he does the teeth and the claws of public opinion. But I must say that I admire his cautious attitude. Most newspaper men are heartless."

"I think preparations should be made at once," said Larry, "for the farm to be patrolled by uniformed detectives. There are agencies which rent them out by the dozen. And I'd certainly have the laboratory surrounded by a concrete or steel fence as soon as you can have one erected."

"I will attend to all that immediately," said Ortola.

"I'd like to drive up to the cabin and be back in time for a night's sleep," Larry went on. "Before starting, I'll get in touch with the office and have the livest wires on my staff up here by to-morrow noon. I think I'll call in Benjamin Sturm, too. He is apt to go off on wild tangents, but he is, after all, the owner of the paper, and he'd be terribly hurt if he weren't called in."

"I'll drive you up as soon as we've had lunch," said Polly. "You men might as well know the worst. It's going to be sandwiches and coffee."

"I'd prefer hiring a car in Brookhaven," Larry protested. "You've been on the go for two days."

"Polly has the constitution of a three-year-old colt," said Professor Morgan.

"It would be wiser," Ortola supported him, "to have Polly drive you up, Galloway. A taxi driver might see more than he was meant to. You can't be too careful."

Larry laughed. "I think secrecy has become an obsession with all of you."

Muller said sourly: "You aren't complaining, are you? If we hadn't made secrecy an obsession, these fields would be black with reporters. I think you've been handed something on a silver platter."

"You mustn't pay any attention to Muller when he's disagreeable," chuckled Professor Morgan. "He has these moods after every experiment. The only time he is really happy is when everything goes wrong."

"Then it's settled," said Polly. "I'm going to drive Mr. Galloway up. I'm simply dying to watch this dog when he sees the cabin."

Professor Morgan lifted his glass.

"Gentlemen, I am going to propose a toast. We will not drink to the happy success which has crowned our labors, because it would be insulting to drink to such an achievement with grain alcohol."

Larry was prepared to see the biologist's boyish grin;

but Professor Morgan was not smiling. Far from smiling, his lips were protruding in hard, squarish little wads, and his eyes, behind the gold-rimmed spectacles, were aglitter.

"God save our livers!" croaked Mr. Muller.

"To the early downfall of prohibition!" cried Professor Morgan, and his voice was startling, so harsh, so bitter it was.

Larry shot a glance of alarmed inquiry at Polly Morgan. Her eyes were downcast. She looked pale and scared.

Jason Ortola met Larry's eyes over the rim of his glass and ponderously winked.

10

THE ETERNAL GALAHAD

HIS POSITION AS final arbiter of all the news stories, features, photographs, editorials and cartoons published in *The Daily It* gave Lawrence Galloway considerable power, but in this power there was little of the stuff which inflates a man's soul. It evinced itself only in the daily neat statements from the circulation department.

For four years he had wielded his power against vice, against greedy transit corporations, against evil-smelling politicians, but in these cases the results were hard to gauge. Once, however, with the resources at his command, he had made an unknown girl famous.

She had been called to Larry's attention by his dramatic critic. She was an actress, playing an obscure part in an obscure play. There, the dramatic critic had declared with gentle indignation, was the bright flower of genius. Larry dropped in to see the play. And his opinion of Bernice Sartwell's talents confirmed that of the dramatic critic.

He promptly put the machinery of *The Daily It* to work upon her destiny. Photographers imprisoned her most telling poses in gelatin. Interviewers and feature writers spent hours with her. *The Daily It* lifted its honest voice, caroled her genius, and was respectfully attended.

Bernice Sartwell, testifying to the magic and the majesty of printer's ink, was at present fulfilling a long-term motion picture contract at two thousand dollars a week and occupying a Moorish castle in Beverly Hills.

It is hardly necessary to add that the managing editor of *The Daily It* was besieged by hosts of theatrical Cinderellas who claimed to be every whit as deserving as Bernice Sartwell, and for weeks his mail was charged with scented note paper and autographed photographs taken through chiffon. But to these wholesale pleas Lawrence Galloway maintained the frozen unresponsiveness of the sphinx, and he never wielded his power in quite that way again. Worthy widows and orphans he would always unsheathe his sword for, yes—but no more actresses.

Now, however, he was preparing to concentrate his power on another beautiful unknown, but with the very opposite results in mind. Polly Morgan must not fall into the hands of the yellow press; must not receive sensational publicity—or any other kind of publicity. She must learn life—but she must remain unspoiled.

He sat, comfortably relaxed in his corner, with Paddy's head between his knees, as the coupé hummed along between fields aglow with goldenrod in the amiable afternoon sun, up and down hills darkly green with pines and over little bridges which spanned little brooks.

In his preoccupation he frowned and steadily gazed at Polly Morgan's profile. At long intervals she darted a glance at him.

She was the kind of driver who kept her eyes constantly on the road.

"Are you angry about something?" she finally asked him.

"I was wondering," he answered, "why Muller was so peevish."

"You mustn't mind him, Mr. Galloway. He growls at everybody. It's just his nature."

"Does he growl at you?"

"N-o-o-o."

"He's in love with you, isn't he?"

"What makes you say that?"

"He was sore because you wanted to drive up to the cabin with me. He was jealous."

Polly withdrew her eyes from the road and gazed at him wonderingly.

"You're awfully sophisticated, aren't you?"

"I have to be."

"Yes, he's in love with me."

"Wants to marry you?"

She nodded.

"And Ortola wants to marry you?"

"Yes, Mr. Galloway."

"Anybody else?"

She laughed softly. "You're so funny. Yes, there are a few others."

"Please be specific," he said sternly.

"Well, there's Professor Hornbrook, for one. And Dr. Corcoran, for another."

"How old are they?"

"Professor Hornbrook is fifty-two, and Dr. Corcoran is about forty-nine."

"And Mr. Muller is about forty-three?"

"Yes—about."

"So that the ages of the men who want to marry you vary from thirty-nine to fifty-two?"

"I—I sometimes wish I could marry them all," Polly exclaimed. "They're so pathetic and helpless. They all are!"

"You mean all scientists, or all men?"

"You certainly aren't pathetic!" Polly cried. "Or helpless. You're the most self-contained, self-sufficient man I ever knew. I can't imagine a woman ever helping you—at anything."

"I've had to make myself self-contained and self-sufficient," the young man informed her. "It's been a case of sink or swim with me all my life. I'm swimming because I've never leaned on anybody."

"I suppose that's why you're so skeptical and suspicious," Polly reflected. "You just have to be, don't you?"

"I do," he affirmed. "What is your father's attitude toward all these elderly scientists who—are so pathetic and helpless?"

"You're not joking, are you?" she said anxiously.

"Indeed not!"

"Well, dad really doesn't seem to care. He thinks I can handle the situation without any help."

"You mean, he'd consent to your marrying any of these men?"

"I'm sure he wouldn't mind."

"He doesn't realize the danger you are in."

"I suppose not," said Polly.

Larry groaned. Paddy whined sympathetically, as if anxious to help. And Polly's glance was troubled.

"You don't understand how serious it is," Larry exclaimed. "You can't understand, because you've never had the chance to make comparisons. Nothing but old men around you all your life! Pawing you!"

"It hasn't been so bad."

"The time is coming," said Larry, "when you will look back upon this period of your life with amazement. You realize, of course, that you can't stay there any longer."

The coupé was just about to cross a little bridge. When it was across she looked at him.

"Must I go away?"

"For more reasons than one," he soberly answered. "That household is not the place for you. And in another week it will be positively unsafe for you. You're too pretty, too alluring, too innocent."

A sharp explosion close aboard interrupted him. Paddy barked. A measured rumbling shook the coupé. Polly pulled up beside the road and stopped. Larry climbed down and investigated. The left rear tire was flat. The spare tire looked none too trustworthy.

"You'll find the jack under the rumble seat," Polly advised him. "Can I help?"

"You can tell me what to do," said Larry. "I'm not much of a hand at this sort of thing. I hope this spare will hold up."

"Why," she asked as she alighted, "will the farm be unsafe for me?"

"Because," he answered, on hands and knees, "it will be swarming with detectives in a few days. They won't be the polite kind you read about either. They're strikebreakers, roughnecks."

"But who'll cook the meals and run the house?"

"Some one will have to be hired," Larry answered. "In a few days the farm will be practically in a state of siege."

"What are your plans for me?"

Larry, with one hand on the handle of the jack which he had pushed under the rear axle, looked thoughtfully up at her.

"Wouldn't you like to go around with men and girls your own age for a change?"

"Of course! I'd adore it!"

"That's what I'd like to have you do, Polly. You're missing things. You are too pretty, too young to be missing things."

Polly was unscrewing the rim nuts.

"But where would I go?"

"Haven't you any relatives or friends in some large city?"

"I know lots of professors."

"Professors," he said, "are out. The scientific atmosphere is what you must get away from."

"I wouldn't consider going anywhere but New York," Polly said gravely. "It scares me to think of going away anywhere, but if I went to New York you'd be there and you could—well, advise me."

"I'd be delighted to," said Larry. "Do you know anybody in New York?"

"I have an aunt in New York," Polly answered, "but she and dad haven't been on speaking terms for years. I wouldn't dream of visiting her unless she invited me. And I wouldn't dream of writing to her suggesting it. So what can I do?"

Larry lifted off the flat tire, hung it on the rack in the rear, and put the spare one on the wheel.

"What sort of woman is your aunt?"

"I believe Aunt Sally is very active socially. Of course, we've been out of touch with her for years."

"I'll have a talk with her," Larry said, "if you'll tell me who she is."

"Will you really?" Polly squealed.

"Indeed I will!"

"I never knew a man like you," the girl marveled. "You aren't afraid of anything. Her name is Mrs. Horace Glen Islington, but I don't know her address."

"I'll find it," the crusader promised.

11

FLAT!

PADDY'S EARS WERE erect and pointing ahead. His stub of a tail wagged frantically. Now and then he whined— now and then he uttered an excited yelp.

The coupé was almost at the end of the lane that led to Larry's cabin. Pines untouched by the axes or saws of man reared themselves to breathless heights and filled the air with a clean fine scent.

The coupé lurched down into the clearing in which the cabin stood. Slanting rays of sunlight sparkled against the windows. Small waves rippled upon the curve of sandy beach. Behind the craggy headlands which formed an entrance into Black Bay the blue Atlantic glistened.

Polly exclaimed in an aching voice:

"What a gem of a spot it is!"

Paddy, with a frantic yelp, scrambled out of the window and bounded across the clearing with nose to the ground.

The Airedale ran in concentric circles, each one larger than the one before; then he stopped, threw up his head, barked and trotted toward the still muddy excavation between the two pines.

Larry sprang out. Polly followed him. In her excitement she seized his arm.

Paddy was sniffing at the moldy oak box, eagerly wagging his tail.

"What," Polly gasped, "do you suppose he is thinking?" They approached him.

"Paddy," Larry said gravely, "do you realize that you slept in that box for two years? In that hole?"

The Airedale looked up at his master, yelped softly and bounded off toward the cabin. He put his forepaws up on the door and scratched, then dropped down and sniffed at the cracks and whined. He looked back over his shoulder at Larry and barked.

Larry unlocked the door, and the dog dashed in. He circled about the room with nose to floor, sniffing and whining.

Larry stole a glance at Polly's eyes. They were moist. His own eyes were moist.

"Paddy!" he called sharply. "Go to bed!"

Paddy stopped his circling and crawled under the bunk; vanished.

"Come out!" said Larry.

The Airedale strolled out; barked.

"Get your collar!"

The heavy brass-and-leather collar still depended from the hook where it had hung since the night when Paddy had died.

Paddy unhesitatingly leaped into the air—and returned to the floor with the collar in his teeth. Larry buckled it about the dog's neck.

"That's all I wanted to see," he told Polly.

"How about a swim before we start back?" Polly

suggested. "I always carry a suit in the back of the car. Have you one?"

He hesitated. "Yes," he said.

"You can wait outside while I dress in here," said Polly, "then I'll wait outside while you dress. Why can't we have supper here? That kitchen is bulging with food."

"Very well," said Larry.

"We can have a swim and supper and be under way by seven. We'll be back at the farm before midnight."

"Fine," said Larry. He was somewhat pale. He told himself, as Polly went to the coupé for her suit, that he had found this innocently reckless child only in time. Supposing some unprincipled rascal had been her companion in these circumstances! She was utterly unaware of the appeal of her slim young beauty; so touchingly ignorant of life!

This impression deepened when, a few minutes later, she issued from the cabin in a black bathing suit that could have been sent to any part of the United States by parcel post, Larry swore to himself, for about six cents.

Polly Morgan seemed innocently unaware of herself. Later, when he knew her better, he would wonder if girls with superb figures, with slim, straight legs, with boyish hips and beautiful shoulders, were ever as aware of themselves as girls whose figures were not so superb.

"You'd better make it snappy," said the unsophisticated child cheerily. "I'll wait for you on the beach. Come on, Paddy!"

But Paddy preferred to remain with his lord.

It occurred to Larry, as he began to disrobe, that she was as naïve as a Fiji Islander.

She was floating far out when he reached the beach.

"I'll race you to the end of the bay and back!" she challenged.

Larry plunged in, although he hated contests with girls.

Polly Morgan was a dozen lengths in the lead when they reached the inlet. She was fifty yards ahead when they returned to the beach; he, spent; she, breathless but radiant.

"Your stroke is pretty good," she said, gasping a little, "but you should take your arms out of the water nearer your head—not so far back. Like this."

She illustrated it, bending forward and looking up at him, while her hands and arms went through gliding, snakelike motions.

"Who taught you?" Larry panted.

"Professor Whaley, the Australian endocrinologist."

"I suppose he wanted to marry you, too," said Larry somewhat peevishly.

Polly laughed. "No; he was married and very, very much in love. He was a marvelous swimmer. I'll hurry and dress, Mr. Galloway, and I can be starting supper while you're dressing."

"No," Larry disagreed, "you're going to rest while I get supper."

Her brown eyes glowed. "You're the first man I ever knew who could cook. You're hopeless."

"Why?" said Larry.

"I'm so used to having men depend on me. It doesn't seem right having a man do things. There isn't a solitary thing I can do for you. I never felt so useless in my life!"

She went into the house. Larry observed that the sun was down and that the pines were fast turning black.

He wondered why he felt so grouchy. In the kitchen, a

little later, as he turned a sizzling slice of ham in a skillet, sleep descended on his eyes like hot sand. He was aware of a bitter, unaccountable resentment of Polly Morgan.

Then he heard her voice. It was a small, sweet, lonely voice. She was singing. Larry went to the door and looked out.

Against the deep crimson of afterglow she was silhouetted, huddled against the center roofpost of the porch, her head back, her eyes fixed upon the sky, where the evening star hung sparkling with the hot brightness of a spark from a blacksmith's hammer.

With sweet melancholy she sang:

> "Have you ever heard about Willie the Weeper?
> Had a job as a chimney sweeper;
> Had the dope habit and had it bad.
> Listen while I tell yuh 'bout a dream he had."

"Where," Larry sharply interrupted, "did you learn that song?"

As if she had not heard him, she continued to gaze up at blazing Venus and the shocking song went on.

> "Went down to the dope shop one Saturday night.
> He knew the lights would all be burning bright.
> Well, I guess he smoked a dozen pills or more.
> When he woke up he was on a foreign shore.
> "The Queen of Sheba was the first he met;
> She called him lovey-dovey and pony pet.
> She gave him a great big auty-mo-beel
> With a diamond headlight and a golden whee-eel.

"Landed with a splash in the river Nile
Ridin' on a seagoing croc-ee-dile.
He winked at Cleopatra. She says: 'Ain't he a sight!'
He says: 'H'about a date f'next Sat'd'y night?'
"He landed in New York one evening late
Asked his sugar for an after-date.
Started to kiss her, and she started to pout
When bang—*bang!*—and—the—dope—gave—out!"

"There's more of it," said Polly, "but I forget it."

"Who taught you that song?"

"It's on a record that Professor Hornbrook brought me for my victrola," Polly answered. "What's an 'after-date,' Mr. Galloway?"

"A girl like you doesn't know about that kind of thing," he rudely answered.

"I think it's marvelous," said Polly. "It's a swell song. Isn't it a glorious night? Do you know it's after eight o'clock?"

"We'll be on the way by nine," said Larry. "That'll bring us to the farm by about one thirty. And I'm going to drive," he sternly added.

"I won't quarrel," Polly sighed. "Is supper almost ready? That ham smells ambrosial."

She was, he discovered presently, in a playful mood. It seemed to strike her as humorous that Larry, that any man, should know how to cook. Where had he learned and why? Larry's grouch grew. He knew that the strain of the past two days had been enough to overtax any girl, but he had never inured himself to that species of humor popularly known as "kidding."

He wasn't used to being kidded. He was a serious, earnest

young man, and he had earned the right to be taken seriously. He forgot how tired she was and became sulkier at her silliness.

He had expected warm praise for the simple supper he had prepared and his reward was merry quips.

He denied her the privilege of drying the dishes for him. When he turned out the lights and locked up the cabin, she was reclining as before against the roofpost, with face tipped toward the evening star, fast asleep.

Reluctantly he awakened her.

"I ache," she informed him, rising, "in every bone. That swim let me down and your supper has taken all the blood away from my brain to digest."

They walked to the coupé with Paddy lagging behind, as if he, too, were spent from the day's eventfulness.

Larry switched on the lights.

Polly gave a sudden exclamation of dismay.

"Mr. Galloway," she wailed, "that tire is flat!"

"Flat!" he groaned.

"And we haven't a spare!"

12

THIS PERILOUS ATMOSPHERE

LARRY INSPECTED THE treacherous tire and, under his breath, relieved his soul of its accumulated burdens.

Then he sagged down beside Polly on the running board, where she drooped with head in hands.

"What are we going to do?" he demanded. "I don't know anything about automobiles. How do you fix tires when they're flat like this?"

"At least," she sighed, "there's one thing a woman can help you do."

"I don't think this is anything to joke about," he said irritably.

"I don't, either," Polly agreed. "Fixing a punctured tube in a worn-out casing in the dark when you're blind for sleep is no laughing matter."

"Have you the stuff to fix it with?" he eagerly asked.

She did not reply. Her hands had dropped limply at her side. Her head had fallen forward. She had simply gone to sleep in the middle of his question.

He shook her shoulder.

"Polly!"

"Honestly," she breathed, "I'm all in."

He shook her again with greater violence.

"We've got to get out of here, Polly! It'll be daybreak, as it is, before we reach the farm."

"I don't care," said the drowsy girl. "I can't go an inch farther."

"Look here, Polly—"

"Please stop shaking me!"

"Where is the stuff you fix the tires with?"

She arose from the running board, a slim ghost against the stars.

"It's in the car somewhere, Mr. Galloway," she answered, yawning. "Can't I call you something else besides Mr. Galloway?"

Impatiently, he said: "My friends call me Larry. Where did you say the stuff is?"

"I didn't say, Larry. I don't know where it is. It may be under the rumble seat. It may be back of the driver's seat in the little compartment. It may be in either of the side pockets."

"We've got to find it and fix this tire!"

"Honestly, Larry, I'm so sleepy I can hardly hold my eyes open. I'll fix it in the morning."

"In the morning!" he barked.

"Larry, I am not going to fix that tire to-night. It's hard enough finding a puncture and fixing it in the daylight. In the dark, it simply can't be done."

"You certainly: don't intend to stay here all night!" he exclaimed.

Polly withdrew her attention from the evening star and gazed up into his glowering face.

"Why not?" she asked, and there was a little edge in her voice.

"Why not!" he repeated. "Are you joking?"

"Why not?" she reiterated, and there was now a decided edge in her voice. "You'd have stayed all night at my house, wouldn't you?"

"You don't realize what you're saying!" gasped the horrified young man.

"I realize," said the stubborn girl, "that I'm simply dead for sleep and that I haven't had my head on a pillow for forty-eight hours and that I'm too all in to fix that tire to-night and that it would be practically impossible to find that puncture in the dark, anyway. I'm going to spend the night right in this car."

"Your father, I suppose," Larry went on with sarcasm, "will be delighted when we drive in around noon to-morrow and tell him we spent the night here. He'll believe the story about the puncture, won't he?"

Polly's answer was to open the coupé door and climb in. She switched off the lights. Her voice issued rebelliously from the darkness.

"You're not worrying about me. You're worried about yourself. You can rest assured, my dear, I will never tell a soul. Now set your alarm clock for five thirty and let's get some sleep."

Larry liked to think of himself as a fighter, but the fight was all gone out of him.

"I won't let you sleep in there," he said. "You'll use the bunk in the cabin. There's a canvas hammock slung between a couple of trees behind the cabin. I'll bunk there."

Polly debouched from the coupé's murky interior.

"You're the nicest man I ever knew," she said, "when you're not scolding."

Gloomily, Larry reopened the cabin; lighted a lamp for her and departed with blankets and a poncho. The character of his emotions as he approached the canvas hammock was not on the side of enthusiasm; he had slept in that hammock before and no matter how tightly it was stretched between the trees, the ropes would yield and the hammock would sag, making a comfortable sleeping posture impossible.

He discovered when he reached the hammock that he had brought along the wrong poncho. He had contrived an ingenious method of sheltering himself from the weather when he camped out overnight. He first slung the hammock between two trees. A foot or so above the hammock he strung a rope taut. Over this he hung the poncho, tent-fashion, so that the hammock was sheltered from end to end. But a foot or more was missing from the poncho he had brought from the cabin.

It was now too late to repair his mistake, for the cabin was in darkness. Polly Morgan had turned out the light and gone to bed and, while she had no doubt fallen instantly to sleep, he could not bring himself to return for the other poncho. The sky, however, was clear, and he was sure there would be no rain before morning.

Larry was in the blackest vale of unconsciousness when, perhaps an hour before dawn, the first drop fell. He was unaware of this drop and of many subsequent ones. His first awareness, in fact, that rain was descending came with a growing conviction that he lay in a bath of cold water. The short poncho was permitting the ends of the hammock to act as small rainsheds; the accumulating raindrops were running down to form a small pond in which, with chattering teeth, he lay.

Sleep permeated his brain like the fumes of an opiate. Sleep clamored for him, yet he could not sleep. He was wet to the skin.

In soft, earnest tones he voiced his opinion of all the contributing circumstances which had reduced him thus to misery. The world was black and wet. He could distinguish no object near or far. Rain came sifting down from an invisible sky, pattering softly on the poncho and his unprotected head.

Larry swung his feet over the edge of the hammock and planted them heavily on the hard, furry, body of Paddy, who, scornful of all weather, lay sleeping as near his master as he could crawl.

The dog came awake with a yelp.

"Heel!" growled Larry, and made his way through the damp darkness to the coupé. Here the dog and the man adjusted themselves as comfortably as they could to the cramped space and when Larry awoke, the rain had stopped, the sky was pale with rising dawn and a crisp, salty breeze was blowing in from the Atlantic.

Mingled with its saline fragrance was the spicy steam from bubbling coffee. Shivering in his damp clothing, stiff in sundry joints from the cramped position in which he had slept in the coupé, dull-witted from insufficient sleep, the crusader made his way into the kitchen, where he found Polly preparing breakfast.

Sleep-faced, she looked twelve; misty-eyed, flushed and disheveled, she in no wise resembled the hopelessly innocent, vixenish young woman who had provided him with a night of woe and what forthcoming complications?

"If you'll finish getting breakfast," she said in her sweetly husky voice, "I'll start work on that tire. What a glorious day!"

Larry, in sulky silence, took over her task. It seemed to him that all was for the worst in this worst of possible worlds.

An hour later they were once more jouncing along through the muddy ruts with Polly at the wheel.

Larry, silently brooding, sat in his corner and watched the road. And presently Polly said:

"You have only two facial expressions, haven't you? One of cynical knowing and one of cynical disapproval. You've been wearing that one ever since you woke up."

"And well I might," retorted the gloomy young man.

"I suppose editing a tabloid makes you cynical."

"I've been thinking," he said stiffly, "about what your father is going to say."

"Dad won't say a thing. He knows me."

"He must be a mighty queer father."

"All scientists make queer fathers. I simply can't understand why you're so upset over my staying at your cabin."

"No," Larry agreed; "I realize now that you simply couldn't understand. That's what makes it so much worse. Your innocence puts all the guilt on me!"

"Guilt," she cried, "for what?"

The young man said nothing. Polly gave him a glittering sidelong glance. It was evident that he puzzled her quite as much as she worried him.

The farm was deserted when the coupé rolled up, shortly before noon, and stopped beside the big red barn.

Polly honked the horn. After an interval the heavy oak door opened and Professor Morgan stepped out. In the gripping anxiety of a young man who has been the victim of uncontrollable circumstances, Larry waited for the biologist to speak.

Professor Morgan came toward the coupé with his boyish smile, squinting through his spectacles. He glanced in at Paddy.

"Well," he amiably asked, "how did the dog react to the old familiar scenes?"

"He simply went wild!" Polly explained. "Larry told him to go to bed—and he went, where he always used to go to bed! Larry ordered him to get his collar—and Paddy jumped up and snatched it from the hook where it's been hanging! Dad, you should have seen him sniffing at his *own grave!* It was so creepy!"

"I expected you'd be home last night," Professor Morgan murmured.

Beads of cold sweat came squeezing through the pores of Larry's forehead.

"We had two punctures," Polly calmly explained. "We stayed all night at the cabin. You didn't worry, did you, dear?"

"I didn't worry, but I was anxious to know about the dog's reactions."

"Where," Polly wanted to know, "is everybody?"

"Jason went to New York yesterday shortly after you left. He's going to bring back detectives, and a gang of workmen, to carry out Mr. Galloway's suggestions. How I dread this part of it! Muller is down at the birch lab. I suppose," he said, smiling ruefully at Larry, "the peace of my declining years will soon be invaded by your bright young men, too. You won't let them misquote me, will you?"

Larry shook his head.

"I had better shave, hadn't I?"

"I think you better had," Polly agreed. "You look ferocious with those whiskers. And you'd better put on a clean coat."

"I'll be up in a few minutes," her father promised.

Polly drove on to the house. Alighting, she paused with one foot on the running board and smiled at Larry.

"Well?" she said.

"Another batch of grain alcohol came off successfully," was his comment.

Polly laughed softly. "You wanted him to be furious!"

"I did!" the young man asserted. "He should have been furious. He didn't care."

"You're mistaken," Polly disagreed. "He loves me. And I love him."

Larry said no more. She must, the crusader to himself declared, be removed from this perilous environment. She must be protected. She must be given a fair opportunity at life. His very first act upon reaching New York would be to interview Mrs. Horace Glen Islington!

13

LIFE RESTORING, A
CORPORATION

LAWRENCE GALLOWAY HAD extended an invitation to the owner of *The Daily It* to be present at this momentous conference because he had not wanted to hurt Benjamin Sturm's feelings. His opinion of *The Daily It's* owner was not a high one. Benjamin Sturm had those objectionable traits which one regretfully finds in the make-up of the go-getter type. Mr. Sturm was a self-made man—and proud of it!

Larry admired him for his aggressiveness, pitied him for his arrogance, and hated him for his sensationalism. Mr. Sturm loved sensationalism. If Mr. Sturm had had his way, *The Daily It* would have handled divorce cases and murder trials with the luridness of those certain other tabloid newspapers with whom *The Daily It* was in bitter competition.

Larry handled divorce cases and murder trials as he felt that they ought to be handled, with honesty and dignity. The success of *The Daily It* since he had been its managing editor had been phenomenal. In four years, he had sent its circulation up from seventy-five thousand to more than two hundred thousand. With honest, dignified methods.

He should have convinced Mr. Sturm that honesty and dignity would build a solid satisfying circulation; but Mr. Sturm was a hard man to convince. He liked his news served up sizzling hot and he frequently declared that Larry was an iceberg. On this rock of policy, the two men time and again split. Larry sensed that another split was coming.

They were seated about Professor Morgan's library— Benjamin Sturm, Jason Ortola, Larry, and two of *The Daily It's* high priced feature writers. Polly Morgan stood in the dining room doorway, smiling inscrutably as Larry briefly summed up the situation. He was not dramatizing the facts; in his firm, rich young voice he was simply stating them.

And Benjamin Sturm, slouched down deep in a leather chair, crossed and uncrossed his legs and fingered his big brown beard. His eyes, like the eyes of the others, shone with excitement; but he was having a harder time keeping it in. He divided his attention between Larry's pale face and Paddy, who lay at Larry's feet, wagging his stub of a tail and occasionally whining.

"I was as skeptical, as incredulous, as suspicious as each one of you were when I first stated what Professor Morgan has done," said Larry. "It seemed to me inconceivable that any man, any scientist—a scientist as celebrated even as Professor Morgan—had successfully restored dead matter to life. You might not even wish to take my word when I say that I saw this miracle performed before my very eyes, but you, Doyle, and you, McWhorter, and you, too, Mr. Sturm, knew this dog before he died two years ago. You

know that no doubt can exist. You know also that I am not carried away by false enthusiasms."

Mr. Sturm deep in his barrel of a chest, grunted. Larry knew that a quarrel was coming. When Benjamin Sturm plucked at his beard and crossed and uncrossed his legs, he was irritated.

"What I'd like to know," spoke up the owner of *The Daily It* in a voice as resonant as an empty cistern, "is why you have been holding back so long on the story. The big story was the guinea pig. You had that almost forty-eight hours ago. You knew that Professor Morgan is one of America's leading scientists, if not *the* leading scientist; you knew that Jason Ortola is one of America's foremost business men. You should not have hesitated."

"It was too important a story," Larry argued. "I did not want the *It* to be made the victim of a hoax."

"Would men of Professor Morgan's and Mr. Ortola's importance try to hoax anybody?"

"I was taking no chances," Larry stoutly answered.

"Newspaper men must take chances," stated Mr. Sturm in his most offensive manner. "This story may be on the streets of New York at this very moment."

"That is unlikely," Ortola broke in harshly. "The story is tightly bottled up. I was at first impatient with Mr. Galloway, but I must admit now that he has acted with the greatest wisdom. As I told you, Mr. Sturm, we selected Mr. Galloway because of his record. We did not want this story to be handled in the usual way. We wanted the public to get the facts straight and we wanted them kept straight. I am convinced that we could not have selected a better spokesman than Mr. Galloway."

Benjamin Sturm's heavy brow was corrugated with wrinkles. There was something as ponderous as himself in the stare he fixed upon the chemist.

"I don't see why you were so afraid that the story might have been twisted."

"That brings us," Ortola quickly took him up, "to the point which we have so far left unsettled. Your advice on it will be most welcome. As I told Mr. Galloway on our drive down from his cabin, this discovery of Professor Morgan's is not to be presented to the world with the usual pretty gesture. Professor Morgan has worked too hard; I have far too much money involved.

"It is up to Mr. Galloway to prove to the public that Professor Morgan has succeeded in restoring the dead to life. For proof, we offer a guinea pig that was dead ten months and a dog that was dead two years; both are now alive and perfectly normal. Professor Morgan will next show the public that he can restore a man to life—any man whose skeleton can be obtained. That will be a demonstration of what we can actually do."

Jason Ortola paused. He swept the pale, eager faces

about him with his burning, dark eyes. Defiantly, he concluded:

"Thereafter, we will take on business. We will charge one million dollars to restore any man to life who weighed two hundred pounds or under. For each additional pound, the cost will be fifteen hundred dollars."

BENJAMIN STURM WAS grasping the arms of his chair; staring across the library table at Jason Ortola with eyes that seemed to bulge.

In a voice thick with excitement, he exclaimed:

"What a story! A corporation to revive the dead at one million dollars a crack!"

"I don't like it," Larry objected.

"You wouldn't!" snorted his employer. "It's a story. It's a whale of a story!"

"Look here," said Larry. "Mr. Ortola came to me with a definite proposition. It was this: In return for giving him and Professor Morgan honest advice, I was to have this story exclusively for *The Daily It* as it developed. My honest advice to Mr. Ortola is that he will be making a great mistake to tell the public that he will not restore the dead to life except at a profit. Doyle, what's your slant?"

Doyle's eyes were glistening and his full lips were moist.

"Never, in all my experiences," he said, fairly panting, "has a story the size of this one come anywhere near me. I am itching to get at it. No matter what you leave out, no matter how you say it, it's the biggest piece of news that ever broke.

"I can't give you an unbiased opinion, Mr. Galloway. From the news point of view, I'd say, by all means shoot in the stuff about the corporation. It would be a crime to leave it out. At the same time, if you consider—"

"That's what I say," broke in McWhorter, who was a reporter of twenty years' experience. "It's hot stuff. A corporation to bring the dead back to life at a million dollars a corpse!"

Benjamin Sturm was chuckling.

"It looks as if you're voted down, Larry."

Larry glanced across the room to where Polly was standing. She was smiling at him mistily. Little imps of devilishness were dancing in her eyes. She was, he knew, looking upon this scene as a battle; he was jousting with the roomful of them. Her smile, her eyes, he felt, were also saying that he was being his overzealous, over-suspicious self.

"I am not voted down," he said firmly. "The contract you and I signed six months ago, Mr. Sturm, gives me the absolute final say on what does or does not go into *The Daily It*. I will not let this story of the corporation be printed in *The Daily It*, not because it is not news, but because I have agreed to handle the story with the best interests of Mr. Ortola and Professor Morgan in mind."

"In other words," Mr. Sturm angrily took him up, "you're putting other interests before the interests of your job!"

"I am simply abiding by the agreement I made with Mr. Ortola!" Larry snapped.

The face of the owner of *The Daily It* was red and it seemed to be swollen. His eyes were black with rage.

"I won't have that story kept out of my paper," he shouted, "because you're bogged down in a lot of silly ethics. As a matter of fact, I won't have you making editorial decisions of this kind. You haven't advanced any valid argument why the story of the corporation should not be run, anyhow."

"My argument," Larry answered, "is simply that, to publish it, would be to endanger the life of Mr. Ortola and Professor Morgan."

"How do you know it would endanger their lives?"

"I know enough about the public mind to be sure that the public, the world, would be extremely resentful. You are dropping a bombshell on the public, anyhow."

Mr. Sturm slowly and ponderously shook his head.

"I don't see how you figure that out. I simply don't see it. You can't tell what the public will do in a case like this. We're shooting off the biggest gun that has ever been fired in the history of newspapers. It's going to be heard a long way. To tell you the truth, Galloway, while I have a high opinion of your ability as a circulation getter, I haven't much of an opinion of your actual editorial judgment.

"You are a quietly aggressive young man. But what you have to learn about newspapers would fill a five-foot shelf. I'm saying in so many words that you aren't old enough, seasoned enough, wise enough, to make this decision. So, naturally, I'm going to make it for you."

"That story," Larry interrupted him, "is not going to run."

"That story," Sturm roared, "is going to run! If you don't want to handle it, you can quit."

"You are forgetting," said Larry hotly, "that I have a two-year contract, giving me absolute authority over what goes into *The Daily It.*"

"You can tear that contract up!"

"I refuse to tear it up!"

"You're fired, anyway! I'll keep you off *The Daily It* if I have to go through every court in the United States to do it!"

"Mr. Sturm," Polly Morgan broke in, "I wonder if I can say just a word." Without waiting for permission, she went on: "I am officially representing my father in this conference. He told me to listen in and to make what suggestions for him I felt were necessary. My father will back me up absolutely to the limit. If you fire Mr. Galloway, my father will not let *The Daily It* have this story exclusively. In fact, he won't let you have it at all."

Benjamin Sturm gazed at her with astonishment. Then he softly chuckled.

"Very well, my dear; Galloway keeps his job on condition that he makes the concession I want him to make. What is your opinion on the corporation feature?"

"I haven't an opinion," Polly confessed. "But I'll abide by whatever decision you arrive at."

"Meaning me?" Mr. Sturm asked, jocularly.

"No; meaning all of you."

"We might take a vote," suggested Mr. Sturm. "Larry, will you abide by a vote?"

Larry looked at Jason Ortola. "I think it is really up to you," he said.

"I," said the chemist, "am anxious for that story to be printed. If it isn't, the public as I've said before, will jump to the wrong conclusion. This discovery positively is not a gift to humanity. I will abide by the consequences."

"Now," burst out Mr. Sturm, "will you play, Larry?"

Larry glanced at McWhorter and from him to Doyle.

"You two men know public opinion as well as I do, or better. What is your honest opinion?"

"I'm for featuring the corporation angle of the story," said Doyle. "It's red-hot stuff."

"That's my dope," McWhorter concurred.

"Very well," said Larry, "I'll concede the point."

"The next one," Mr. Sturm boomed, "is, who is the man we are going to have restored to life? Have you selected a man, Ortola?"

"We have deliberately left that to your discretion," the chemist answered. "All we insist on is that Professor Morgan be provided with the complete skeleton. And we must be sure that we are not being hoaxed."

"My suggestion, for what it is worth," Mr. Sturm said, with a covert glance at his difficult managing editor, "is that we let the American public decide that question by a voting contest."

"Too cheap," Larry promptly decided.

"Well, wait a minute. Is it too cheap? Who is going to decide, anyhow? I think the man Professor Morgan brings back to life ought to be some famous, historical American, like Lincoln or Washington or maybe Roosevelt. Who are we going to let decide that? I don't want the responsibility. Maybe you want it, Larry."

"No," said Larry, "I don't want it. I'd prefer to have a committee of the most important living Americans decide it."

"Who's going to appoint the committee?" Mr. Sturm inquired in a jeering tone. "Are you going to let it get into the hands of politicians? Are you going to let a flock of old

ladies, like the Senate, decide? I'm for keeping Congress
and all politicians out of it.

"*The Daily It,*" he explained to Ortola, "is actually the
head of a feature service supplying eighty-seven of the
leading newspapers in America with features, mat service
and boiler plate. I'm for arranging with our clients by wire
to spring this story simultaneously in eighty-seven cities
and towns. Was that your idea, too, Larry?"

Larry nodded.

"I was planning to release the story in small daily doses,"
he answered. "The guinea pig story the first day; the dog
story the next day; the man story the third day."

"That," Mr. Sturm agreed, "is more like it. And on the
third day, when the announcement is made simultaneously
by these eighty-seven papers, that Professor Morgan is
willing to bring a dead man back to life, we'll spring the
news of the contest. There will be a coupon printed on the
front page of every paper, entitling the buyer of the paper
to one vote. If that won't be a circulation builder— Well,
shall we take a vote on *that?*"

"I call it red hot," declared McWhorter.

"Same here," agreed Doyle.

"Larry," said Mr. Sturm with a mocking solicitousness,
"are you with us or against us?"

"I'm against it." Larry announced himself, "on the
grounds that it cheapens a subject which should be handled
with the greatest dignity. But it will be a wonderful circulation builder."

"Then you're with us!"

Larry smiled wanly. "Yes; I'm with you."

"Who," Ortola put in, "do you think will win such a contest?"

"Theodore Roosevelt!" said McWhorter without hesitation.

"Abraham Lincoln!" cried Doyle.

"George Washington," asserted Mr. Sturm.

"My only objection to Washington," said Ortola with one of his rare, grotesque smiles, "is that he weighed well over two hundred pounds and—I am putting up the money!"

"This story," said Doyle in a voice that was almost a pur, "has more sweet angles—oh, more sweet angles! When do we tear into it, boss?"

"We'll collect Professor Morgan and get busy," Larry answered. "Where's Bronson?"

Bronson was *The Daily It's* star photographer.

"He's out shooting everything in sight," Doyle informed him. "I would suggest—if I may make a suggestion—that he shoot about ten film packs of Miss Morgan. You will want plenty of side angles on this story, and you can use her in all sorts of ways—how she helps her father, how she runs the farm, her opinion on jazz and modern dancing, her opinion on who ought to be brought back to life; what her interests are."

Polly withdrew.

"That suggestion," Mr. Sturm cried, "is a dandy!"

"But it is not going to be acted on," said Larry. "Miss Morgan is to be left entirely out of this."

"You don't seem to be doing anything," his employer complained, "but throwing monkey wrenches in the machinery. I never saw you act so negative, Larry. You've been dead set against every good feature the story has."

"Miss Morgan," said Larry, grimly, "is leaving here as soon as arrangements can be made with her relatives. She will remain in seclusion until the excitement is over."

He went out into the kitchen, where he found Polly at the sink, washing dishes. She dried her hands on a dish towel.

"I told dad about your plan for shipping me away. The poor dear almost broke down and cried, but he agrees with you that it's best. Look down there! It just isn't home any more."

Larry looked out the kitchen door. The ground in the vicinity of the red barn was swarming with laborers. They would work night and day erecting a fence that would isolate Professor Morgan and his coworkers from storming mobs. Lounging under the apple tree were a half dozen men in pale-blue uniforms.

"There'll be a dozen more detectives," Polly said in a doleful voice, "on the morning train. You—you aren't going to let your men photograph and interview me, are you, Larry? Because if you are," she hastily added, "I want to put on another dress."

Larry smiled. "You will not be photographed or interviewed."

Polly seemed a little disappointed at his decision.

"It would be fun, sort of, to have my picture in the papers," she said wistfully. "And I'd love to give an interview on modern dancing. I'd say that a law ought to be passed compelling boys and girls to learn to dance before they're five. But that wouldn't be in keeping with your dignified policy, would it?"

"Or wise," Larry added. "I came out here, Polly, to thank you for saving my job. It's rather a curious situation. Did you ever hear the old story of the traveling salesman who had a stroke of luck, selling his factory's entire output for years to come to one concern? He wired the good news to his boss, and his boss wired back, 'Fine! You're fired!'

"My contract with Sturm calls for the payment to me of five thousand dollars for every fifty thousand increase in *The Daily It's* circulation. This story ought to boost our circulation to well over a million. The story will do that—I won't."

"But you're responsible for getting the story. If you weren't so honest, dad and Jason wouldn't have selected you."

"Nevertheless," Larry went, on, "having stumbled on the biggest circulation building idea in the history of newspapers, my boss is tempted to say, 'Fine! You're fired!' I don't want to be fired. Thank you for preventing it."

Polly sighed. "You can thank me in New York by taking me out to tea or something. And I'd love to see your office."

"You shall."

"I can come any time," said Polly. "The Gores will move up here, and Mrs. Gore will take charge as soon as I'm gone. What are your plans?"

"My immediate plans are to familiarize Doyle and McWhorter with the lay of the land. As soon as that's done we'll start for New York in Sturm's car. We'll spring the story in the first edition to-morrow. McWhorter will stay here to cover this end."

"I have to go to Brookhaven on some errands for dad," said Polly. "I probably won't see you again before you go. So I'll say so long now."

She held out her hand and looked up at him soberly.

"You're so sedate, Larry, and so poised and so—so sophisticated. You think that I'm just an untutored little savage, don't you?"

"I think you're charming," Larry answered.

"But dumb," said Polly.

"No!" he cried. "Naïve."

"I'm going to learn not to be naïve," she declared. "Will you look up Aunt Sally soon?"

"To-night," he promised.

14

FROM THE FRYING PAN
INTO THE FIRE

THE TAXICAB HE had taken from *The Daily It* building deposited Larry before an apartment building in what is probably the smartest section of the smartest avenue in the world. The building was of some rough white stone, so tall that to look upward at it was to invite dizziness. The rent of a comfortable apartment in this edifice, he had heard, was thirty thousand dollars a year.

Vague misgivings assailed him even as he crossed the sidewalk to the amber-lighted foyer. This foyer bore the same relation to the foyer of an ordinary apartment building that a great cathedral bears to a little country church. The rich strains of an orchestra floated from an unseen dining room. Sleek-haired young men in mauve uniforms moved about on mysterious errands.

Larry, soaring upward in an elevator to the thirty-seventh floor, reviewed the brief telephonic conversation that had brought him here. He had found, without difficulty, the address of Mrs. Horace Glen Islington. He had talked to her from his office; had told her that he wished to see her privately on a matter of some importance connected with her niece, Polly Morgan. And she had cordially urged him to call at his earliest convenience. To-night.

He had been carrying in his mind a picture of Aunt Sally, and he wondered now if that picture bore any relation to the actual Aunt Sally. He had pictured her as a woman of great charm and poise and culture, in her late fifties; a woman who was widely read and widely traveled; who would instantly grasp the problem presented by Polly Morgan and willingly undertake to aid him in solving it.

Aunt Sally would have softly waving gray hair, and calm, fine gray eyes. She would, in short, resemble closely the perfect lady of another time.

The elevator stopped with an abruptness that fairly lifted him from his heels.

He was presently pressing a mother-of-pearl button set in a panel of rose and ivory.

The door was opened by a maid whose appearance was pert, whose manner was French, and whose accent was Brooklyn.

Larry yielded his hat to her and followed her down a short hall into a studio living room. It occupied vertically two stories, and was somewhat less in area than a baseball diamond. The largest Bokhara rugs he had ever seen lay upon the floor. Tapestries adorned the walls, and the kind of furniture he had seen in the more ambitious of high society motion pictures stood about the room. No doubt lingered in his mind concerning Mrs. Horace Glen Islington's affluence. She must have an income of a hundred thousand a year at least.

His inspection was cut short by the entrance of a tall, slender girl of perhaps twenty-five. She was a golden blonde, and she wore a dress of pale blue-green. Its color, as she advanced toward him, reminded him of a lightning flash.

Larry corrected his estimate of her age as she came nearer. She was, he judged, a perfectly preserved thirty-five. She had sparkling blue eyes, and a quick smile.

All of this he absorbed in the little interval before she spoke. It had not occurred to Larry that Aunt Sally might have children of her own.

She was holding out a slender white hand to him.

"You are Mr. Galloway, of *The Daily It*," she said, putting it in the form of a statement rather than with a rising intonation.

Larry waited for her to say: "My mother will be in in a moment." Instead of which, she said: "I am Mrs. Islington. I am simply dying with curiosity. What has Polly Morgan been doing, and how can I in any way be connected with it?"

Larry was shocked almost beyond words. He invariably looked before he leaped. He had with some care prepared the speech he would make to Aunt Sally; it was too late now for him to shift.

Perhaps this sophisticated blond girl would be a good influence for Polly, but the evidence was all against her. She and her environment stood for the smartest of smart New York. Would this environment be the proper one for the education of Polly Morgan?

"Professor Morgan has recently made a discovery of world importance," he heard himself saying, somewhat stiffly. "The first announcements will be published tomorrow in *The Daily It*."

"Do sit down, Mr. Galloway! I can't tell you how thrilled I am. Or how devoured with curiosity. Professor Morgan may be a wonderful scientist, but he is the world's worst and most difficult brother-in-law. We haven't, as you probably know, been on speaking terms since he dragged my sister off to that God forsaken farm."

She was seated close beside Larry on a small overstuffed settee upholstered in a rare shade of pink. Negligently, she had crossed her knees. She was, he gathered, devoid of any modesty. She had beautiful rounded knees.

A taboret stood beside the settee. On this, with the paraphernalia for smoking, reposed a little silver bell. This she now rang. The maid who had let him in came trotting into the room.

"Highballs, Marie," said Aunt Sally. "You look like the kind of man who takes Scotch. Or will it be rye?"

"Scotch," said Larry.

Aunt Sally inserted a cigarette into the end of a long purple holder. She lighted it. It was scented.

"Do go on, Mr. Galloway!"

She had a suave, silken voice. She was, he thought, a suave, silken person.

"Because of the startling nature of the discovery your brother-in-law has made," Larry obliged, speaking sternly while he realized that those beautiful sparkling eyes were already testing him out, "the Morgan farm has been placed under an armed guard, and it will be necessary to get Polly away as soon as possible."

"How perfectly thrilling!" Mrs. Islington cried. "I suppose the papers will simply be full of it, and you've come up to interview me because everybody related to Hendricks will be of news value. Well, what can I say? What *can* I say?"

"The reason why I thought Polly should leave the farm," Larry enlightened her, "is because she must avoid publicity."

"How old is Polly? About fourteen, isn't she?"

"She is twenty," said Larry.

"Great grief!" the beautiful blonde exclaimed. "How time flies! I've always thought of her as a child. I haven't laid eyes on her since she was—um—about six. They do shoot up, don't they? My husband has been dead five years, and it seems only yesterday that I wore black!"

Larry's attention had been caught by her cigarette holder. It sparkled. He guessed that it was inlaid with diamonds. It had probably cost five hundred dollars at Cartier's, in Paris. To himself he groaned: "She is one of these gay New York widows!"

"I suppose you're an old friend of the family."

"Not exactly," he said. "In fact, I've known the Morgans only a few days."

"I see," said Aunt Sally.

"But it wasn't necessary to know the Morgans long to discover Polly is unbelievably innocent. You have no idea, Mrs. Islington, how innocent that girl is. She is absolutely unsophisticated."

"How odd!"

"She has been brought up in the most unnatural way," the crusader plunged on. "She is nothing but a household drudge. There are a dozen good reasons why she should leave that farm. She has been, for years—in fact, since her mother died—hardly more than a servant girl to a houseful of selfish scientists."

"Selfish, as applied to a scientist," she warmly agreed, "is putting it most mildly. Is Polly good-looking?"

"She is beautiful!" said Larry with more fervor than he really intended.

"Ah!" said Aunt Sally. "Now we're getting somewhere. You're in love with Polly, and you've come to her aunt for advice. My dear boy, I am all sympathy. You can count on me to the limit!"

Larry was aware that his face was fiery hot. Marie returned with a silver tray, sustaining tall glasses filled with a golden liquid. He accepted the one tendered to him and swallowed a third of it.

"I am not in love with her," he denied. "I simply realized that she is too fine a girl to waste herself any longer in that weird environment. That is why I've come to you."

Blue, thoughtful eyes regarded him over the rim of a glass.

"I thought," he recklessly plunged on, "that, inasmuch as you are Polly's aunt, you might consider—might like—" He faltered. "I am merely interested in seeing that Polly is given the proper opportunities."

Larry might have gone on to say: "But I've changed my mind. I don't think you are the proper person for Polly. You are too far the other extreme. You would do everything wrong."

"The proper opportunities," Aunt Sally was murmuring. "What you thought, Mr. Galloway, was that I would bury the hatchet and give them to her. Was that why you came to see me?"

"I haven't gone about it very tactfully," said Larry. "I asked her if there were any relatives she might visit until the excitement blows over, and you were the only one she could think of."

"Does my brother-in-law know about this? I mean, is it his scheme?"

There was no laughter in the blue eyes now. She was deadly serious.

"He is not interested," Larry answered, "in anything Polly does. He has let her grow up—like Topsy. By pure good luck, she is a fine girl—but absolutely unsophisticated."

"And beautiful," murmured the gay widow.

"And beautiful," Larry affirmed.

"How about clothes?"

"I don't know about clothes," Larry confessed. "Clothes? Well, the kind of clothes a girl living under those conditions would wear."

"Has she a good figure?"

"I—I suppose so,"

"Of course," she said dryly, "you didn't notice."

"She is slender and about your height," said Larry huskily.

"She could wear my clothes."

"I hadn't thought of that."

"Now let me think," mused Aunt Sally. "You have absolutely no interest in Polly but an altruistic one."

Larry waited. He was wondering how he could wiggle out of it. He had forgotten all about an aunt of his own in Boston. Perhaps—

"I always look for people's motives," the silken voice

was saying. "I can't quite fit you into the picture. I don't believe in altruists or Santa Claus any more. Yet you seem to be an honest, earnest young man. How old are you, Mr. Galloway?"

"I am twenty-eight."

"M-m-m-m-m! And you want Polly to be sheltered from publicity."

Again he nodded.

"Tell me something about her personality," she requested. "Is she the scientific type?"

"No," said Larry. "The contrary. She is bright and—and quite charming, but exceedingly naïve." He took a deep breath. "I've been so full of the idea," he went on hurriedly, "that it hasn't occurred to me until now how—how forward all this must seem to you, Mrs. Islington."

He stood up and placed his empty glass on the taboret.

"Blundering in on you like this." He would, he decided, wire his aunt Maude as soon as he could reach a telegraph office.

"But I'm really terribly interested, and I don't think you've blundered at all. It is the greatest compliment you could have paid me, Mr. Galloway. Really, I'm not offended. I'm beginning to warm up to your idea. I think you *are* an altruist. I like you, and I'm ever so grateful to you for coming up."

"I understand," he helped her eagerly, "the position it places you in. But it would be an imposition. You're too busy. Something else can be arranged."

"But I don't want something else to be arranged," she cried. "I love the idea. And I'm not busy. I have nothing but time. If Polly is the kind of girl you say she is—why, I can hardly wait to see her."

To his inner self Larry groaned: "How *can* I wiggle out of this?"

"But it would be an imposition—" he began.

She wailed: "My dear boy, do sit down! Marie, bring Mr. Galloway another highball. I'll wire her tonight! No! I'll telephone."

Aunt Sally was halfway across the great room before Larry could say a word. She, picked up a French telephone from a table.

"Jimmy," she said, "I want you to get long distance right away. Have long distance put through a personal call for Miss Polly Morgan, at Lake Shallon— Wait a minute, Jimmy."

She whirled about. Larry had crossed the room.

"It's Brookhaven, isn't it?" Her eyes were dancing with excitement.

He nodded.

"It's Brookhaven, Jimmy. Brookhaven, Connecticut." She replaced the telephone on its standard.

"It isn't fair," Larry protested. "The expense—"

"Expense!" she cried. "I have money enough to dress and entertain a dozen Polly Morgans!"

She began to pace up and down the largest of the Bokhara rugs, the restlessness of New York, of her kind, expressed in every motion of her long, slim, supple body. Her feet were small, really trivial feet. He started worrying about the turns. She would come to one end of the Bokhara rug and pivot about on her high heels. But every time she missed the fringe.

He stood at one side and watched her as she paced up and down, back and forth, her short blue-green skirt softly billowing out behind her. From time to time she placed, a single finger over her lips, as thoughts came, were considered, rejected or accepted.

This gay young widow—plotting Polly's future. There was nothing he could say now. Nothing. She had taken all initiative from him.

"Is she dark or light?"

"Dark," he said feebly. "Dark hair, brown eyes."

"Complexion?"

"Well," he faltered, "it—it's creamy, I suppose you'd say, with high color. She's outdoors a lot. She's tanned."

Aunt Sally halted abruptly and faced him with large, serious eyes.

"Does that girl wash the dishes?"

"She does," Larry confessed.

"That means her hands are red, rough, and swollen."

"I—I'm afraid they are."

Aunt Sally took up her pacing where she had left it off. Once again that slim, elegant finger flew to her red mouth as she dealt with the many fascinations of this welcome problem. He had lost all hope. Red, rough, and swollen hands were not an obstacle to Mrs. Horace Glen Islington. They were merely one detail in an absorbing, delightful task.

She paused again, with a hand resting upon one slender hip. Her suavity was all gone now. She had become merely the acme of herself, a restless New Yorker to whom had been tossed a new toy to play with.

"I think you are a dear to have taken all this trouble." The voice was no longer silk, but honey. "At first, I was terribly suspicious. I have done nothing that the papers could possibly use. I was afraid you were making an oblique attack. I see now that you are really a splendid young man with—with ideals. You *are* an idealist. Idealists, altruists, and Santa Claus I put out of my life years ago."

Larry smiled ruefully. Aunt Sally was a neurotic. She was, however, the kind, of woman he enjoyed being with: poised, sophisticated, subtle. But she wasn't for Polly.

The phone bell tinkled discreetly—a little silver apology of a sound. Aunt Sally raced to the telephone, as if, perhaps, some one might reach it first.

She said: "Hullo, hullo, hullo!" And turned an eager smile to the managing editor of *The Daily It*. "A business man once told me to keep on saying hullo until they got your connection. Hullo, hullo, hullo! Yes; calling Miss Morgan. Hullo, hullo, hullo! Polly? Darling, this is Aunt Sally."

A pause. "Yes, really! I am phoning from New York, my dear; my apartment. A charming young man has been telling me everything. I want you to come and stay with me as long as you can—months and months. How soon can you start?... Really? I had no idea trains started at such ungodly hours.... What? You are? Isn't that marvelous? We'll have such fun, darling.

"Of course, I'm dying to see you.... No, no, no, it isn't an imposition; I am absolutely delighted; I am simply tickled, I'll meet your train, then.... Yes, dear. I'll be at the gate to meet you. I'll wear—um-m-m-m—a bright blue hat, a largish one, and a white coat. If you miss me, come straight to the apartment.... Yes; darling; he's standing beside me."

She banded the telephone to Larry. He said "Hello!" heavily.

Polly's voice, thrilling with excitement, cried: "Larry! You're a perfect dear! How did you ever do it? Is she as lovely as she sounds?"

"Why—yes," Larry said.

"Mr. McWhorter has just gone to bed. He was awfully funny. He insisted on washing all the supper dishes. He—he wants to marry me. You newspaper men are awfully fast workers."

"Are we?" said Larry stiffly.

"Will the story be in to-morrow's paper?"

"The guinea pig story—yes."

"You'll look me up as soon as you can, won't you, Larry? I know I'm going to die of lonesomeness."

"Of course I'll look you up. Good-by, Polly."

"Good night, Larry."

He put the telephone down and turned to find that Aunt Sally was again pacing from one end of the great Bokhara to the other. Her excitement had shorn years from her.

"Don't you think," she said, "that Polly and I will set each other off?"

"Perfectly," he laughed.

"She was so excited she could hardly talk! She's taking a train that leaves Brookhaven at five to-morrow morning. Did she tell you?"

"No; she didn't mention that."

"Will you have photographers at the station—or will they come to the apartment afterward."

"Perhaps I neglected to mention," Larry patiently

answered, "that one of my reasons for wanting Polly to leave that farm, was so that she could easily avoid publicity."

"No, you didn't forget to mention it," Aunt Sally corrected him. "But why should she avoid publicity?"

The beautiful woman gazed at him with a finger to her mouth.

"But what a shame it would be to let such a glorious chance slip by. I *love* publicity."

Larry started to speak, but the impulse was perverted into a gulp. His good intentions had all been wasted. Nothing, he realized, would penetrate Aunt Sally's present glowing self-satisfaction. She was about to play a rôle that all women love and she was immeasurably thrilled.

"What possible harm could it do, Mr. Galloway?"

"She has never been exposed to that sort of thing," he argued. "You simply can't realize, Mrs. Islington, how unworldly she is."

"I'm beginning to realize," she replied, "that you are a terribly serious young man."

He flushed. People were all the time telling him how seriously he took life, his work, everything, and he always resented it.

"Polly," he said, "is apt inadvertently to let slip certain information that would be embarrassing to *The Daily It*. We have the story exclusively. Some reporter may rattle Polly. I want her kept away from reporters for my own self-protection."

"I can handle reporters," the beautiful lady serenely assured him. "They can't rattle me and they can't bully me. I'll handle the reporters."

"I'd rather you'd keep her away from them."

"I'll tell you what I'll do," Aunt Sally exclaimed. "I'll simply use my best judgment! What is this story?"

"Professor Morgan has recently been conducting some extraordinary experiments. I'm afraid I can't tell you what they're about."

"You said guinea pigs. He's been torturing guinea pigs again! He drove my sister to her grave with his brutal experiments on guinea pigs and dogs and cats!"

"It will all come out in *The Daily It*."

"And it really will startle the world?"

"It will."

The long purple cigarette holder was drooping from a corner of her lovely mouth. She was gazing at Larry broodingly.

"You are a very strange young man," she said softly. "You are very stubborn and terribly serious. Ordinarily, I don't like serious men. Why take life so seriously? It doesn't get you anywhere. I know. All it gets you is bumps. But, of course, you are a molder of public opinion. Well, I like you, anyhow. Will you come up often while Polly is here?"

"I'd like to very much."

"But you'll have to promise not to reform me. I very much suspect that you are trying to reform Polly. Somehow, she doesn't quite suit you, so you are going to have her made over. My dear, you may be able to mold public opinion, but you can never mold human nature. I'll warn you that I am not going to make Polly over in any way. I am simply going to give her the time of her young life!"

Larry did not answer.

"I am going to make her another Cinderella! Here! You're not going!" she wailed.

"I have to work all night," he explained.

"But I must talk to you. You're the most interesting man I've met in ages. And I feel like talking to you. I know! You're offended because I said you were serious! Oh, I'm so sorry! I didn't mean that I didn't like you. I like you ever so much. You—you're so impervious!"

Larry saw himself settling down to hours of argument with this beautiful, fascinating woman. He had to get back to the office. She was dangerous, too. She was the kind of woman who wasn't satisfied unless every man she met fell in love with her. She had, he resentfully admitted, quantities of sex appeal.

"I must go."

"You'll have one more highball, Marie!"

"I have to work all night."

It took him ten minutes longer to get away from Aunt Sally. It struck Larry, as he was carried to the ground floor by an elevator that lowered him as suddenly as if he were falling freely in space, that he had, with his desire to do a great service for Polly Morgan, become the helpless coauthor of a scheme that would probably ruin her life.

Polly, in going from the drudgery of the farm to the apartment of the woman he had just left, was leaping from the frying pan to the fire.

15

BITTER FRUITS OF TRIUMPH

ON THE FRONT page of *The Daily It*, the following morning, appeared a photograph of Professor J. Hendricks Morgan bending over a bench which was littered with chemical paraphernalia. Appropriately large and startling type announced that Professor Morgan, one of America's greatest living scientists, had discovered, in his laboratory, the secret of restoring life to the dead.

More photographs and details on page three.

Eighty-seven other newspapers, scattered over the United States in as many communities, simultaneously published the startling announcement and the accompanying photographs, which were transmitted to them electrically over the wires of the American Telephone and Telegraph Company.

Every other newspaper in New York carried rewritten versions of the guinea pig's resurrection as hearsay. The subject was promptly leaped upon by agile columnists. A guinea pig is a funny animal. The columnists made the most of this.

But the story in *The Daily It* somehow carried the ring of truth. Handled under Larry's orders, the guinea pig was treated with the dignity befitting the profound importance of the experiment.

Sensational details were promised in tomorrow's issues of *The Daily It*.

Larry was besieged by reporters from other papers. They had made the painful discovery that the Professor Morgan story was exclusive with *The Daily It*—and was going to remain exclusive.

"For two more days," Larry informed a roomful of impatient and sarcastic young men. "I dug up this story. It's going to grow bigger and bigger. Professor Morgan and his co-workers have promised me to let no one interview them until the fourth day. Get at them, then, if you can. For the time being, I am their spokesman."

"It's a frame-up," snapped a young man from the *Evening World*.

"It's a hoax," growled a *Sun* reporter.

"What is Morgan going to do next?" demanded an *Evening Journal* man.

"Read to-morrow's *It*," said Larry.

"You can't get away with it!" snarled a reporter from the *Evening Telegram*.

"At least," Larry laughed, "I'm going to try."

He put in a call for the Morgan farm, and his secretary informed him, at the end of an hour and a half, that the wire was still busy.

At four o'clock in the afternoon McWhorter called him.

"The place is crawling with reporters," he told Larry. "They're coming by the automobile load. Two have just dropped down into the lower meadow in an airplane. There are eighteen detectives policing the barn where Professor

Morgan is hiding. If you know where Ortola is, don't say so on this wire. The fence is half finished. What happened in town?"

"We printed a half million," Larry informed him, "and the circulation department says that newsdealers are calling up every minute, yelling for more. It broke just about the way we expected. Wire me a color story for to-morrow."

McWhorter laughed. "There are twenty reporters in this room, as sore as that many boils. I think they're planning to tar-and-feather me if I don't talk. But it's airtight up here, boss. They are trying to ply me with booze, but I don't ply very well. They've tried bribery, threats, and cajolery. Hey—you!"

The telephone had evidently been snatched from his hand. A harsh, angry voice came booming down the wire.

"Look here, Galloway, you haven't any right to bottle up this story this way."

"Who is this?" Larry cordially inquired.

"It's Riley, of the *News*. Everybody we talk to refers us to you. Don't be such a hog. What's Professor Morgan done?"

"Read *The Daily It*," Larry laughed, and hung up.

He called Polly Morgan at her aunt's apartment. The voice of Marie irritably assured him that Miss Morgan was not in to any newspaper men, nor would she talk to them on the wire.

"Tell her Mr. Galloway is calling."

"Ah!" cried Marie.

But it was not Polly who came to the phone. It was Aunt Sally, a golden voice at the other end of the wire.

"Mr. Galloway, I've been trying to reach you all afternoon. Polly is lying down. The poor child is exhausted.

Reporters discovered that she is here. She talked to none of them. They called her on the phone. You are the tenth Mr. Galloway who has called in the past two hours. How resourceful you newspaper men are!

"You see? I obeyed your orders! Besides, I don't want her photographed until she has some clothes. When are we going to see you?"

"Soon, I hope," Larry answered. "But I'm terribly busy—and going to be busier."

"Did that brother-in-law of mine honestly bring that guinea pig back to life?"

"He did."

"What else has he brought back to life?"

Larry laughed. "*The Daily It* for tomorrow will contain, as we say, sensational disclosures."

"I want to know if he has brought a man back to life!"

"*The Daily It* will answer all your questions."

As he replaced the receiver on its hook his secretary entered with a stack of telegrams a foot high.

"Mr. Galloway," she wailed, "I'm simply snowed under. There are inquiries here from every State in the Union, from universities, newspapers, and cranks. What shall I say to them all? Most of them have asked for answers collect."

"Sift out any that are important," he instructed her, "and I'll answer them. To the rest of them simply say: 'Further details of Professor Morgan's researches will appear in *The Daily It*.' Condense that to ten words."

"The outer office is full of people who want to see you, Mr. Galloway."

"I'll see no one else to-day," he said, "but reporters. You're going to need assistance, Miss Hanson. You'd better collect three more girls."

Larry worked until after midnight. He read the early editions of the morning papers on his way home in a taxi-cab. There were references, some respectful, some other-wise, to Professor Morgan's celebrated guinea pig on the front pages of them all. Every paper carried an editorial on the guinea pig. There were interviews with other scientists.

Dr. Woolsey, of Harvard, said in the *Times:*

> I have not the slightest doubt but that, if Professor Morgan says he has perfected a laboratory technic whereby dead matter once animate may be restored to life, he has actu-ally done so. Scientists through the ages have puzzled over the problem. Carrol, of the Rockefeller Institute, has kept membranes from a chicken's heart alive for nearly twenty years. If Professor Morgan says that he has solved the riddle of resurrection, I, for one, am confident that he is telling the truth.

Professor Lombardi, of the Boston Institute of Tech-nology, said in the *Herald-Tribune:*

> The fact that Professor Morgan has made himself so inac-cessible leads me to a suspect that the whole story may be a hoax. I have the very highest opinion of Professor Morgan. I have known Professor Morgan for a great many years. All my attempts today to reach him by phone have been unsuc-cessful. On the surface, I am inclined to be highly skeptical of this report.

Other scientists sided with Dr. Woolsey, of Harvard, or with Professor Lombardi, of the Boston Institute of Technology.

The prevailing tone of all the editorials was, however, skeptical, if not downright bitter. *The Daily News* was scathing in its comments on *The Daily It's* attitude.

The *News* said:

> It is evident that the methods of the stock market have at last sunk their claws into the fast declining glory of journalism. Our esteemed contemporary has cornered the revived guinea pig market. No one is permitted to whisper into the sensitive ear of Professor J. Hendricks Morgan but representatives of *The Daily It*. We are inclined to be incredulous. We are inclined to suspect that the story has been cut from whole cloth.
>
> Why has Professor Morgan selected this relatively obscure journal as his mouthpiece?
>
> Why is he blinking all the rules of common sense and fair play by refusing to answer the legitimate questions of other press representatives?
>
> One of our reporters, in attempting to gain an entrance into Professor Morgan's laboratory, was thrown into a brook. Is this just? Is it fair?

An editorial in another paper went even further.

> Has Professor Morgan sold his scientific standing for a mess of potage? Has this distinguished biologist followed in the footsteps of notorious preachers and prominent murderers, selling his world important discovery for so many dollars

per column?

Larry grinned as he turned, in each paper, to the full-page advertisement he had written and caused to be inserted. Large black but dignified type stated that Professor Morgan, internationally renowned scientist, would disclose further of his startling experiments in restoring the dead to life exclusively in forthcoming issues of *The Daily It.*

How those newspapers had hated to run that advertisement!

Larry was smiling happily as he turned the key in his apartment door. Paddy, whining and whimpering as the lock grated, leaped upon him with a rapturous welcome. The telephone bell was ringing.

"By this time to-morrow night, Paddy," the young man gravely said to the excited dog, "you are going to be the most famous dog in the world. I hope you appreciate the honor that is coming to you." Paddy yelped.

The busiest young man in New York put the receiver to his ear and said hello.

"Is this you, Galloway?" a voice snarled.

"It is."

"This is Bates, city editor of—"

"Make it snappy," said Larry.

"I want to know what Morgan is up to."

"Read *The Daily It!*"

"It's a dirty, low-down trick to hog this story this way," Mr. Bates stormed. "Look at it reasonably, will you, Galloway? If we don't get in on this story, we all lose our jobs."

"On that basis," said Larry, "every newspaperman in

New York, with the exception of those working for me, are going to lose their jobs."

"For the love of Mike, be reasonable, Galloway. Don't be so tight. We've always played with you. You know how reporters are. You used to be one yourself. No one ever hogs a story as big as this one."

"Nobody's ever had a chance before!"

"The hell they haven't! Look how we work ship news and the police courts. You were in the ship news ring yourself. If you got a story, you spilled it to the gang."

"But I was working on this one alone, I'm not violating any promises."

"All right!" roared Mr. Bates. "Wait till another piece of news breaks and you'll see how near any *Daily It* man gets to it!"

"I'll have to run the risk."

Mr. Bates, assumed a wheedling tone. "Come on, Galloway, give us a tip, will you? What's the dope for to-morrow?"

"Read *The Daily It*," said Larry wearily, and hung up.

He had hardly replaced the receiver on its hook when the bell began ringing again.

"Hello," he said.

"That you, Larry?" cried a brisk, jovial man's voice.

"Yes, this is Larry."

"Well, this is old Bill Holden, Larry. You certainly have done well by yourself, kid. I am as proud of you as if I were your own father. It's the story of the ages. Who dug it up?"

"I did," Larry answered, warming a little. His memory of Bill Holden was vague. Bill Holden, it seemed to him, had worked with him on *City News* at one time.

"I'm with the *World* now, Larry," went on the jovial one. "You can do your old pal a great big favor, Larry. I know you wouldn't turn an old pal down, either. You're not that kind. What's to-morrow's dope on Morgan?"

"Bill," Larry answered in a tired voice, "this story is a beat, and it's going to stay a beat."

"You don't mean that!" cried old Bill Holden. "You're not going to be as selfish and mean as that."

"I'm sorry, Bill."

"You—you—you—" sputtered his old pal. "You go to hell, you big—"

Larry sighed as he hung up the receiver. He wadded up a sheet of paper and stuffed it into the bell just as it began to ring again. The magnets continued to hum resentfully.

Another old pal probably wanted to tell him to go to hell. Larry was discovering that the fruits of triumph were not entirely sweet. Some were sour and others were bitter. They were destined to grow bitterer.

16

THE BUSIEST MAN IN NEW YORK

WHEN LARRY STARTED out for the office next morning, he found, waiting for him in the lobby downstairs, thirty-five or forty reporters. They were sitting on chairs, lounging against the walls. The air was sour with cigarette, pipe, and cigar smoke.

Larry was promptly surrounded. Each man had a well-read copy of the first edition of *The Daily It* in his hand or protruding from his pocket.

The lobby roared with questions.

To all their inquiries, Larry answered:

"You'll find the whole story in *The Daily It!*"

"We'll blow up your damned plant if you don't come across!" shouted one irate newsgatherer.

Larry laughed at him, but he was beginning to feel nervous. If a guinea pig and a dog had created all this confusion, what would to-morrow's announcement do?

They were plucking at his arms, shoving him this way, and that; the farther ones trying to get nearer; all of them shouting. Never, in his experience, had he seen such a disorderly crowd of reporters. Generally they appointed one or two men to do the questioning. He realized that they must be desperate. A reporter, driven by a heartless city editor, would stop only this side of murder to get a story. They were going to get that story or tear him to pieces!

One man thrust under his nose a copy of *The Daily It.* The first page contained an excellent likeness of Paddy. Above it, in large type, ran the streamer:

ANOTHER OF PROFESSOR
MORGAN'S TRIUMPHS

The man shouted: "Come on, Galloway. What's the rest of the story? Has he brought a man to life?"

"Read to-morrow's *Daily It,*" Larry answered.

"You're saying he has!" shouted three men in one breath.

"I'm saying nothing!"

"Then you're denying it?"

"I'm not talking," said Larry.

"You big hog!"

Larry's remaining color departed. He was tired of being called a hog.

"Look here," he said. "I'll answer any questions you want to fire at me about to-day's story."

There was something like a cheer at this.

"Did you actually see that dog restored to life from his own skeleton?"

"I did."

"How do you know it's your own dog?"

"Because I knew his tricks and his mannerisms. You'll find all that on page four. I drove back to my cabin with him from the laboratory. He sniffed at his own grave."

"How did he act?"

"Bewildered. Then he ran to the cabin and I let him

in. You never saw a dog so tickled to get home. It's all on page four."

"How much did that stunt cost?"

"The cost of resurrecting the guinea pig and the cost of resurrecting the dog will come out in to-morrow's *It*."

"How much will it cost to resurrect a man?"

"See to-morrow's *It*."

"Is it costly?"

"Very."

"Did it cost as much as a thousand dollars to resurrect the guinea pig?"

"I can't answer that."

"You mean you won't?"

"That's what I mean. I won't."

"You're admitting in so many words that Professor Morgan has not yet resurrected a man."

"I am admitting nothing that doesn't apply to to-day's story."

"We'll get it all before noon."

"Goto it!" said Larry.

They reluctantly let him go. He walked away from them with that unpleasant tingling in the spine one experiences in leaving a mob from which bricks or bullets may fly.

Entering a taxicab, he found that he was exhausted. If forty reporters awaited his appearance this morning, how many reporters were and had been trying to pry information from others who possessed it? So far, it had remained bottled. But would it stay bottled?

He checked off on his fingers the people who might bring to an end this incalculably valuable suspense: Ortola, Professor Morgan, Polly, Muller, the Gores, McWhorter,

Doyle, Bronson, and Sturm. Each of them would be hounded as he had been hounded. Would there be a leak? Could he keep the story air-tight until to-morrow morning?

With three days' lead on the rest of them, the triumph of *The Daily It* was assured. For weeks to come, people would look to *The Daily It* for the true story as it developed.

If those others would only keep their mouths shut! He checked them off again, estimating their powers of keeping silent. Ortola would not talk. Professor Morgan would not talk. Muller? Muller might. Polly wouldn't, unless they somehow rattled her. The Gores were an unknown quantity. McWhorter, Doyle, and Bronson he would have banked his life on, unless the reporters at Lake Shallon somehow managed to get McWhorter drunk. Sturm liked to see his picture and his name in other papers, but he would be discreet.

If they would all say absolutely nothing!

As he drew within sight of *The Daily It* Building he thought at first that it was afire, then that it had been bombed. The street was black with people.

Drawing nearer, he saw that newsboys were selling papers to them, and that they were leaving when they had secured them. Policemen were trying to keep the crowds moving. Larry counted a dozen policemen.

A riot squad to scatter mobs who wanted only to buy *The Daily It!* Every dream that he had ever had as a newspaper editor was coming true.

Larry pushed his way through the crowd and entered the building. He heard the hum of the presses, and found Burke, his pressroom foreman, and Carlyle, his circulation manager, in his office waiting for him. His secretary, pale and drawn-looking, was sorting telegrams and cables in a corner. She made a grimace of despair when she saw him.

"What's the print order going to be for to-day?" Burke, the pressroom foreman, wanted to know.

"I said seven hundred and fifty thousand," put in the circulation manager.

"I'd say a million," said Larry. "Can you handle it, Burke?"

"I can handle it, Mr. Galloway. I can handle up to two million, but I'll need more men. I ought to have twenty more men anyhow."

"Go ahead and get them."

"How many editions will you run, Mr, Galloway?" Carlyle asked.

"We won't run editions to-day," Larry decided. "Simply change the plates as often as they wear down. We won't alter the make-up except for Wall Street closing prices and race track and baseball results? Just turn 'em out."

"How am I goin' to deliver them, Mr. Galloway?" the circulation manager wailed. "Up to yesterday we were geared for two hundred thousand. I'm going to need more men and two dozen more trucks, anyhow."

"Order them."

Burke and Carlyle withdrew. Miss Hanson came wearily ever.

"I've called an employment agency to send over four of the best girls they have," she said.

"Can you handle them, Miss Hanson?"

She smiled wanly. "I think I can. I'll try. I'm simply snowed under, Mr. Galloway."

"You can have a month's vacation when the excitement's over," he promised her.

"How long will it last?"

"Perhaps a month."

The girl seemed to sag. "I'll be in a sanatorium with a nervous breakdown before that vacation comes around. I left word a few minutes ago with the switchboard girl not to put through any more calls here. The phone was ringing every second. Long distance calls are piling up from every city I ever heard of, Mr. Galloway. And will you look at that pile of telegrams?

"Practically every newspaper in Europe has cabled for stories. And there are at least two hundred inquiries from American papers. Oh, yes; your London, Paris, Rome, and Berlin correspondents have all cabled. There are cables here from Congressmen and Senators and Governors, and colleges and broadcasting stations and churches."

"Tell Mr. Gaynor to come in."

Gaynor was the manager of *The Daily It* feature service, which supplied mat service to eighty-seven newspapers scattered throughout the country.

Gaynor, pale and perspiring, followed the haggard Miss Hanson into the managing editor's office.

"Mr. Galloway," he groaned, "I'm going to need more help. I've had three hundred telegraphic requests since last night for exclusive regional rights to this guinea pig story."

"Hire all the help you need," Larry instructed him. "I'm going to turn all foreign requests over to you. Let me have that pile of foreign telegrams, Miss Hanson."

The tired girl placed a pile of telegrams six inches thick on his desk. He began to thumb them over.

"Every country," Larry commented dryly, "has been heard from. Here's one from Cape Town, Africa. Here's one from Shanghai, and here's one from Bombay. Here are—let's see—five from South America. Take them all, Gaynor, and use your judgment. I want you to handle all out-of-town stuff.

"Hire all the help you want. In all cases in which personal requests for information by cable stipulate a collect reply, refer them to the paper nearest them to whom the story is being sold. If they don't stipulate a collect reply, don't bother with them. Miss Hanson, send Doyle and Bronson into me."

"Yes, sir." She fluttered out.

Doyle was the first to appear. The tall young Irishman looked as if he had spent a sleepless night.

"Boss," he pleaded, "do you mind if I crawl off somewhere and hide until this thing is over? A gang of reporters got me out of bed last night and stayed there until breakfast time. There were fifteen of them.

"They found where I hid my liquor, and by four my apartment was turned upside down and inside out. Furniture is all smashed. Booze is spilled over everything. And you know what modern booze does to furniture and carpets! The wife is up in the country with the kid. When she gets back my name is going to be bologney!"

"Did you say anything?" Larry asked him.

"No, boss, I didn't peep. They tried to make me drink. They tried to bulldoze me. They did everything but ride me out of town on a rail."

Larry's grin was sympathetic. "I'm relying on you to work up to-morrow's story. I'm going to have you locked in a room where you won't be bothered. Estimate the damage that gang did to your apartment, and I'll O.K. a voucher for the full amount."

Bronson, the *It's* star photographer, entered at this juncture. He was white, and his black eyes were flashing.

He was cursing. He continued to curse. With the verbal pyrotechnics of which only telegraph operators and newspaper photographers are the masters, he vividly consigned well specified and detestable insects to impossible regions.

It appeared that some one had broken the lock on his darkroom door during the night and had wrecked it.

"They kicked cans of metol around—and do you know how much metol costs an ounce? They smashed plates and opened boxes of new film. They ruined two Graflexes. They stove in my enlarging machine."

"And stole all your Morgan negatives and prints?" Larry helped him.

"Them? Hell, no, Mr. Galloway! I wouldn't leave *them* lying around. I had them locked up in the business office safe last night. They were just sore. When they couldn't find those, they just wrecked my darkroom."

"Well, fix up your darkroom as best you can, and keep your Morgan negatives and prints in the safe. Have reporters been after you, too?"

The Daily It's star photographer laughed rather wildly.

"A fat chance that bunch of typewriter lizards has of getting anything out of me! Sure, they've been trying! They've been following me around as if I was the President."

"What did you tell them, Bronson?"

Bronson glanced across the room to where Miss Hanson,

who had returned, was bending over a new basket of telegrams.

"I hate to use that kind of language in the presence of a lady," he answered.

"They didn't make you talk, then?"

"Huh! Any reporter living should make me talk!"

"What are you shooting to-day?"

"People mobbing each other, trying to buy the *It*," answered Bronson. "Will Morrisy O.K. a requisition for a complete new darkroom?"

"Morrisy will. On your way out tell him I want him."

Larry glanced at the clock on his desk as he lifted the telephone receiver. It was not yet ten o'clock. The busiest day of his life had hardly begun.

"Miss Jenkins," he said to the switchboard operator, "I am interested only in calls from Professor Morgan, Jason Ortola, Bill McWhorter, Miss Morgan, and Mr. Sturm. Sidetrack all others to the city editor's desk."

"For which," boomed the deep voice of Morrisy behind him, "I ought to be duly thankful."

Larry hung up and wheeled around to face him.

"Anything in the news we ought to play up?"

"Nothing," answered the city editor, "but the usual crop of murders, holdups, and suicides. I'll chuck them all into the back. I've got practically every man at work on sidelights of this Morgan story. I'm getting expressions of opinion from every scientist I can think of. I'm going to run a symposium of scientific opinions."

"Play up the way the public is mobbing newsboys for the *It*," Larry instructed him. "Bronson will have some pictures of them soon."

"How about editions?"

"There won't be any changes until the Wall Street final and the late sports."

"Do I keep Paddy in front all day long?"

"Yep."

"Does another bomb break to-morrow, chief?"

Larry nodded, and Morrisy grinned.

"You know," said the city editor, "I've dreamed all my life of being in on a beat as big as this. I never thought they came this big. And I don't see how you're keeping it corked up."

The phone rang, and Morrisy departed. Larry picked up the receiver, and the voice of Jason Ortola crackled in his ear.

"How are things going, Galloway?"

"Perfectly," Larry told him. "Everybody in the world is frantic for more news. I've had cables from every country in the world and telegrams from every State in the Union. So far there hasn't been a leak. Have you seen the *It?*"

"I have. I think you are handling the story splendidly."

"Where are you?"

"At my Newark plant. I spent the night here. You haven't mentioned my name, so far, and of course there haven't been any reporters around yet. I'm making arrangements to have this plant guarded, and I intend to have a personal guard of five men, two in uniform and three in plain clothes."

"Have you talked with Professor Morgan?"

"He had me on the laboratory extension a few minutes last night, but he wasn't coherent. I imagine he was slightly intoxicated. He says he is in a state of siege and doesn't dare go near a window. But the detectives are handling the crowds well. Is it your idea that I am to talk to reporters to-morrow?"

"I'd prefer," said Larry, "that you'd tell them as little as possible. They will go straight to the worst feature of the corporation story. My advice is to be extremely discreet. I am featuring the tremendous expense you have undergone. I'd harp on that, Mr. Ortola."

There was a pause. Then: "Have you seen Polly?"

"Not yet. She is in town with her aunt. By the way, will it be all right to send a photographer around, and take some pictures of you in the plant?"

"Any time," said Ortola, and hung up.

An office boy came in with copies of the early editions of all the afternoon papers and laid them on Larry's desk. He quickly looked through them. The Professor Morgan story, without exception, occupied the important right hand double column, and in most cases carried a streamer across the page.

There were pictures of a guinea pig and of an Airedale dog. One tabloid went so far as to print, on its cover page, a "synthetic photograph," a highly imaginary conception of the apparatus with which dead animals were restored to life. This was an elaborate affair of many levers and wheels and electric coils. An Airedale dog was seen leaping from a hole in one end of the Goldbergian contraption, while at one side, with his hands on levers, stood a recognizable Professor Morgan. Larry, grinning, laid it aside for Professor Morgan's edification.

McWhorter called him a little before noon. His voice was weary.

"Everything is still air-tight up here so far, boss," was his report, "but it's been an awful struggle. The workmen have finished the fence and they're wiring it now for high voltage, so that anybody who tries climbing over will get the surprise of his life. The farm is swarming with curiosity seekers. There are cars parked as far as the eye can reach and five State policemen are trying to handle the traffic. One enterprising hick is trying to charge everybody a quarter for parking privileges, and they tell me he is cleaning up.

"Professor Morgan is sticking tight to the lab. It took five detectives to get a tray of breakfast down to him. The reporters decided to starve him out, but they didn't get away with it. There isn't a name I haven't been called and my epitaph is going to have to be written on asbestos with a blow torch!

"The Brookhaven telegraph office is swamped. I got a color story through last night. Did it get there?"

"It did," Larry assured him.

McWhorter suggested: "You'd better try to piece out something from what I've given you. I can't get anything through on the wires to-day. I understand the Associated Press is stringing a circuit up here. A truck arrived with a load of tents awhile ago. The place looks like an army camp. How is the paper selling?"

Larry told him. "We are running every press all day long. Our day's run will be close to a million. To-morrow, somehow, we'll try to double that. Can you switch me to the laboratory?"

"I'll do my best, boss, but I'm warning you that the professor isn't in a speaking mood."

There was a clicking and a buzzing. The irritable voice of Professor Morgan presently barked: "Well, what is it?"

"This is Galloway."

"Oh, it is, is it?"

"How are things going, professor?"

"How are things going?" snarled the usually genial biologist. "They couldn't be going much worse, could they? I'm penned up in here like a criminal. I'm sick. Where is Polly?"

"With Mrs. Islington."

"Have you seen her, Galloway?"

"Not yet."

"When you see her, tell her that I wish newspapers had never been invented. Tell her I miss her like the very devil. What have other biologists said?"

"That you have made the most wonderful advancement in the history of science."

"And I suppose the New York papers are full of it."

"The story is being featured by every New York paper, and I presume it is being featured in every newspaper in the world. Why shouldn't it be? It's the biggest news story in history."

"And I suppose you're simply delighted," growled Professor Morgan.

"I am," Larry laughed.

"Good-by," snapped the professor, and Larry's receiver became alive with that hum heard when long distance lines are empty.

Miss Hanson brought in another pile of telegrams, and he plunged into the task of answering the important ones. Until noon he received disgruntled reporters, told them nothing, and sent them away again. Then he called Polly Morgan.

She was breathless with excitement.

"I never was so busy in my life, Larry! We've been going to milliners and dressmakers all morning. Aunt Sally is simply a darling! I can never thank you enough for making it all possible."

"I talked to your father," said Larry.

"How is he?"

"Peevish."

"The poor old dear!"

"He's penned up in the lab. The farm is swarming with reporters and souvenir hunters. You haven't talked to reporters, have you, Polly?"

"Not yet," she said. "But Aunt Sally insists that we talk to them soon. And I think we should, too. They simply hounded us this morning wherever we went."

"But you said nothing."

"I simply ignored them. I pushed right on past them. It was so thrilling! When will you let me talk to them, Larry?"

"What," Larry rudely inquired, "have you to say to them?"

"Why! Loads of things! Aunt Sally thinks it would be wonderful for me to give them my views on the modern generation."

To himself Larry groaned: "Oh, Lord!" And aloud: "Does she?"

"A reporter," Polly bubbled on, "followed us into Cecil's this morning and suggested it. He wants me to write it and sign my name to it. I think he was from the *Graphic*.

And the *Mirror* wants me to write my life story. I've been offered twenty-five hundred dollars for it!"

"I'll pay you three thousand," said Larry. "If you feel that you must write your life story."

"Oh, Larry!" she squealed. "I'll start writing it immediately!"

"I suppose," he said sourly, "nothing can persuade you not to give your views on the modem generation and to write the story of your life."

"But what harm will it do?" she wailed. "Aunt Sally thinks it's a wonderful idea—and I can't very well offend her, can I?"

"Evidently not," agreed Larry.

"She thought you were awfully nice," Polly told him; "but she agreed with me that you're too serious."

"I gathered that," Larry growled.

"She doesn't see any reason why I shouldn't enjoy all of this excitement I can squeeze myself in on. She thinks it's all terribly romantic—all these reporters chasing us and—and everything. Will you help me write my life story, Larry?"

"I am too busy," said Larry.

"But—but you're going to see me, aren't you?"

"I am working from early morning till midnight," said Larry, "and I'm going to be busier."

"But I want your advice!"

"You have Aunt Sally's."

"Oh, Larry, you're sore! What have I done? I must see you. Will you take me to dinner this evening? Larry, I've got the sweetest new hat—"

"I'm having dinner with Benjamin Sturm," he stopped her.

"Very well," she said. "Will you call me up some time, when you're not so busy?"

He hesitated before he uttered a begrudged "Yes."

Then there was a long silence at her end.

"Good-by," she said coldly.

"Good-by," Larry answered, quite as coldly—and slammed down the receiver on its hook.

He didn't want to see her. He didn't want to see Polly Morgan again—ever! She wasn't worth it. Or—she wouldn't be worth it by the time Aunt Sally got through with her. All of the fine plans he had made for her were ruined. Damn Aunt Sally!

17

FAME HAS ITS PRICE

THE BIGGEST NEWS story that had ever appeared upon the horizon of the publishing world continued to grow. People everywhere talked of nothing but Professor Morgan and his epochal discovery.

A mail train was robbed between Chicago and Omaha. A favorite motion picture actress took her life with strychnine. An aviator made a non-stop flight from New York to Rome.

These events and others as epochal were forced to the obscurity of newspapers' interiors. Nobody in the world was interested in anything but the wonders of the laboratory which Professor Morgan had revealed and continued to reveal. In all quarters, opinions of skepticism and doubt were heard.

The attitude of the world had at first been one of incredulity. Then, perhaps because people believe only that which they wish to believe, the reports from the laboratory on Lake Shallon were listened to with some respect. There remained, of course, doubters everywhere.

People said that the story was a hoax. People said that Professor Morgan was a lying scoundrel. But whatever they said and whatever they believed, they bought newspapers as they had never bought them before.

On the day when *The Daily It* made the announcement that Professor Morgan was prepared to restore to life any man the American people would select, the circulation department reported a sale of one million nine hundred and fifty thousand copies.

That afternoon Professor Morgan emerged from the seclusion of his laboratory and permitted reporters to ask him questions and photographers to click their shutters at him to their hearts' content.

The descent of the reporters upon the unhappy man was comparable to that of a starving wolf pack upon a lone and helpless stag. He shot back answers to their questions as fast as they were fired at him; without hesitation, crisply.

"Is it true that you will restore to life any man the American public may select?"

"It is true."

"Are you sure that you can restore to life a man who has been dead fifty or a hundred years?"

"If his skeleton is intact."

"You don't fear a failure?"

"I don't see why I should."

Telegraph instruments in all parts of the United States began to clatter as men with scraps of paper rushed to tents where instruments had been installed. Professor J. Hendricks Morgan was talking at last!

"Is it true that you are not going to follow the precedent of giving your discovery freely to the world?"

"It is true," he answered.

"Are you going to patent your discovery?"

"There is no need for patenting, even if it were patentable. The secret of the process is in my head."

"Is it true that you plan to make a charge of one million dollars per resurrection for a man weighing two hundred pounds or less and fifteen hundred dollars for each additional pound?"

"That is Mr. Ortola's estimate. He is handling the business end."

"What will you do with your millions, professor?"

"That is a silly question."

"But the public will want to know."

"You can tell the public that I plan to go on with my experiments. All of the money I receive I will put into that."

"Can you restore to life a man who has been dead two hundred years?"

"If the skeleton is complete."

"Can you restore to life a man who has been dead five thousand years?"

"I can."

"You are quoted in *The Daily It* as saying that you will not tell how it is done."

"Mr. Galloway saw the experiment performed. He saw

me transform the bones of his dog into the living animal. He was at liberty to describe what he saw. From a scientific point of view, his description is amusing. I told him, and I will tell you simply that the process is chemical and electrical."

"What dead American would you personally prefer to bring back to life?"

"I have no preferences."

"What dead American do you admire above all others?"

"I say, I have no preferences."

"Washington?"

"He was a great man."

"Lincoln?"

"He was another."

"Roosevelt?"

Professor Morgan kept his lips tightly closed. He answered another volley of questions, in which the attempt was made to force from him some description of his revivifying process.

Then some one cried: "Why did you select *The Dally It* as your mouthpiece?"

He answered: "Because it has a reputation for honesty. I have read the *It* for years. I wanted the story told straight and kept straight."

"What was the matter with the *New York Times?*" indignantly demanded a *Times* man.

"What was wrong with *The World?*" a New York *World* man wanted to know.

"Why didn't you pick *The Herald-Tribune?*" a reporter from that flourishing journal peevishly inquired.

"It did not matter who published the original stories,"

was Professor Morgan's answer, "so long as they were not garbled. I wanted to deal with one man who had a reputation for honesty. Before I selected him, I made a thorough investigation. Mr. Galloway met those qualifications better than any other man I could find. He handled the story, as I said, perfectly. It was the first news story I have ever read on a scientific event that was not mangled."

"How is the decision as to what dead great American shall be resurrected to be made?"

"That is in the hands of Mr. Galloway."

One hundred reporters groaned. The name Galloway had become so much gall and wormwood on the lips of all newspapermen.

"He must have paid you a fancy price for the exclusive rights to all this," one cynic remarked.

"On the contrary, he did not pay me a cent. He did not come to me, in fact. I sent for him. We made a simple business agreement. In return for his handling the story with dignity and honesty, I gave it to him on an exclusive basis for three days.

"You can have one more hour of my time, in which I will answer to the best of my ability all intelligent questions. At the end of that period, I am going to be pestered by no more reporters. You will have to go to Jason Ortola hereafter."

"What can you tell us of the rumor that your daughter is engaged to marry Galloway?"

"It is news to me. She can marry whom she pleases."

"Have you any objections to Galloway as a son-in-law?"

"I know Galloway only casually," the biologist answered,

"He struck me, in the little time I saw him, as a splendid young man. Why don't you ask him?"

There was a growl from the assembled reporters.

"The only answer he has to anything," one of them barked, "is, 'Read *The Daily It*.' Damn *The Daily It!*"

Then they again concentrated on the process whereby the dead were restored to life.

The rumor of Larry's engagement to Polly was already occupying front page prominence in many newspapers. Larry, for perhaps the tenth time that day, was saying into his telephone:

"There is absolutely no foundation for it. I am not engaged to Miss Morgan. I am not contemplating an engagement to Miss Morgan or any one else."

"You're so busy denying everything you're asked," responded the surly reporter at the other end of the wire, "that it has become a habit."

"If you doubt me, why, ask Miss Morgan."

"She has been referring all inquiries to you."

"We are not engaged and we are not going to be engaged," Larry angrily told him. "We are nothing but casual friends."

"How casual?"

"I have known her less than a week," Larry snapped.

It occurred to him, as he terminated the connection, that, since the big beat had fallen into his hands, no newspaperman, except those on his own staff, had had a kindly word for him. He had become the most hated man in journalism. Throughout newspaperdom he was bitterly referred to as "that big hog."

This constituted the only cloud upon his peace of

mind. By corralling the biggest news story ever known and handling it as he had, he had become journalism's outstanding figure. The highest position in the newspaper world was automatically opened to him. He had, in three days, sent up the circulation of his paper from two hundred thousand to almost two million. He had realized the most fantastic dreams of all newspaper editors. He only wished that his brethren did not hate him so.

THE STAFF OF every department of *The Daily It* had been doubled and trebled. Five secretaries were working overtime to handle Galloway's telegrams and correspondence. Miss Hanson had brought order out of chaos. Burke had miraculously geared up the presses; Carlyle has superhumanly managed the tremendous task of distribution.

But Lawrence Galloway, twenty-eight-year old managing editor, was the genius who inspired it, was responsible for the units functioning as a smooth-working whole.

Perhaps the most impressive moment of his experience so far occurred when the police commissioner of New York paid him a visit in person.

"I don't want to know what you're going to spring next, Mr. Galloway," he said. "All I want to know is, are you going to spring anything bigger than you already have?"

"I am," said Larry.

"Then certain arrangements must be made for your protection. I understand that Mr. Sturm has placed one of his limousines at your disposal. My suggestion is that you let me select a police department chauffeur for you, and that you let me assign some men from my department to accompany you wherever you go.

"Word has come to me already that cranks have tried

to get at you. If you intend to have anything to do with a scheme whereby a man is brought back from the dead, my opinion, for what it is worth, is that your life will be in constant danger.

"Beginning to-morrow, I will have a motor cycle escort for your limousine, and a personal guard of two men who will accompany you. And, with your permission, I will station a half dozen men about the office. If you care to have me, I will post one man, who is versed in secretarial work, in this office."

Larry gave his approval to the commissioner's suggestions. A little later in the day a quiet-voiced, gray-eyed young man was added to his secretarial staff, and that night, when he rode home from work, two muscular young men rode with him in the limousine.

Crowds stared at him now when he appeared on the street. If he wasn't popular, he was at least famous! He was not only the man who had scooped the world on the Morgan story; he was the owner of the dog that had been resurrected after two years in the grave! He was, incidentally, a comfortably well off young man, as a result of the bonus accruing to him for *The Daily It's* increased circulation; five thousand dollars for each fifty thousand additional circulation—a total of approximately eighty thousand dollars!

If his voice took on a new assertiveness, if he was crisp and curt with people with whom he had formerly been amiable, if he, in short, took to thinking of himself as a young man of great talent and vast importance, who, really, could blame him? The wine of success almost made him reel. And there were greater triumphs to come!

The most exciting moment of his life occurred a few days after the police commissioner's visit, when a madman somehow slipped past the guards in the outer office and did his best to stick a knife nine inches long into Larry's back as he sat bent over his voluminous correspondence.

He was not aware that an attempt had been made upon his life until, hearing oaths and the sounds of a violent struggle, he sprang up to see the gray-eyed young man from central office wrestling on the floor with a wild-eyed, black-haired man who foamed at the mouth.

Jujutsu in the end triumphed. The man with the knife suddenly became inert, and Dennison, the secretary-sleuth, seated on his heaving chest, quietly said:

"Would you mind sending out for a man to put cuffs on this wild Indian, Mr. Galloway?"

It was unnecessary for Larry to follow out Dennison's suggestion. The office was promptly filled with indignant employees and detectives, who hustled the maniac away, but not before Bronson had permanently recorded his frothing image upon celluloid.

This attempt upon Larry's life was, of course, good "copy." It was featured in subsequent editions in columns paralleling the life story of Miss Polly Morgan. A pretty girl in pigtails smiled out from the same page from which glared the frenzied visage of the murderous fanatic.

Larry gazed at these features a little later with acute distaste. Morrisy had not consulted him about running the madman story; hadn't deemed it necessary. It was news. Lawrence Galloway was an important personality; an attack upon him by a maniac was hot stuff.

But, to Larry, the story was dull. It offended his dignity.

And the life story of Polly Morgan, which she was sending down by messenger day by day, offended his finely developed sense of delicacy. It was a fairly well written, bubbling, girlish story of a life spent among scientists, profusely illustrated with photographs from her album— Professor Hornbrook's handiwork!

It was not an "I confess" type of story, but it had that flavor somehow, and Larry was depressed whenever an installment of it met his eye. In it he saw the neurotic inspiration of Aunt Sally.

It was, of course, good news, because it supplied the avid readers of *The Daily It* with the background against which Professor Morgan had worked. It gave them intimate glimpses of his life, of his daily routine. And, despite its copyright line, it was being shamelessly seized upon and rewritten by other journals in America and abroad. Later, Larry would have the pleasure of seeing that life story in twenty-six different translations.

He disapproved of Polly for writing it; he disapproved of Aunt Sally for permitting it to be written.

Aunt Sally had, after that famous third day, been basking to her heart's content in reflected limelight. With Polly, hugging her arm, she had been photographed innumerable times; had seen her chic self flashed on the screens of motion picture theaters; had gladly given out interviews on her renowned brother-in-law, in which she tempered justice with mercy and spoke only of his finer qualities.

Aunt Sally was, in the vulgar speech of the photographic world, a lens lizard. You could not fatigue her, no matter how many times you clicked your shutter at her. And Polly, it seemed to Larry, was fast falling into the same detestable category. He came to look, in the clippings that piled hourly on his desk from all parts of the world, for Polly's "camera smile." It was becoming the fatuous, artificial smile of the motion picture celebrity.

It made Larry sick. Polly, too, was a lens lizard, smiling sillily at you from every newspaper; and she was likewise publicity mad. She gave out interviews on the modern generation, on dancing, on transatlantic hops, on any subject the reporters suggested.

Larry successfully withstood a week of "The Story of My Life," by Polly Morgan, Daughter of the Renowned Biologist, and a week of Polly's professional camera smile and inane interviews. He found that he could stand it no longer. He instructed one of his secretaries to get her on the telephone. At the end of one hour, his secretary reported that the attempt to establish communication with Miss Morgan had been fruitless, but that a woman would take the message.

"I'll talk to her," said Larry. And into the telephone: "Is there any particular reason why I should not talk to Miss Morgan?"

"Miss Morgan," came back the suave voice of a woman, "is always engaged between the hours of eleven and twelve writing her memoirs."

"Her memoirs," Larry repeated disgustedly. "Are you, by any chance, referring to the story of her life which she is writing for *The It?*"

The woman admitted that the designations were inter-changeable.

"Who," Larry demanded, "are you?"

"I am Miss Morgan's secretary."

"Her secretary!"

"Who is this?" snapped Polly's secretary.

"This is Lawrence Galloway. Will you kindly tell Miss Morgan that I wish to have a word with her?"

"But Miss Morgan gave me the strictest instructions—"

"As the publisher of her memoirs," Larry interrupted heatedly, "I should have the privilege of consulting her, if you'd like to put it that way."

"I'll see what can be done," said the woman with dignity. "But I promise nothing."

Polly's voice, however, came down the wire a few minutes later.

"Oh, Larry?" she said, drawling it. "I almost expected that you were never going to phone me again. You're always the one exception to my rules about not being bothered. Hereafter, I'll leave word that you are to speak personally with me whenever you call."

"That's terribly good of you," said the sarcastic young man. "I trust I didn't break your thread of thought. I called because it seems to me that the time has come for me to deliver a little of that advice that you wanted."

"Larry, I do appreciate your thoughtfulness in calling. When would you like to see me?"

"How about dinner to-night?"

"Dinner to-night!" she wailed. "I meant sometime about ten days from now."

"Ten days from now!" he repeated. "Are you going away?"

"I'm going to be terribly busy. I am terribly busy. I'm dated up, literally, for every minute of my waking time for the next—um-m-m—let me see. Miss Jordan, will you let me have my appointment book? Larry, will you hold the line while I look?"

Larry fumed in silence while the investigation was carried on at the other end of the line. Her voice, contrite, apologetic, was presently heard again.

"The very first time I can let you have, Larry, is from two to three in the afternoon, a week from next Thursday."

"A week from next Thursday!" he roared.

"But, Larry, if you'd only spoken sooner, you ought to know that you could have had every date I have between now and doomsday. But you didn't phone. You were peeved. I thought you weren't ever going to see me again."

"I'm going to see you to-day," he stated.

"There isn't a chance, Larry," she wailed. "Oh, why didn't you call sooner?"

Larry glanced at his date pad and mentally drew a line through an appointment to confer with department heads at four-thirty to five-thirty.

"I'm going to see you," he said grimly, "at four-thirty this afternoon. You can name the place. Name it!"

"But, Larry—"

"Name it!"

"This afternoon at four-thirty," she answered in a quavering voice, "I have an appointment for tea with the secretary for the British embassy. He's coming all the way from Washington—"

"Break it!" Larry snapped. "I don't care if he's coming all the way from Mars!"

"I'll meet you in the lobby of the Ritz at four-thirty," said Polly in a hurt voice.

18

WHEN THE WORLD GOES MAD

IT WAS STRANGE that, despite the numerous photographs he had seen of Polly Morgan in the daily press, Larry still carried in his mind the picture of her as he had last seen her—a sweet, merry girl of the outdoors with a certain naïve charm that had left a deeper impression on him than he would care to admit.

This afternoon, when she met him, only fifteen minutes late, he recognized her, not as the girl he had known, but as the artificial personality created by flattering reporters and ubiquitous flash lights. She was become a radiant creature. She was all the things you could apply—in a nice way—to the season's most popular débutante.

She was poised; she was beautiful; she was with the costly assistance of the city's most exclusive modistes and milliners and masseurs and coiffeurs, a girl of elegance. She was simply attired in dark blue silk. A blue-fox scarf rested nonchalantly upon her slim shoulders. And she exhaled the subtle and alluring aroma of a perfume that probably cost seventy-five dollars an ounce.

She was really exquisite; but Lawrence Galloway didn't see her that way. If he had been meeting her for the first time, he might have been infatuated; certainly, fascinated. But such a spell as she might have cast upon him was ruined by the things that tormented his mind: her camera smile, her interviews, the silly story of her life—her "memoirs."

But her fine brown eyes looked up at him and wanted approval. He had none to give her. His expression was sour. He was aware that nearly every one in the lobby was looking at them, talking about them; and this irritated him the more.

There was a queer, actual hurt in his heart as he looked down into her upturned face, her smile fading, her eyes losing their glow of expectancy.

He knew—anybody with intelligence would know—that a fine girl had become a little sap.

"Have you reserved a table?"

He had, of course, neglected to reserve a table and they were, as a result, relegated to a stuffy corner.

Polly said rebelliously as they seated themselves:

"I don't see why you take the attitude that you do with me, and it puzzles me just as much—why I let you take it. You've been sore as blazes ever since that night at your cabin. You disagree with everything I say and disapprove of everything I do. You made all arrangements for me to come to New York—and you haven't been near me. What have I done? What do you want me to do?"

Larry gazed across the table at her perfect hat, her perfect face, and what he could see of her perfect dress. The words that came most naturally to his grieving mind were: "You're perfect." He said just those.

Polly seemed to stiffen.

"If you're going to be sarcastic I'm going to leave this table!"

"I didn't mean to be sarcastic," the young man apologized. "You are perfect. You're perfectly dressed. You're a perfect beauty. Every man for yards around is staring at you as if he'd like to eat you up. But some of it just doesn't happen to be the kind of perfection I was aiming at when I—when I—"

"When you found me," she dryly finished. "I've changed, have I?"

"Changed!" he hollowly echoed.

"You were going to give me advice," she said. "Why don't you do it?"

He glanced at her hands. They were no longer rough, no longer red, no longer swollen. They were tanned, but they were slim and elegant. And they were defiled by no jewels. At least, he approved of her hands.

She spoke again before he had stopped hesitating.

"I suppose you are sore about the story I am writing for *The It*. I'm not a literary person. I'm simply doing the best I can."

"I don't see why you wrote it."

"I wrote it," Polly informed him, "because I needed the money. Dad hadn't much to give me for this trip. You have no idea how badly I needed clothes. Aunt Sally would have loved to buy them, but I had to draw the line somewhere, didn't I? Everything I have I've paid for. My status is simply that of a house guest. You wouldn't want me to be an object of charity, would you?"

"These interviews on the modern generation—" Larry mutteringly began.

"Have you been reading them?" she asked.

"Have I!"

"You may have noticed, then," Polly spiritedly went on, "that the generalities I'm handing out to the modern generation are darned sensible. Have you a cigarette?"

He opened his case and handed it to her. A waiter brought the tea service, and Larry watched her. She hadn't forgotten how many lumps he took or his preference for lemon over cream. But the hands that yielded his cup to him was trembling.

"I've had an offer to go into vaudeville."

"My God!" Larry groaned.

"What do you advise?"

"What does Aunt Sally advise?"

"She urged me to accept it—also an offer I've had from the movies."

"Why not?" Larry asked.

"That means you disapprove."

"Does it really make any difference?" Larry softly wanted to know. And it was the softness of an iron fist in a velvet glove.

Her eyes suddenly became moist and her chin trembled.

"Nothing I can do pleases you!" she cried. "I think you're cruel and selfish."

He retorted:

"I've wanted you to be what you might be. You're a million miles off the track. That's what I'm sore about. You're going to be another Aunt Sally."

"She's a marvelous woman!" Polly declared. "She's been as kind as if I'd been her daughter. I think she's perfect. I'd like to be just like her."

Larry compressed his lips and said nothing. She watched him as if she were a little afraid he would say something more unkind.

"Larry," she began again in a hopeless voice, "I wish I knew what it was you wanted. I've been saving this hat and this dress especially for you, and you—you haven't even said you like them. Won't you tell me what you'd like me to do instead of always taking the attitude that I've made another mistake?"

Larry started to answer her. But he had become conscious that he had no earthly right to dictate to this girl. His criticisms were presumptuous. He had constructed an ideal of her and he wanted her to grow into it. He was, he realized, nothing but a meddlesome jackass.

"I think your dress and hat are beautiful," he said, and was pleased at the quickness and gratitude of her smile. "Up on the farm I thought you were pretty. You're beautiful, Polly."

That made him feel much better. She was inclining toward him. Now she placed her elbows on the cloth and her chin on her clasped hands, in the attitude of a woman who has become tremendously interested in a topic.

"That's the first nice thing you've ever said to me," she told him. "It almost makes up for all the dirty cracks!"

"I've probably been going along on the assumption," he answered her, "that everybody else is saying nice things."

"But a girl never gets tired of hearing them."

"Doesn't every man you meet tell you you're beautiful—ravishing—irresistible?" he laughed.

"What if they do? I've wanted you to."

"Well, I have."

Polly smiled. "I suppose that entitles you to go ahead and say some more nasty things about me. What a little idiot I'm making of myself. Do you really want me to stay out of vaudeville and the movies?"

"I haven't anything to say about it."

"There," she groaned, "you go again."

"No," he disagreed. "I'm through being your severest critic. From now on, I'm going to be the soul of appreciation."

"Will you tell me that the story of my life is pretty well done—for an amateur?"

"I'd rather not talk about that."

"Or that my interviews are intelligent and constructive?"

"Or those. Tell me about the men you've been meeting. How many of them have proposed since I saw you last?"

"Eleven," said Polly solemnly. "Not counting the one I stopped before he started. Or Jason. It wouldn't be fair to count him."

"How many times have you seen Jason since you've been here?"

Polly looked thoughtful. "I've had lunch with him twice and dinner with him twice, and theater afterward. I had tea with him here yesterday. You probably saw our pictures in the papers. The reporters mobbed us. He insists that I'm going to marry him. He thinks the difference in our ages isn't important. What do you think?"

He answered: "What does Aunt Sally think?"

"That's another dirty crack, isn't it?"

"No."

"She thinks he's well worth considering. He's worth millions."

"Do you love him?"

Polly looked more thoughtful.

"I've had a taste of nice things. I'd like more. I'd like everything. He could give them to me."

"That's looking at it practically."

"Why not look at it that way?" Polly took him up. "That's what people marry for nowadays, isn't it? I used to think I was romantic. I thought I'd like to give all for some poor, struggling man who needed me. But that was before I rode in a Rolls Royce. Larry, you were going to look up Jason for me. Did you?"

"I did," Larry answered. "All I can tell you is that his private record is in keeping with what you know. The newspapers have been featuring his blackest side, because of his insistence on turning your father's discoveries into profit. You've seen the editorials."

"They're dreadful," Polly breathed. "He must have a shell an inch thick. But he only laughs about them. I asked him if it was true that he had bribed his way out of trouble that time they arrested him for selling reclaimed alcohol to that bootleg syndicate. He admitted that he had 'arranged matters with certain powerful officials.' But he didn't think he was doing anything wrong. What do you think?"

Larry answered carefully:

"I think Ortola is in a position to be a pretty dangerous citizen. I agree with his individual views up to a certain point, but I feel uneasy about him when I hear that he sold over a million gallons of reclaimed alcohol in a year."

"But you think, taking him by and large, that I might as well marry him?"

"I'd rather have you ask Aunt Sally that."

She gazed at him, broodingly, for several seconds. Her color was high. Her brown eyes were softly asparkle. Her long lashes drooped as she glanced down at her cigarette. And Larry was filled with a vague discomfort.

It struck him that any other man in his position would have been making love to this attractive girl. It occurred to him that the subject had been in the offing almost from the moment he had met Polly, and that he himself had been pushing it into the background.

Certainly, Polly Morgan had more appealing traits than any girl he had known. She had a winsome personality.

The reason behind his present unresponsiveness, he reflected, was Aunt Sally. He might have fallen in love with Polly if she had made some effort to live up to his ideal of her.

Her simplicity, which he had found so charming, would soon be lost. She was becoming materialistic. Soon she would be only another blasé New Yorker, feeding her greedy soul upon sensations.

"How," she asked him, "did that story start about our engagement?"

"Such rumors," he answered, "don't start. They just are."

"You denied them so flatly I almost felt I'd been jilted."

"I didn't want to spoil the good chances I knew you were going to have."

Polly gave a slight shrug.

"You're awfully funny," she said. "You're so darned suspicious."

This, Larry reasoned, demanded an explanation, but he did not ask for one. They were silent a few seconds. Polly presently said:

"Tell me about the voting contest."

"It's attracting more attention," Larry responded, "than any contest in newspaper history. Yesterday's sale of *The It* was a million nine hundred and eighty-five thousand. We've had, so far, more than a million votes in to-day's mail. We have two hundred clerks opening letters and assorting coupons. Day before yesterday's returns amounted to more than eighty per cent of our sale.

"The same averages apply pretty nearly all over the country. The total of three days' voting, based on the telegraphic reports from the hundred and seventy-six papers subscribing to *The It* service and thereby entitled to participate in the contest, is over fifteen million. That's about an eighth of the entire population of the country. More people are voting in this contest than have ever voted for a President."

"Some people are voting more than once," Polly suggested.

"I don't care how many times they vote," Larry laughed. "They're having a battle and all our papers are profiting by it. I don't care who wins, and I don't want to have anything to do with the decision. If George Washington comes back to life, I don't want him to point an accusing finger at me, if he doesn't like the life he's brought back to.

"That's what one body of cranks are arguing: maybe the man selected will resent being brought back to life. And some people, of course, are saying that we haven't the right to monkey with life and death. I'm getting about a thousand letters a day from cranks. I don't believe the country has ever been worked up to a higher frenzy over any issue.

"Our most difficult problem is the politicians. Here's a national issue they aren't in on—and can't get in on! My

Washington correspondent tells me that the work of state has been practically suspended until the excitement dies down. Congress is sore because we didn't put the decision up to them. A delegation of Senators is taking me out to lunch tomorrow!

"I knew this story would be an explosion, but I didn't dream there would be so many incidental explosions. There have been several riots. Well, you're reading the papers."

Polly nodded. "I'm reading every scrap. Is George Washington going to win?"

"Without question," Larry answered. "The returns, when I left the office at four o'clock, gave him a lead of two million votes over Lincoln, and his gain is increasing by the hour. Roosevelt still holds third place, and Robert E. Lee fourth. The Southern States are still voting heavily for him. Woodrow Wilson and Benjamin Franklin come next. There are still surprisingly big returns for McKinley, Harding, Grover Cleveland, Paul Revere, Alexander Hamilton, Thomas Jefferson, and George Dewey.

"Hundreds of names I've never heard of—regional heroes—are still coming in. Hollywood has sent in over two hundred thousand votes for Rudolph Valentino. I don't remember what Wally Reid's total is. A good many old-timers are still casting ballots for John L. Sullivan.

"In another day or two, though, I think it will settle down to a race between Washington and Lincoln. What do you hear from your father?"

"I had him on the phone a few minutes this morning," Polly answered. "He's very irritable."

"He refuses to talk to me," Larry told her.

"I don't think he dreamed things would be so hectic.

He's shut up there in the lab with nothing to do but drink. Reporters have tried every conceivable scheme to get in there. He won't talk to a soul but me, and he takes my head off every time we do talk. He says there are two hundred detectives patrolling the grounds now, shooting away cranks and reporters. Jason is going up to-night. I think dad is getting scared. He says he can't sleep at night. The poor old dear!"

Larry said nothing. He was more worried over Professor Morgan than he would care to admit. He knew that the manifestations of public opinion were preying upon that once genial man. Throughout the world he had been bitterly condemned for not giving his secret to all scientists. And he was being stormed, as Larry had anticipated, by people who wanted husbands, wives, fathers, mothers, sons, daughters, aunts, and uncles brought back to life; who appealed to him by mail, by wire, by telephone, and in person.

Upward of a thousand telegrams and ten sacks of mail were being delivered to the Morgan farm daily, McWhorter had reported.

More hopeful or more determined supplicants had brought or shipped the skeletons of their loved ones by train and by automobile. Two hundred skeletons had, so far, been shipped back to consignors by the Brookhaven express office. More than a dozen people had attempted to present Professor Morgan with cremated remains, and word had trickled out of the laboratory, via detectives, that science was unable to deal with ashes.

The newspapers had seized upon this story and given, it

great prominence, whereupon crematories all over America promptly became idle!

There had been two attempts by cranks to bomb the laboratory.

And Professor Morgan, hiding in his big red barn from this Frankenstein monster that he had not dreamed of creating, was beginning to crack under the strain.

Larry wondered if Polly was concerned about her father. If so she was most successfully concealing it.

"You look as if you're not getting enough sleep?" she told him.

"I'm not," he admitted. "When I ought to be sleeping, I lie awake wondering where this thing is going to lead."

"Worrying," she corrected him.

"I knew there would be more excitement over it than over anything that had ever happened before," he answered. "In fact, I said so. Everybody was accusing me of being too cautious. You can understand now why I was so opposed to Ortola's determination to announce that they'd restore life on a factory basis. That has become a boomerang. Everything is out of control."

"Don't you think that things will calm down, once the voting is over and whoever wins is brought to life?" Polly asked.

"I do not," he replied. "The country is going to go mad. Have you ever gone to an old-fashioned revival meeting? There you had a relatively small number of people going into hysterics and having convulsions. When George Washington is brought to life—simply multiply that by a million."

"It scares me," Polly admitted.

"And it's keeping me awake nights," said Larry.

She glanced at her wrist watch and rose.

"I have a date at six. Any time after this you want to see me, I'll break any date I have for you. I think it does you good to talk to me. I have always prided myself on my soothing influence."

There was something, Larry admitted, in that.

"When this is all over," she went on, "I think we all will need a vacation."

"When will it be over?" he wanted to know. "Will it ever be over? I can see life getting more and more complicated years and years into the future. I can't quit. Your father might save the day by refusing to go on."

"Dad will see it through," said Polly. "You may think he's cracking, but I know him. He's drinking too much, that's all. Every eye in the world is on him. He's probably the most hated, feared, and tormented man who ever lived. But I'm not worried about him. He has tremendous will and an iron constitution."

At least, Larry reflected, she was aware of the true situation in the big red barn on Lake Shallon.

19

DISTURBED IN HIS LAST SLEEP

RETURNING TO HIS office in one of the largest of Benjamin Sturm's limousines, Larry reluctantly agreed that Polly Morgan's influence was soothing. She had somehow enabled him to clear his mind, to give him a new grip on a situation he had felt was slipping.

The truth was, of course, that events were happening too rapidly for the mortal mind to keep pace with. He had perceived the effect of Professor Morgan's announcement upon the world as an abstraction. He had not foreseen a mob frenzy that would sweep the nation, precipitate riots, arouse the antagonism of Congress.

As a newspaper editor, he had seen the circulation of *The It* shooting to dizzy heights. But he had not seen people destroying news stands and trampling upon newsboys or that daily amazing spectacle of mounted policemen, like Cossacks, charging upon the mobs who clustered about *The Daily It* Building. He had, he realized, imagined an excited but polite public. He had not pictured a public that would cluster in knots, arguing, quarreling, coming often to blows, to knives, to pistols!

Business throughout the United States had reacted woefully to this mob frenzy. People would not work.

In shops, in offices, in factories they discussed Professor Morgan. It was as if America had been convincingly informed that the world was coming to an end.

People were emotionally clutching at the realization that, provided you were rich enough, all the sting had been removed from death; that, in weeks or months, one would enjoy the incredible sensation of gazing upon a living man who had walked upon this earth when the American hemisphere was an unknown wilderness; of other men who had known the world when we lived in caves; when Egypt was a strident young empire. The riddles of ten thousand years would be answered, and time would cease to be.

Confronted by these stupendous realizations, how could ordinary mortals be expected to perform their trivial daily tasks? How much more important to discuss an election in which every nominee was dead? How much more vital to consider this new world, created by one scientist, in which one must revise his entire list of values! How, indeed, could one grasp, without endless discussion, that death, the specter of the ages, had finally been vanquished?

Larry glanced, almost with apprehension, at the latest editions of New York newspapers lying upon his desk. He was in constant suspense over some vague but dreadful happening that impended. Headlines announced that to-day's toll of dead, resulting from arguments over Professor Morgan, was, in New York alone, nineteen; that Wall Street, the stock market, would close its doors until further notice; that the brigade of State militia called out to maintain order along the roads leading to the Morgan farm, had been augmented; and that the outcome of the balloting was now certain.

With the hourly growing certainty that George Washington would win the contest, agitation was rising in new quarters. A minority declared that the indignity of this scientific experiment should not be visited upon a man so venerated by the American people.

Let Professor Morgan experiment with the bones of some ordinary man! Let the mortal remains of the Father of our country repose in peace! What good could possibly come of bringing George Washington back to life?

In this staccatic clamoring was heard the rising protest of those who held that God's work should not be tampered with.

An armed mob of passionate volunteers was hourly growing in Mount Vernon. Men bristling with rifles and shotguns were guarding George Washington's tomb, prepared to destroy with holy fervor any one who attempted to tamper with it.

This was the most important development in the day's news. Larry read on, and learned that historical societies were rising in their wrath, but in the ranks of these there was dissension.

In all places where chapters or branches or posts existed, debate was going on in the American Legion, the Sons and Daughters of the Revolution, the Descendants of the Signers of the Declaration of Independence, the Spanish War Veterans, the Civil War Veterans, and even such organizations as the New Jersey Council of the Junior Order of United Mechanics. All were in a state of furious agitation.

The issue was becoming, in short, more and more tremendous. The majority of American people, perhaps eighty per cent of them, were in favor of the project of restoring George Washington to life. The minority were, however, the more fanatical. They would be more violent; would put up a fierce resistance.

How, then, in the face of tremendous and armed opposition, could the bones of George Washington be removed from the vault at Mount Vernon? It began to look as if the experiment could not even be attempted!

Larry received a delegation of newspaper men in his office that evening after dinner to discuss this important and unexpected development.

Frankly, he admitted, he did not know what was to be done. In his position as Professor Morgan's mouthpiece, he was expected to say something.

"Professor Morgan," he told the reporters, "is waiting in his laboratory until the skeleton of the man the American people select is brought to him: None of us foresaw this contingency. What are we going to do when a mob of armed fanatics will shoot down any man who goes near that tomb?"

"It is up to you," one of the reporters replied, "to decide what is to be done. You have taken it upon yourself to be the ringmaster of this show. No one else has had a chance to give advice or offer suggestions. You're up a tree and a gang of bears is crawling up after you, waiting for your first false move."

The remark was characteristic of newspaper men's attitude toward him. They would never forgive him for his selfishness; they hated him.

Another one asked: "Are you going to appeal to Congress?"

"I am not going to appeal to anybody," Larry snapped.

"I am not going to do anything about it. If the skeleton of George Washington is delivered to Professor Morgan, Professor Morgan will bring George Washington to life. I'm doing nothing but covering the story."

"The hell you aren't?" one man snarled. "You took it on yourself to decide who was to be brought back to life, didn't you? You started this darn fool contest, didn't you? If you hadn't been such a hog for circulation, you'd have picked any skeleton that happened to be handy. You've got yourself into a beautiful mess, and we want to know how you're going to wriggle out of it."

"I have nothing to add to what I said."

"What are you going to do if Washington's skeleton can't be obtained?"

"I don't know."

"You aren't going to try to get it by force?"

"Certainly not!"

"Do you realize there's apt to be a pitched battle at the tomb and that a lot of people are going to be killed?"

"I hope it doesn't happen."

"Do you realize that Washington's remains are contained in a sealed marble sarcophagus that would have to be blasted if you secured the skeleton?"

"Yes," Larry wearily admitted. "I know all about that."

"Had you thought of obtaining permission from the Mount Vernon Ladies' Association which controls the tomb?"

"I had not," Larry answered. "I had considered my relation to this whole affair that of a reporter. Why don't you talk to Jason Ortola? He is managing the practical end of it."

"Ortola sent us to you."

"All I have to say," Larry promptly took up the questioner, "is that I will have nothing to do with any attempt to obtain Washington's bones from his sarcophagus. If they are brought to me I will deliver them to Professor Morgan."

"You will?"

"I will."

The reporters presently left him—left him to his renewed contemplation of the fact that all newspaper men, with the exception of the little handful in his employ, cordially detested him; wanted him to make some false move so that they could crush him, punish him, humiliate him.

He had not foreseen this either. He had seen nothing but glittering triumph, the realization of a fantastic dream.

He was, naturally, seeing as little of reporters as possible. His tilt with them to-day was his first contact with them since the announcement of the voting contest was made, save for a random inquiry now and then by telephone.

It seemed to him that their attitude was very unfair. He had done what any newspaper man in the same circumstances would have done. They were, he argued as he had done before, simply jealous of his good luck, his great success, his ability.

His pride in his achievement presently returned. He *was* a great success! He *had* performed the greatest achievement in the history of journalism! And it was not his fault that people were being killed. He had either printed facts as they had been presented to him, or acted under orders.

Newspapers on the following morning prominently featured his answers to the reporters' questions. They were unfair stories. In them he "hedged," "backwatered," "stammered," and "passed the buck."

People, he read, were going to Mount Vernon from every part of the country to join the armed mob that was protecting Washington's tomb. The police did not know what to do about them. They did not dare attempt to disarm them; their numbers were so great.

Congress was taking up the matter, but Congress was already divided. By evening, Congress was still quarreling. A resolution to empower the President to send soldiers to drive the mob from the tomb was shouted down.

Filibustering was going on in the Senate Chamber. A Senator from the South, with strong anti-resurrection tendencies, possessed the floor and read all day long from books on Washington's life.

The President, pressed for his opinion on the entire matter, refused to commit himself.

Two days later the contest closed. The results, given in round numbers in the next morning's papers, were as follows:

George Washington	12,500,000
Abraham Lincoln	7,750,000
Roosevelt	3,000,000
Robert E. Lee	2,750,000
Woodrow Wilson	1,500,000
Benjamin Franklin	1,000,000
McKinley	750,000
Harding	750,000
U.S. Grant	750,000
Rudolph Valentino	600,000

Admiral Dewey	500,000
Grover Cleveland	400,000
Paul Revere	350,000
Alexander Hamilton	275,000
Thomas Jefferson	250,000
Wally Reid	225,000
John L. Sullivan	150,000

More than one hundred names were represented in the list. A total of approximately fifty million votes had been cast. Throughout America, people congregated on street corners and heatedly argued.

The deadlock in the House of Representatives continued. The filibustering in the Senate continued. The President issued a statement to the effect that he had nothing to say.

Bulletins from Mount Vernon reported that the armed mob was being swollen by steady streams of automobiles. It was estimated that one million people had swarmed to the banks of the Potomac.

Police were unable to cope with the problem. The greatest traffic jam in history was occurring. It would require, it was estimated, several days to untangle it.

A bulletin from Lake Shallon contained the information that more militiamen had been called out to prevent a growing army of citizens, which surrounded the farm, from trespassing.

Professor Morgan was reported to have spent the night in conference with Paul Muller, his assistant, and Jason Ortola.

Three men carrying infernal machines had, during the night, been apprehended and arrested.

An attempt had been made to poison Professor Morgan's supply of drinking water with cyanide of potassium.

At eleven-fifteen a flash came from Mount Vernon that electrified the nation. Airplanes, flying low over the tomb, were dropping tear gas bombs!

The voluntary defenders of Washington's last sleep were flying before the yellow clouds!

Bulletin:

> Two of the planes, after circling like hawks, have swooped down near the tomb. Men wearing gas masks are climbing out of the cockpit. Companion planes continue to deluge the tomb's vicinity with tear gas bombs!

For fully fifteen minutes the entire nation waited in breathless suspense for more news.

Bulletin:

> Three unknown men entered Washington's tomb, blasted open the sarcophagus, placed the bones of Washington in a sack, reëntered their planes and have vanished toward the north!

Less than an hour later, Baltimore reported that five planes, in close formation, flying high and fast, had passed over, headed north.

Then the five planes vanished as if they had soared upward and away into space.

Later they were sighted, as five infinitesimal specks,

above New York. Subsequently they were reported flying above New Haven, Conn.

Reporters who had been permitted to remain at the Morgan farm presently began sending bulletins. The five planes were reported circling about overhead, as if seeking a field in which to land. One of them darted down with motor idling, skimmed treetops.

He alighted in the meadow below the laboratory.

A man leaned from the cockpit and swung outboard a canvas sack. Reporters and detectives raced toward the plane.

A detective was the first to reach him.

He dropped the bag in the detective's arms. His face was spattered with oil from the motor.

Reporters agreed unanimously that he was grinning when he crisply jerked out:

"Present this to Professor Morgan with my compliments. It contains the skeleton of George Washington!"

The mysterious flier ducked his head as a camera clicked.

The motor raced. The plane moved; rolled ahead; gained momentum, and swiftly joined its companions wheeling about above.

Fifty voices shouted: "Who was that?"

No one knew. The plane had no markings. They had, it was later advanced, been painted out for this reckless exploit.

Tenderly indeed the precious sack of bones was carried to the laboratory. Jason Ortola met the excited procession.

Graflex shutters clicked and motion picture cameras whirred as the chemist, with his twisted smile, accepted the sack from the man in pale blue.

A moment later the iron door in the concrete wall clanged shut, and the reporters gazed into the sky. The planes were gone.

In the laboratory, Professor Morgan and Mr. Muller were bending over the canvas sack. Mr. Muller withdrew a white skull.

Jason Ortola was rasping into the wall telephone: "Galloway? The fliers have just come. We have the skeleton. Is your plane ready?"

He replaced the receiver and said to Professor Morgan: "Galloway will leave Belmont Field in five minutes."

20

"BRADDOCK! WHERE ARE YOU?"

A FOKKER CABIN-PLANE coasted into the meadow below the laboratory a few minutes after the sun had set and was quickly surrounded by newspaper men, photographers, and "Professor Morgan's Constabulary," as his hired guardsmen were lightly referred to by the press.

One man alighted from the cabin. It was Lawrence Galloway. He lifted out a large black suitcase and faced the crowd.

A reporter seized him by the elbow.

"I suppose," he growled, "you think you're going to hog this, too?"

Larry stared back into his hostile eyes and groaned. His face was gray and drawn and haggard. Under his eyes were smudges of darker gray.

"If George Washington comes out of this experiment alive, he isn't going to be hounded to death by reporters."

"We aren't going to let you whole-hog the rest of this, if that's what you're getting at," one of the men answered.

"Where are you going to take him?" another asked.

"To the farmhouse," said Larry. "As soon as he's got his bearings, eight of you can come in and talk to him. That's my proposition, and you can take it or leave it. Decide who the eight will be, and let me know."

"How long will this resurrection business take?"

"I don't know how many hours from now it will be finished. I don't think much will happen before ten o'clock."

"How about getting into the lab while it's going on?" an Associated Press man asked.

"I'll ask Professor Morgan."

"And that'll be the last we'll see of you?"

"Whatever he says," Larry said wearily, "I'll make an agreement with you to tell you immediately afterward every detail of the experiment I can remember."

"You mean, you'll hog it as usual. We've been trying for days to get permission from Morgan and Ortola to get in there while it's going on. We're always referred to you. Take your feet out of the trough awhile, will you, and give somebody else a chance?"

"If I can get anybody in there, I will," Larry promised.

A volley of jeers gave him a fair estimate of how highly his promises were held by newspaper men. Larry made a tired gesture with his hands, eloquent of his inability to make himself understood.

He was surrounded now by uniformed detectives. They formed a slowly-moving wedge that delivered him presently at the iron gate in the concrete wall.

Muller admitted him. He, too, bore evidences of the strain he had been under.

"Be careful of the old man," he warned Larry. "He's ready to blow up."

Larry went into the laboratory. Professor Morgan looked up from the long white cylinder and glared at him.

The most talked about man in the world was a shocking spectacle. He had not shaved for at least a week. His eyes were bloodshot and fiery. His face was as gray as lead. Since Larry had last seen him he had aged, in appearance at least, ten years. The stalwart, genial scientist was gone. In his place was a petulant old man. He seemed even to have shriveled.

The glare was his only recognition of Larry's entrance. Larry spoke to him, but he did not answer.

"Jason, test out that C-coil."

Larry glanced at the cylinder. It was only partly opened. He saw what he believed was the top of a skull. He shuddered.

It struck him suddenly again that all of this was too preposterous for intelligent belief. He had, he told himself, been sleeping all this time before the fire in his cabin; dreaming. No living man would, could possibly emerge from that cylinder.

He said crisply: "Professor, will it be possible for a few reporters to witness this experiment?"

The biologist turned about from the cylinder.

"Aren't you capable of handling this matter without help?" he peevishly demanded.

"I am capable enough to handle the story," Larry answered, "but I can't, with any justice, be the only newspaper man to watch the experiment. I have been called a hog ever since this story broke. It would make things easier for me if you would permit eight men to see the experiment."

"It's too many!"

"Oh, for God's sake, let him have them!" Ortola snarled.

Larry took Professor Morgan's bristling silence for

assent. As he started for the door, the wall telephone rang. Muller answered it.

"Polly?" he exclaimed and turned from the instrument. "It's Polly," he said. "She and her aunt and Benjamin Sturm have just flown up from New York. They're at the house."

Professor Morgan took the receiver from his hand.

"Positively not," that irritable man said after a few seconds of listening. "You should not have come here. You had no right bringing her here. I will not let either of you in here to-night. We have no room for any more. Very well, Mr. Sturm will have to stay disappointed."

Larry slipped out. He found Detective Sergeant Walker and a dozen or more of his men lounging about outside the iron door.

"Pass the word along," Larry told him, "that eight men will be permitted to watch the experiment,"

Larry returned to the laboratory. Muller met him at the door.

"I'll let you know when we're ready. The old man doesn't want you or anybody else snooping around. It will be a big surprise to me if this thing comes off at all. You saw the shape he's in, didn't you?"

"I hardly knew him."

"He's been on the verge of D.T.'s for a week. He won't eat. He can't sleep. All he does is drink that rotten stuff and walk—walk—walk. He's cracking. He hardly knows what's going on. And Ortola is wild. All he can see is the possibility of the old man's spoiling three-quarters of a million dollars' worth of his damned precious chemicals."

Larry said thoughtfully: "I wonder if anybody has thought of having a doctor handy?"

The osteologist replied: "Do you suppose we haven't thought of everything? Run along and I'll let you know when we're ready. And for God's sake keep your friends quiet. Drum it into them how touchy the old man is."

The oak door closed. Larry lighted a cigarette and found a well-worn path which ran along one side of the building. It was perhaps thirty feet in length and beaten hard and deep. How many miles had "the old man" paced off on this runway since two weeks ago?

The drone of an airplane drew his eyes aloft. Dusk had fallen and the sky was a soft purple haze shot with bars of rose and silver. He could not see the plane, but suddenly espied a glittering light on either wing tip; one red, one green. It was, he knew, the Boston-New York air mail.

He pondered: "Boston—New York—Chicago—Washington— Everywhere in this country, people are sitting at their radios, packed about newspaper bulletin boards, waiting for news to come from this old red barn. Waiting for word that George Washington is alive again!" It made him feel weak, sick. Everybody in the world, almost, waiting to hear that George Washington was alive again! And that drunken, bleary-eyed old man all ready to crack!

Larry resumed his pacing. He was tired. He had never been so tired. His eyes burned and his head weighed tons. No man in the world had ever been so tired. And the future was chaos. He tried to think back to a time when life was uncomplicated; when the dark shadow of some vague impending doom did not hover over him, and wondered if he would ever again have a month to himself in the cabin.

He wondered what the symptoms were of nervous breakdown. He was sure he had five or six of them; this queer twitching of his eyelid muscles, his inability to sleep, his way of jumping at the slightest unexpected sound, the annoying pressure at the back of his head.

The iron door clanged. Men's voices rose around the corner. Larry turned back. Men were filing through the gate. He counted them. One—two—three— There were, in all, eight.

They came to meet him, eight pale, nervously grinning, half-scared men.

"When is it going to start?" one of them quavered, speaking in a low, husky half-whisper.

"Muller will let us know."

The eight men stared at the oak door as if, behind it, lurked some awful monster.

"How are we going to get our stuff out of there?"

"It can't be done," said Larry firmly. "It's only twelve minutes from start to finish, anyhow."

"Oh, yes," one of the reporters muttered, huskily, "twelve minutes."

They were all lighting cigarettes or cigars or pipes as an outlet for their agitation. It was so dark now that match flames lighted their faces.

"I think we should have a clear understanding of what we're to do afterward," Larry said, his voice, too, hushed. "I suppose it's occurred to all of you that if George Washington—"

One of the men tittered. The others softly swore at him.

"George Washington!" he giggled. "Good Lord, it's too much!"

"Shut up!" growled Grenville Brown, a *Sun* man.

"If this thing comes off," Larry went on, firmly, "we are

suddenly going to find ourselves with a delicate problem on our hands."

"Mr. Washington," the man with the thin voice began, mockingly, "it gives us great pleasure to welcome—"

"For God's sake, bottle it," snapped Brown.

The giggler subsided.

"I don't think any of us can stretch our imagination far enough," Larry proceeded, "to grasp what his reactions may be. We have got to take that into consideration. My suggestion, if it does come off, is to give him, say, fifteen or twenty minutes to get his bearings, while we are outside giving the stuff to the others."

The reporters argued it. In the end, they agreed to support Larry's suggestion and the discussion drifted off into a whispered debate about George Washington's age, were he to be revived.

They smoked and whispered. Stars came out. A faint rumbling filled the air, a distant, many-voiced tumult, made up of automobile horns, of automobile exhausts, of people's voices. All roads leading to the Morgan farm were choked with cars.

A voice on the other side of the concrete wall cried:

"Has anything happened yet?"

Brown called back: "They're still getting ready."

The voice impatiently cried: "Can't you let us have something?"

"We don't know any more than you do. Pipe down!"

"Another point I want to talk over," Larry said, "is the condition Professor Morgan is in. No one must ask him questions. If he talks, let him. But don't irritate him with questions. He's almost ready to crack."

"That's news!"

"Wait a minute. You'll discover something when you see him that you may have suspected."

"You mean, he's tight?"

"He's been drunk ever since he shut himself in there," Larry answered. "You'll see it yourselves. I know how you feel about granting any request I make, but I'm not asking a personal favor."

"His secret is safe with me," one of the men said promptly.

There were varied remarks upholding Larry.

"Is he so drunk he's apt to fumble it?" Brown wanted to know.

"We're worried about that," Larry admitted.

"But if he fumbles it, we'll have to tell why."

The oak door opened. Against hazy amber-green light the head of the osteologist was silhouetted.

"Galloway! Now, listen to me, you men. You are to file in quietly. I mean quietly! Watch your step! If you touch any piece of apparatus, knock anything over, I'll kill you. Professor Morgan is to be asked no questions. Ortola is to be asked no questions. I am to be asked no questions.

"I have arranged benches for you to sit on. There is to be no jumping up or running around—and no comments. Professor Morgan is in a serious nervous state. He is just able to go on with this. Now—follow me."

Cigars and cigarettes were cast to the ground; pipes were tapped out on heels. With white faces and sharp, darting eyes, the reporters filed in behind Muller.

On tiptoe they entered the laboratory.

Larry, seating himself, glanced critically about the high,

whitewashed room. It was, he concluded, unchanged—
this made-over wagon room on which the attention of the
world was focused to-night.

Work tables against the walls and in the middle of the
room were littered with the same confusing array of paraphernalia he had seen on that tumultuous morning when
Paddy had been miraculously restored to life. He tried to
photograph the scene upon his memory. Later to-night he
would require that photograph. If all went well, the biggest
story of his career would be written to-night.

The high voltage cabinet in the far corner was hissing.
Behind a peephole, a green light waxed and waned.

Professor Morgan was bending over the long white
cylinder, adjusting a heavy wire to the electrode at the left
end. Ortola was moving the Z-ray tube nearer the cylinder's aperture. Muller went from burner to burner, lowering
the blue licking flames under some retorts, raising them
under others.

The man beside Larry hoarsely whispered in his ear:

"That thing the cylinder he comes out of?"

Larry nodded. The men were staring with large,
half-frightened eyes about the room, following with slowly
moving heads the confusing system of glass and rubber
tubes which flowed out from the contributory pieces of
apparatus to the tangled ganglia above the great white
cylinder.

Larry wished that his heart would not beat so hard. It
was shutting off his breath. He glanced at the row of faces
beside him. Every man's teeth were clenched; every man's
eyes were popping; every man's face was pasty and gleaming with sweat.

Their attitudes and their expressions suddenly reminded him of his only visit to the death chamber in Sing Sing. As a cub, he had been sent to cover an electrocution. The same fear he had seen in the faces of the men about him then he saw in these faces about him now. The man who giggled put his hand over his mouth, in the gesture of a frightened woman.

Professor Morgan said in a creaky voice: "We'll start at eight-thirty, Jason."

Nine pairs of eyes flew to the wall dock. It was eight twenty-four.

"Heat up this tube, Jason."

The chemist walked to the switchboard as the executioner at Sing Sing had walked to the switch which had sent, with a single horrible convulsion, a man to his death. He closed a double circuit. The tube glowed, a frosty heliotrope. Professor Morgan wheeled it closer to the aperture and it threw a flickering ghostly light into the rafters.

The hissing in the cabinet and the steaming of the retorts seemed to grow louder.

The man beside Larry said, "Phew!" and mopped his forehead with a silk handkerchief.

Professor Morgan croaked: "Are you ready, Jason—Muller? Are we all ready? Are you sure of that C-group, Muller?"

"Yes, sir; the temperature is one forty."

"Start at nine thousand volts, Jason. All right, Muller. Now!"

The hands of the clock pointed to eight-thirty.

The electrical machine in the corner began to rumble. Ortola, watching the Z-tube, quickly manipulated levers on the switchboard. The tube's emanations became intensely violet tinged with yellow. Muller, limping about, carefully adjusted burners. Professor Morgan, with face averted, spun the steel wheel which controlled the gigantic tube.

A great retort near the reporters blossomed rosily. The line of men swung their heads to stare at it. Its luminosity increased until that end of the room was bathed in soft rosy effulgence.

Larry wondered, as he had done before, which stage of the experiment was so dangerous.

Vapors began to charge the atmosphere with a fine, pale-blue mist. It seemed to him that this irritating blue fog came earlier than it had in the other experiment, earlier and thicker, and he presumed that this was due to the greater quantity of chemicals being employed.

The mist tickled his throat and burned his eyes. The man beside him began to cough convulsively into his handker-chief.

Still the blue fog increased. Professor Morgan, cursing softly under his breath, became a dim and preposterous figure, the emanations from the tube lighting only one side of his face and body, the other side seeming to be non-existent. Muller and Ortola were gnomes, laboring in this rising artificial blue haze that was beginning to shut off the rafters.

A thick white spark came crackling to life on top of the cabinet, and all other sounds were silenced by its savage snappings. It bruised the senses with short periodic crashes.

To himself Larry confided: "I can't stand any more of this."

The scene and the actors in it, moving about in the dense

blue atmosphere, had become monstrous, horrible. Science, bringing its intricate mysteries, its awful powers to bear upon the task of creating life from death, had gone too far.

He wanted to cry out "Stop!" It was wrong. In this azure fog, stinging his eyes and parching his throat, he found the very essence of immorality.

He would never again, he knew, be the same man.

Somehow he had to write the story of this. He would say:

"Last night, in the red barn on Lake Shallon, occurred the most romantic moment in the story of humanity since the miracles beside the Lake of Galilee."

He shuddered. That would not do. To mention the Saviour in any relation to this meeting would be not only sacrilegious, but hideous.

"Last night, in the red barn on Lake Shallon," he would say, "science reached, a goal toward which it had been grop- ing for a thousand years.

"I have seen George Washington, living, breathing, in the white casket wherein he was created—"

He dropped his face into his hands and groaned.

A soft puff of an explosion occurred at the other end of the room. A sickening odor, suggestive of silver paint, crept through the blue atmosphere.

Then Professor Morgan's voice: "Cut out that group and use your emergency retorts!"

And Muller's snarling reply: "I have! I have!"

"Twelve minutes!" gasped the reporter, and began to cough.

Where the retort had cracked, a sudden crash was heard.

Particles of glass came showering through the air. Rising to his feet, Larry heard the biologist shout:

"I can't stand it!"

In horror he saw Professor Morgan lifting a club or a bar of metal above his head and bring it smashing down on a retort a foot in diameter. The retort vanished and a thick black fluid began running in a viscid stream from the bench.

Muller cried: "Grab him!"

An interval of shocking silence followed.

"Open that cylinder!"

None of the reporters moved. They were standing where they had risen. Professor Morgan began to curse in a low, terrible voice.

The man who giggled started toward him. His knees seemed to give way. He went to the floor on hands and knees and slowly rolled over on his back.

Larry stepped over him. Ortola was tugging at the copper terminal which sealed one end of the cylinder.

"Loosen those wing-bolts!" the chemist directed.

Larry touched one of them. It was warm. He ran his hand along the white round wall. It was warm.

The cylinder suddenly flew open along its upper seam, and he saw the pink body of a large man lying face down.

The man who lay in the cylinder gasped out in a thick, desperate voice:

"Braddock! Where are you?"

21

THE FIRST AMERICAN

ONE OF THE numerous dispatches sent from the telegraph tents on the shore of Lake Shallon that night contained the following:

> While a delegation of eight reporters stood frozen with terror in the famous red barn, watching Professor Morgan, his mind temporarily deranged by strain, smash valuable apparatus with a club, Lawrence Galloway, managing editor of *The Daily It,* rushed to the still hot cylinder and tore it asunder, freeing Washington, who lay within, gasping for breath.
>
> Paul Muller, the great biologist's assistant, stated to Associated Press representatives that Galloway's prompt action had undoubtedly saved Washington from returning to that dark vale whence Professor Morgan's genius had recalled him.

Lawrence Galloway's account of the event was admitted, even by the men who most detested him, to be the most graphic and thrilling of any that went out over the telegraph and telephone wires from Lake Shallon that night.

With the headline and drop Morrisy placed over it, the Galloway story is reprinted here in full.

IT EDITOR SEES WASHINGTON REBORN!

Opens "White Casket" to Greet Re-created "Greatest
American"—Washington Dazed But Well—Age Is Twenty-three—Has Full Mental Powers

BY LAWRENCE GALLOWAY

Managing Editor of *The It*

Copyrighted by *It* Features

(All rights reserved)

Special to "The It."

LAKE SHALLON, AUG. 12.

I HAVE SEEN GEORGE WASHINGTON! I HAVE
SHAKEN HIS HAND! I HAVE TALKED WITH HIM!

At 8.43 p.m., in an inferno of strangling blue mist, amid
the hissing of retorts and the crackling of high voltage apparatus, the "greatest American" was miraculously reborn.

At 8.43 p.m. I opened the white casket wherein science in
twelve minutes, at a cost of seven hundred and fifty thousand
dollars, had created him.

He was lying, face down in the cylinder, gasping for breath.

His first words were:

"Braddock! Where are you?"

This voice that had been hushed for one hundred and thirty
years was choking and desperate.

I helped him from the cylinder and to his feet. George
Washington stared at me for full thirty seconds, then said,
sharply:

"What are you doing here? I must—"

His voice broke off as he became aware for the first time of
surroundings which must seem as fantastic to him as some
nightmare.

Standing beside the white cylinder, he looked in stupefac-

tion through the dense blue vapor at the chemical paraphernalia and the electrical apparatus surrounding him.

Professor Morgan had disappeared. Paul Muller, his assistant, and Jason Ortola, followed by eight reporters who had
been permitted to watch the experiment, now crowded
around Mr. Washington.

He stared at them in bewilderment, with his head jutting
outward from his broad shoulders. In the same dazed state,
he permitted them to shake his hand.

GEORGE WASHINGTON'S AGE IS TWEN-
TY-THREE. THIS CONTRADICTS PROFESSOR
MORGAN'S EXPECTATIONS. HE BELIEVED THAT
WASHINGTON'S AGE WOULD BE BETWEEN
TWENTY-SEVEN AND THIRTY.

The first questions shot at him by the semicircle of reporters concerned his age.

He bewilderedly answered: "I am twenty-three."

Washington soon became aware of his nudity. To the
bewilderment in his blue eyes was added resentment.

Ill-considered questions were put to him, causing Washington to grow more bewildered and more resentful.

"Do you know that you have been dead more than a
century?"

Washington did not answer. He looked angrily at the questioner.

"Do you know that you have been dead one hundred and
thirty years?"

He answered: "Where are my clothes?"

His voice has a decided English flavor.

The suitcase of clothing I had brought by airplane two
hours earlier was opened. He was helped into the clothes it

contained. How strange these garments must seem to the gentleman of 1775! He is now wearing black Oxfords, a gray tweed suit, a white shirt with a soft collar, and a dark blue four-in-hand tie. They were selected in a department store this morning according to Washington's old measurements and fit him fairly well. It was decided not to heed the many suggestions that he be attired in the style of the eighteenth century.

He appears to be a grim young man. He has a long face with high cheek bones; blue, penetrating eyes set wide apart under a heavy overhanging brow. His hair is dark brown. His large mouth is kept firmly closed. The muscles of his face are under constant control. His lower jaw is massive.

His resemblance to familiar portraits of himself in his former existence at that age is startling. Most closely he resembles the ivory miniature of J. de Mare's.

While we were dressing him, he asked repeatedly where he was, but to all explanations he grew only more dazed and more resentful. He refuses to grasp the fact that he has been dead one hundred and thirty years.

He said time after time, in a distressed voice: "I do not understand."

He stared at an electric light bulb hanging by a cord from the rafter above him and asked what kind of light it was.

"An electric light," he was told.

Paul Muller attempted to explain. "All branches of science have made great strides, Mr. Washington, since you were on earth before. That is a glass globe from which the air has been exhausted. It contains a filament of fine metallic wire which is heated to incandescence by the passage of an electric current."

George Washington shook his head and made his familiar

comment: "I do not understand."

A reporter asked: "Mr. Washington, do you think some one is playing a joke on you?"

His answer was prompt: "I do."

Questions flew again.

"Mr. Washington, do you remember that you were the first President of the United States?"

He answered: "The United States?"

The reporter said: "The United States of America, formed of all the Colonies that existed during your time and States that have come into the Union since?"

Washington shook his head. "Governor Dinwiddie" he began, and stopped, staring at us.

"Governor Dinwiddie," he was told, "died in 1770. You don't remember his death?"

Washington did not answer.

"Do you remember the Revolutionary War?" No answer.

"Do you remember throwing a dollar across the Potomac?"

Washington's eyes brightened somewhat, but he did not speak.

"Did you ever throw a silver dollar across the Potomac?"

"No," he answered.

More questions, mostly senseless ones, were fired at him. He did not reply until a reporter asked:

"Is it true that, when you were a child, you cut down a cherry tree, and when your father asked you if you had cut it down, you said: 'Father, I cannot tell a lie; I did it with my little hatchet?' "

Washington did not smile. His answer was: "Absurd!"

"It isn't true?"

"No."

His anger was rekindled when reporters began asking him questions concerning his love affairs. His blush, of anger or embarrassment, deepened.

He was asked: "Who was the 'Lowland Beauty'?"

Washington stared at the questioner without replying.

A reporter asked: "You are credited with having been in love with Betsy Fauntleroy, Mary Cary, Lucy Grymes, Mary Philipse, and Sally Fairfax."

"You are insolent!" Washington said angrily.

The attack was shifted.

"What is your last recollection—the last thing you remember before you found yourself in this room?"

Washington answered: "I was encamped on the Monongahela above Fort Duquesne. Where is General Braddock?"

I answered: "General Braddock died more than one hundred and seventy years ago from wounds received in the battle near Fort Duquesne."

Washington turned his piercing blue eyes upon me. They were puzzled, angry.

"One hundred and seventy years ago?" he repeated.

I added: "In the year 1755."

Washington said firmly: "This is the year 1755."

Reporters clamorously corrected him.

Washington shook his head. "I do not understand."

A reporter asked: "Do you remember your wife?"

He answered sharply: "I have no wife. I am not married."

"Her name," he was told, "was Martha Custis."

He stated, more sharply: "I am not married to Martha Custis."

I asked: "Do you remember any occurrence after General Braddock's troops crossed the Monongahela on July 9, 1755?"

"How can I?" he replied crossly. "They will not cross until to-morrow morning!"

"You cannot grasp," I said, "that 'tomorrow morning' was more than one hundred and seventy years ago?"

His eyes flashed with anger. It was obvious that he still believed himself the butt of some elaborate, cruel practical joke, for he suddenly exclaimed: "You are Contrecoeur's men!"

A reporter laughed and said flippantly: "George, we are all one hundred per cent Americans like yourself!"

Washington stiffened. His eyes blazed.

He snapped: "I am Colonel Washington, sir!"

Jason Ortola at this juncture interrupted with: "You have asked this young man enough questions. Give Colonel Washington a chance to collect himself. Perhaps he will talk to you later."

The newspaper men, agreeing, left the laboratory to purvey to the waiting world the greatest news story of all time.

The picture I carried with me from the laboratory was of a tall, haughty young man gazing in pathetic bewilderment from his trouser legs to the complex machinery which had made him, once again, a mortal.

22

THERE IS NO DEATH!

LARRY WAS THE last of the newspaper men to file out of the big red barn. He was so weak he could hardly walk. He leaned against the side of the barn.

A clamor was rising outside the iron door, beyond the concrete wall. Later he learned that impetuous citizens had made a gap in the fence of State militiamen surrounding the farm; that upward of a thousand men and women had forced their way in before the gap was closed.

Days ago, a platform had been erected fifty feet from the door. On this platform powerful searchlights had been mounted. Beams whitely flooded the mob that milled about the iron door.

Larry fought his way into the crowd. He found Detective Sergeant Walker and shouted into his ear:

"You have to clear this crowd away."

"Is Washington alive? Did you see, him, Mr. Galloway?"

"He is in the laboratory. We must get him up to the house as quickly as possible. You'd better have fifty or more of your men surround him. And drive this crowd back!"

"Yes, sir; I'll do the best I can, Mr. Galloway. Does he look like his pictures? How old is he?"

Larry hastened to the house. He selected a typewriter and wrote his story.

The roaring of the crowd was abruptly hushed as he neared the end of it. He tapped out the final sentence and, with the copy in his hand, hastened outside.

In the crowd, under the blinding beams of the searchlights, he thought he saw Polly Morgan; then the crowd churned and he lost sight of her.

A space had been cleared at the iron door. Jason Ortola and George Washington were coming out. Guards were fighting back men and women. Larry saw the silhouettes of cameras.

McWhorter shot out of the crowd and ran up the kitchen steps.

"Boss, I missed you at the door as you came out. I've shot in all the stuff I could pick up. Is it true that—"

Larry handed him the typed sheets.

"Where's Doyle?"

"He's phoning a story of his own. I'll get this right off." And McWhorter ran toward the press tents.

Detective Sergeant Walker, Larry perceived, was finally bringing some semblance of order out of the awful confusion.

George Washington, looming above Ortola, was surrounded by a dense ring of guards. Other men in pale blue, detaching themselves from the crowd, were running toward the house. Systematically, they posted themselves in squads of six and eight at every door and window.

Larry saw a police club rise and descend on a man's hatless head. The man sank from view.

There were, a count later revealed, six arms and two legs

and a collar bone broken in that march from laboratory to house.

Dust was rising in a thin cloud. The searchlights, piercing it, followed the dense mass of guards and their nucleus. The frenzied roar of that crowd would linger in Larry's ears for hours. It was his first glimpse of true mob hysteria.

Throughout America, he supposed, in fact, throughout the world, mobs were doubtless acting as madly; people hugging one another; hats flying into the air; people on their knees, praying, chanting, blubbering. It was awful!

The searchlight beams, striking through the floating atoms of dust, gave to the scene a fantastic aspect that struck him as monstrous.

He thought: "Humanity lifted to a madness of rapture because death is conquered. George Washington is only a symbol. He is nothing but proof after the fact. But they will adore him! Good Heaven, how this hysterical, hero-worshiping country will adore him! The poor young devil!"

How long before America, the world, got back to an even keel? A blue-white beam played upon Washington's tousled hair. His face was white. His eyes rolled. The young man seemed terrified.

"It's cruel," Larry thought. "It's devilish. Did Indians resemble this mob when they did a war dance? He must be thinking of that. What *can* he be thinking? The poor kid! He thinks he's gone to hell. No picture of infernal regions could be as dreadful as this. What *are* we going to do with him?"

Then: "Think of the unhappy old men who will commit suicide—to be rejuvenated!" was his next reflection.

Larry saw that Jason Ortola was supporting the reborn Washington by an elbow. The young man was collapsing.

Larry turned and ran into the dining room. He called: "Polly! Polly! Mrs. Gore!"

There was no answer; or he heard no answer. Nothing but the shrill uproar outside. The house, except for himself, was empty.

He returned to the kitchen doorway. The slowly moving wedge of guards had shifted its course. They would take George Washington in the front way.

He ran through the house to the veranda and found a small war being waged there between photographers and guards. The guards were trying, with flailing clubs, to force them from the veranda, and the photographers were defending their position with pieces of chairs and folded tripods or anything that came to hand.

A battery of Kleig lights had been mounted midway down the veranda and they blazed brilliantly upon the fray.

A Pathé cameraman with a bleeding cut over one eye came staggering toward Larry.

"Mr. Galloway," he panted, "for God's sake tell these

boneheads to let us stay. We've got to get this. We haven't had a decent shot at Washington, and it's our only chance."

Larry threw himself into the mêlée and presently managed to make himself heard. The photographers were to retire behind a wide crack in the veranda floor directly in front of the battery of Kleigs; the guards were to line up along the railing and prevent a general invasion.

He retreated to the doorway as the phalanx of guards opened to disgorge George Washington and Ortola.

The face of the hero was paper-white. Drops of sweat formed upon it and trickled down in rivulets. He seemed to steady himself, however, when he saw Larry. He shook off Ortola's hand and faced the Kleig lights with lips slightly parted; tried to stare past their blinding brilliance at the whirring cameras.

NEVER HAD LARRY felt so sorry for any man. The historic steadiness of George Washington's character would be rudely shaken before he made any kind of adjustment to the chaos into which science had hurled him.

George Washington, with little jerks of his head, was peering dazedly about him, his expression woefully bewildered.

Larry heard him mutter: "These lights. All these lights."

"They want your photograph," Larry shouted, and realized that the camera, as a practical instrument, had not come into the world until after the middle of the last century.

"I do not understand."

Larry heard men calling his name. Reporters, beyond the rigid wall of guards, were trying to get his attention. Beyond them were faces, faces, faces, an endless sea of upturned faces, glimmering, undulating in waves under the hot white radiance of the Kleigs.

Little balls of white fire floated up over their heads. Flashlights. The air was acrid with the fumes of burning magnesium.

Larry's knees were trembling. There was hardly enough strength in his legs to support him.

"Colonel Washington—" he began.

A woman he at first did not recognize broke through the guards. Her bobbed hair was disarrayed. Her white dress was torn off at one shoulder.

Under his breath he groaned: "Polly Morgan!"

Another woman followed her, likewise disarrayed, wild-eyed. Not until minutes later did he identify her as the chic Mrs. Horace Glen Islington, otherwise Polly's Aunt Sally.

To Larry's horror, Polly Morgan, staggering to the bewildered Washington, seized his hands and, before he could resist, pulled him down, reached up on tiptoes and kissed his cheek.

His worst anticipations for her were realized in that revolting moment.

She turned from Washington with the girlish fixed smile with which Larry had already been made painfully familiar and gazed as sweetly as her wild condition would permit into the banks at Kleigs. Then, slowly, as if she had been rehearsed, she turned and walked into the house.

He said hoarsely: "Mr. Washington, if you will come into the house with me—"

"We'll take him into the library," Aunt Sally shrilly offered, but Larry still did not recognize her, so disheveled

she was, with a bleeding scratch along one side of her aristocratic nose and a long smudge of dirt across her forehead.

Placing her hand at Washington's elbow, Mrs. Islington
urged him into the house. Jason Ortola limped after her.
One of his Oxfords was missing.

The door closed after them.

In the front line of the mob that pressed about the
veranda Larry saw the faces of Grenville Brown, of the
New York *Sun;* Riley of the *Daily News;* Orcutt of the
Philadelphia Inquirer; Billings of the *Baltimore Sun.* All
were calling to him and gesticulating. Larry bent down
and shouted into Brown's ear:

"What can I do? He can't stand any more of this!"

"Let us in!" Brown shouted back. "You've framed this
the way you framed it from the start!"

A red-haired man behind Brown cupped large hairy
hands about his mouth and called up:

"Mr. Galloway, I'm in charge of the Radio Corporation's
field installation here. I can run a line to a microphone in
the room you use. I'll hook up the line to loud speakers on
that searchlight platform and the crowd can listen down
there. I'll hook up another loud speaker at the press tents.
Every broadcasting station in the country is connected on
a loop from my tent over there. I'll plug in the whole works
on one circuit, then everybody can hear all that Washington says."

Larry asked: "How long will it take?"

"Not more than ten minutes," the radio man answered.
"Most of the wires I need are already up."

Larry decided without hesitation: "Go to it! I'll open

that window at the end of the house and you can pass the microphone in."

Brown shouted, as Larry turned away from the veranda rail:

"How about the rest of us?"

"Isn't that arrangement satisfactory?"

"Like hell it is! What right have you to hog the whole works?"

Jason Ortola came limping out on the veranda.

"Galloway," he said, "Washington wants you."

"Wants me?"

"Yes, you. He wants to talk to you. He's somehow got it into his head that you're in charge. He wants to talk to you alone."

Larry, for the first time that evening, smiled. To Grenville Brown he said:

"Did you hear that?"

"No!"

"Washington wants to see me alone."

"Apple sauce! You framed it up."

Larry's triumphant little smile vanished.

He leaned over the railing and snarled into Brown's face:

"You can go to the devil!"

23

A TALK TO MILLIONS

GEORGE WASHINGTON WAS seated at the long table in the library when Larry went in. There was a glass of milk in one hand and a sandwich in the other. Bewilderment lingered in his face.

Aunt Sally was bending over him solicitously.

"Isn't he too marvelous for words?" she demanded.

Washington frowned, but did not acknowledge her presence otherwise. Polly fluttered about behind his chair, as if she longed to touch him.

"He simply doesn't realize a thing," Aunt Sally exclaimed. "Mr. Galloway, was there ever such a moment in the history of the world? Aren't you positively thrilled to the core? You poor boy, you look absolutely all in."

"I am all in."

For perhaps the first time in her life, he realized, Aunt Sally was satisfying her greed for sensation.

"I was just asking President Washington about his wife, but he doesn't remember her. Isn't it weird?"

"I am not married," Washington said wearily.

"Her name," Aunt Sally reminded the dazed man joyously, "was Betsy Ross."

"Her name," Larry wearily corrected her, "happened to be Martha Custis."

Aunt Sally's laughter was silver sleigh bells on a frosty night.

"History never did like me."

A tapping occurred at the window. Larry raised the shade and peered out. A man in khaki overalls raised a nickeled microphone into the light. A black wire attached to it vanished among the trees.

Larry lifted the window. The man, grinning nervously, said:

"It's plugged in, Mr. Galloway. Just put it on the table between you and—um—Mr. Washington. About fifty million people will hear every word you say, so don't do any cussing or we'll have to yank you off the air!"

Larry pulled in a dozen feet of the wire, shut the window and lowered the shade.

He placed the shining instrument on the table a few feet from George Washington.

The bewildered young man stared at the microphone. And from the microphone he glanced quickly at Larry.

Larry seated himself across from him.

He said: "You wanted to talk to me, Mr. Washington?"

Washington answered: "I want an explanation. I want to know what I am doing here. I want to know who these ladies are. You are the first one I can remember seeing when—when—" He stopped.

"When you came back to life?"

"I do not understand. I understand nothing of what is happening. What is that thing?"

"That," Larry answered, "is called a microphone."

"What is its purpose?"

Larry drew a deep breath. How could one explain the abstruse mysteries of radio to a man who had died before any practical application of electricity had been attempted; to a man who had died before the telephone, the telegraph, the electric light, the electric motor existed?

"This," he slowly replied, "is a device by which your voice and my voice are being transmitted to all parts of the American continent."

Washington interrupted: "Who are you?"

"My name is Lawrence Galloway. I am the managing editor of a New York newspaper."

"Will you explain my presence in this place?"

"I will attempt to," Larry returned. "And I assure you, Mr. Washington, that I am being truthful. We are not Contrecœur's men. We are Americans of a new and, to you, a bewildering age."

Jason Ortola limped out of the room.

Aunt Sally had, this time, been pacing up and down behind Washington. Now she whirled about, but Larry lifted a hand to stop her before she could speak. He did not want the dignity of this interview spoiled by her frivolousness.

Polly, seated at the end of the table, was staring intently at Washington.

Aunt Sally resumed her pacing.

He went on: "You will have to grasp the unbelievable fact, Mr. Washington, that you have been dead for one hundred and thirty years."

"I cannot grasp that fact," the young man said stubbornly.

"I will try putting it another way. Your memory stops with General Braddock's fight with the French and Indians on the Monongahela below Fort Duquesne, which began on the ninth of July, seventeen hundred and fifty-five.

"You will simply have to take my word that you have been brought to life again, in another age, one hundred and seventy years after your last memory."

The blue eyes of Washington were fixed intently upon his face. For the first time, bewilderment was absent from them. They were clear and piercing and, Larry thought, extraordinarily cold.

"I think you are telling the truth," he said.

"I will give you a very brief sketch of what has occurred since that time," Larry went on. "The battle at which your memory stops is known by us to-day as one of the engagements in the Colonial wars. In a subsequent attack on Fort Duquesne, the French surrendered to you."

Washington's eyes were glistening now.

"I returned to Virginia?"

"You did."

"And attacked Fort Duquesne again?"

"You did."

"By what road?"

"The one known as the Pennsylvania road."

Washington's mouth settled into its long, stubborn line.

"Not the Virginia road?"

"No, Mr. Washington. The French surrendered. And you returned to Mount Vernon and married Mrs. Martha Custis. In seventeen fifty-nine."

Washington's eyes narrowed. His jaw muscles hardened, but he made no comment.

"The American Colonies united in the early seventies of that century," Larry continued, "and in seventeen seventy-six declared war against England, partly because of burdensome taxes. You were tendered the post of commander-in-chief of the Colonial forces—and accepted."

"And fought England?" Washington incredulously demanded.

"And won."

"But I am a loyal British subject!"

"You were—in seventeen fifty-five," Larry hastily reminded him. "From seventeen fifty-five onward, one unpleasantness after another arose between England and the American Colonies. You and other Colonial leaders agreed that the Colonies must have independence. The war is now known as the Revolutionary War or the War of Independence. It ended in seventeen eighty-one."

Washington folded his arms upon his broad chest and sank his chin into his collar. His cold blue eyes remained unwaveringly upon Larry's.

"The united Colonies became known as the United States of America, and you were elected the first President. The capital of the United States was then at Philadelphia. In eighteen hundred it was moved to Washington, District of Columbia—a city named after yourself. It has been there ever since. The city is on the Potomac River, in accordance with a wish you once expressed."

Bewilderment was returning to Washington's face again.

"You served two terms of four years each as President," Larry hastily went on, "then retired to your plantation at Mount Vernon."

Washington interrupted in a thick voice: "When did I—die?"

"In seventeen ninety-nine. You have since been honored as the Father of your country."

The young man slowly shook his head. His eyes dropped to the microphone. His hand reached out and he touched it gingerly with the tips of his fingers.

"You say that this silver thing is carrying the words that we are saying to fifty million people?"

"Yes, Mr. Washington."

"It is beyond my comprehension. Let me ask you some questions, sir. Have these United States of America prospered since my death?"

"The United States has become the richest, most powerful nation in the world."

"Richer and more powerful than England?"

"Yes, Mr. Washington."

"Than Spain or France?"

"Than any nation."

Washington again slowly shook his head. And Larry recalled, from his recent prodigious reading, that Washington had always been grave, just short of being sad; that he seldom shook hands or gossiped; that he would listen to jokes with a straight face; that he so seldom smiled that once, when he had laughed in a theater, the newspapers were prompt to record it.

"The population of the United States," Larry enlightened him, "is now estimated at one hundred and twenty-five millions."

Washington's eyes grew round again, and again he wearily shook his head.

"My dear boy, the population of New York City alone—" Aunt Sally impulsively began, when Larry's angry gesture silenced her.

She hastened to Polly and whispered into her ear, and Polly, who had been dividing her attention between Washington and Larry, suddenly bit her lower lip.

Larry, with Washington's fascinated attention, went on expounding the glories of the United States of America. He told him pithily of her successful wars, her industrial development, he graphically described to his absorbed auditor the invention and perfection of the steamboat, the railroad and the telegraph.

He spoke in a clear, incisive voice as a man well might who realized that fifty million listeners were paying the closest heed to his every syllable. And he was glad that this opportunity had been given to him.

In the laboratory, the situation had all but escaped from his control when the reporters began asking ridiculous questions. He was proud to be in this position, introducing to the American people their greatest hero; doing it with dignity, with intelligence, keeping this stern, admirable young man on the pedestal where he belonged.

How easily might Grenville Brown or some of those others have reduced him again and again to angry bewilderment; perhaps made of him a laughing stock!

Repeatedly Washington commented: "It is beyond my comprehension." Or, "I do not understand."

Once he said: "Modern America, as you have drawn it before my eyes, is nothing to me but chaos.

"This au-to-mo-bile"—he pronounced the word slowly, hesitantly—"I cannot picture it at all, darting over the roads faster than the fastest horse can run. Or this machine that flies into the air. Or the other machine that goes so swiftly along two rails. Or vessels that cross the Atlantic in six days without sails. How were these miracles achieved?"

"By years of patient endeavor," Larry replied. "In each case, the man who sponsored it was laughed at by the public. In each case, it was a crude experiment. The inventive genius and the patience of man has perfected each one until, now, our civilization is built upon them; would collapse without them."

"I cannot comprehend," Washington repeated.

"This instrument I am touching now," Larry went on, "is called a telephone. It came into existence perhaps sixty years ago. There are millions of telephones in constant daily use. The voice, when you speak into this small rubber mouthpiece, is carried over wires to the man you wish to converse with.

"Many American business deals are transacted over the telephone. America is a vast network of wires, connecting all cities. If the telephone were taken away, American business would go into a panic."

Washington shook his head wonderingly.

"I do not understand how the human voice can reach out over so many miles."

"This device, this microphone," Larry went on, "is, with the complex machinery of which it is a part, perhaps the most wonderful development of them all. By means of this strange invisible energy, which we call electricity, our voices, as we speak now, are sent through the air without wires, across continents, even across oceans. People as far-away as England, even as far-away as Australia, clearly hear every word we are saying. By the same agency, in connection with the telephone, a business man in New York may talk to a business man in London."

Washington commented: "It is an age of incomprehensible wonders. It is an age of scientific miracles. And you say that science is responsible for my being here, upon this earth, again."

"Your being upon this earth again," Larry told him, "is considered the scientific triumph of all ages. Practically every branch of science has contributed its part to make the miracle possible. And this mysterious power, electricity, was applied in perhaps three of its different forms."

"I understand that least of all," said Washington. "I am, frankly, in a daze. So many of your words are meaningless. What a strange vocabulary the American nation must be using! What strange laws must have been passed in keeping with all the changes! We did not realize how simple life was—one hundred and seventy years ago! I must see all of the wonders you have told me about. I must see the places that were familiar to me—one hundred and seventy years ago! What has happened to my plantation?"

His voice was wistful and eager.

"It has been preserved as it was left when you died."

"And Fort Duquesne—now?"

"Is the site of blast furnaces in the city of Pittsburgh, Pennsylvania."

"Why," Washington suddenly cried in a voice of desperate sadness, "was I brought back to this?"

"The American people," Larry throatily explained, "wished you, more than any American who ever lived, to be brought back. You are their greatest hero."

"But what good can come of it? One hundred and thirty years, you say, have elapsed since my death. I can remember nothing later than one hundred and seventy years ago. I find myself in a bewildering new age, founded upon strange inventions which are beyond my ability to understand. You are talking a new language. You are faced, doubtless, by queer and baffling problems. What will be expected of me?"

"All America will want to see you. America will want your opinion on practically everything you see."

"I am too tired now even to contemplate that prodigious task," said Washington. "My head is aching. I cannot think. My brain can take in no more. Will I sleep in this house to-night?"

"A room has been prepared for you. Before you retire, do you wish to say anything to your millions of listeners?"

Washington gazed bleakly at the microphone.

"It is too soon. Later, when I have collected my thoughts, I will perhaps speak to America over this strange, incomprehensible instrument. I will say this now: America must not look upon me as the figure you say I became after the conquest of Fort Duquesne.

"I have been addressed to-night as 'General Washington' and 'President Washington.' I am certain that I wish to be considered only as the man I was at the time of my last recollections. I am Colonel Washington. It will please me to be addressed simply as Colonel Washington."

He arose quickly from the microphone. Larry watched him with shining eyes. How the American people would love this grave, unaffected man; would admire and respect his sincerity, his frankness, and his pride!

This youthful Washington, Larry reflected, was the embodiment of all those qualities the American people demanded in their heroes. It struck him that the American people had been using this very man as the pattern to which all their heroes must conform.

A sparkling in the darkness of the dining room doorway attracted his attention and he saw, standing there, Mrs. Gore—the mysterious, hostile woman who had taken up Polly's abandoned duties as housekeeper. The woman who tortured cats in the interests of biology!

Her pale-gray eyes were fixed coldly upon George Washington in a stare not unlike that of a reflective feline.

She had, Larry thought darkly, tortured, vivisected cats, helped her husband, the aloof Professor Gore, to analyze their nervous systems, in the elaborate preparations which had gone into the remaking of George Washington.

She was not looking upon him as the object of a nation's, a world's, emotions, but as the product of laborious years spent with test tubes and scalpels.

The great diamond on her hands, as mysterious as the essence of her own personality, glittered and flashed.

"I will take him to his room," she said, in her slurring Southern voice. "It is ready." And she went to the stairway.

George Washington placed his right hand, lightly clasped, over his heart and bowed deeply, first to Polly, then to her aunt, in what is sometimes described as "the continental manner." He did not smile.

Bowing more briefly to Larry, he accompanied Mrs. Gore up the stairs.

Larry, following him with glowing eyes, did not see Aunt Sally gesturing frantically to Polly. He turned only in time to see Polly seize the microphone from the table and lift it to a level with her trembling gray lips.

Breathlessly she spoke to those tensely listening millions:

"Good evening, everybody! This is Polly Morgan. Hasn't it been simply thrilling? Colonel Washington has gone up to bed. We all hope that he will feel much more at home with us by to-morrow, don't we? The poor boy was simply all in. I want to wish everybody good night and to tell you that my thrilling experiences will be made into a film by the Classic Features Corporation. Good night, all! Polly Morgan signing off!"

"Good Heaven!" Larry moaned.

He removed the microphone from her hands, took it to the window, which he opened, and hurled it into the night.

24

THE OLD STORY

AUNT SALLY, WHEN he turned about, was holding Polly in her arms, rapturously hugging her. Her face was flushed and her large blue eyes were excitedly shining.

So furious he almost sobbed, Larry cried: "How dared you do that?"

She retorted enthusiastically: "It was the greatest publicity stunt in history!"

"Publicity!" he groaned. *"Publicity!* Debasing a great moment with that cheap, horrible speech!"

Polly burst into tears. She dropped into a chair and covered her face with her hands.

He raged: "I was trying to avoid just that kind of thing. You've spoiled everything!"

Aunt Sally ran her slim long fingers through her tousled blond bob. She said angrily:

"Don't take things so deuced seriously. What Polly said was no worse than the stupid, dull, pompous things you said!"

Wretchedly, he shook his head.

"Running up to him. Kissing him like that. Oh, my God!"

"You're acting like an ass. It was good publicity. They

were both fine stunts. The first woman to kiss him! Millions of women will be furious with envy—and they'll all flock to see her picture!"

"Polly," he groaned, "how could you?"

"Don't blame her," Aunt Sally snapped. "Both ideas were mine. What are you kicking about? I didn't see you galloping out of the limelight! I've noticed that you've kept in the center of the stage ever since things started! Are you jealous?"

"Jealous!" repeated the wretched young man. "All I wanted was—was dignity. It's all I've been fighting for from the start. He mustn't be cheapened. I won't let him be cheapened!"

"Oh, stop being so silly. People don't like so much dignity. They like thrills Polly gave them two lovely ones. Here! Drink this milk and stop being hysterical!"

Larry ignored the glass of milk and sat down.

"You're a meddlesome, dangerous woman," he told her.

Aunt Sally laughed. "What I want to know is, what have you got against Polly?"

"What have I *got* against her?" he gasped.

"Yes; what have you got against her?"

"I think," he answered in a controlled voice, "that you and I understand each other perfectly, Mrs. Islington. You know what I wanted for Polly. You have deliberately gone against every wish I expressed. You seized her merely because she was an opportunity to gratify your greed for sensation!"

Aunt Sally laughed wildly. "Go on, go on!"

"I wanted to see her become what she promised to be—a fine woman. What is she becoming?"

"Oh, you reformers! What? What? I'll tell you, you pathetic deluded thing! She's becoming the only thing she could possibly become—a fine woman! You are simply obsessed with the notion that she mustn't enjoy her youth. Just as you are obsessed with the notion that George Washington must be made deadly dull."

She was pacing again, up and down, forth and back, from him to the end of the long rug, pivoting on one heel, returning as if she intended to attack him. Her blond, short hair stood out in wisps, in tags, in tangled knots.

One of her transparent stockings was torn and hung down below her knee in a long tongue. Her white kid slippers were almost black.

"Never have I heard such deadly conversation! Didn't you realize the poor fellow was dead already from excitement? You and your hellish dignity!"

Polly looked up. Her face was streaked with dirt and tears.

She stuttered: "Larry, w-why didn't you s-stop me?"

"Stop you! Stop you from racing up and kissing him? Stop you from grabbing that microphone when I wasn't looking and making that horrible speech?"

Polly was huddled over, her arms crossing upon her breast, her hands clasping her shoulders.

"It makes me sick to have you th-think such th-things of me!"

Aunt Sally paused beside her chair:

"Polly, for heaven's sake, if you must fall in love, can't you pick some man who's amusing?"

"I'm not in love!" Polly gasped.

"You're both in love. You've been in love since you clapped eyes on each other. If not, why do you quarrel so?"

"Mrs. Islington, I want you to understand—" Larry began frigidly.

"I understand everything," she interrupted. "That's why I'm so wretched. You're wearing yourselves out fighting each other. If you weren't kneeling down and worshiping your dignity every solitary minute, you'd take her in your arms and—and have it over with! She adores you."

"Mrs. Islington, I assure you—" Larry thickly tried to head this impossible woman off.

"She weeps every time she talks to you on the phone. Her only desire in the world is to please you—as if any woman alive could please a man like you! Tell her you love her! Get it over with! And then please, please let her enjoy herself a little while!"

"Good Lord, Aunt Sally—" Polly began.

"I won't say any more," Aunt Sally assured her. "You two can fool yourselves, but you can't fool me."

She had stopped before a mahogany mirror. She was staring into it.

"Merciful Heaven, is that me?" Her hands flew to her hair, but did not touch it. They remained suspended beside her head as she gazed at her image fascinated.

She spun about.

"I've just learned that I'm going to spend the next four-teen hours in bed. I'll leave you to fight it out. *Hasn't* it been a thrilling evening!"

Larry and Polly were gazing at her resentfully.

The gay widow laughed sadly. "Larry, my dear, you're really a marvelous young man. I admire you greatly. If I had my life to live over again, I'd marry a man exactly like you. Polly, don't stay up too late. You're really a sight. You—you look at least twenty-two! Good-night, children."

They murmured good night and watched her until the last battered slipper had dragged itself from view up the stairs.

Then they examined each other. Larry presently arose and went over to Polly. With hands in pockets, he stood over her.

"Polly," he said, "I don't want you to think too harshly of me."

Polly did not raise her eyes.

"I don't think harshly of you. I think harshly of myself."

"You mustn't. Your aunt is probably right. I can look at life, as she says, from only one point of view. It's my worst shortcoming. I realize it. I'm wrong oftener than I realize. I don't want to hurt you."

She burst out miserably: "Why didn't you tell me not to go into the movies? You said at tea that day—the *only* time you've been near me—to take her advice."

"Why not?" he said stonily.

With large, tearful brown eyes she looked up at him.

"I'll do just what you tell me to do."

"Why should you?" he insisted.

Her eyes were suddenly wet. Impulsively she rose. She placed her hands on his shoulders and laid her cheek against his chest with a weary sigh.

"I—I don't know," she whispered. "I—I've been so damned bewildered ever since this all started. I'm not used to excitement. I want somebody to tell me what to do. I adore Aunt Sally, but I—I respect your opinion more than hers—anybody's. You aren't bewildered or dazed. You know what I ought to do."

Larry put her gently away from him, but retained her hands.

"Polly," he said soberly, "my life hasn't been like hers. I've never had any time to play. I've had to be serious, and it hurts when people kid me about it. Believe me, you and she aren't the only ones. I want to be honest with you. I try my best to be honest with everybody. That's why I'm up in the air now. I don't know what to advise you—and I haven't the right to advise you, anyhow."

Polly averted her eyes; said nothing.

"Take her advice," he went on. "She knows how to play, how to get the most fun out of life. Stop worrying about my opinion and have a good time."

She glanced up at him brightly.

"Go ahead with my picture contract?"

It hurt him to say "Of course!" but he managed it. And added, qualifying, in spite of his intentions: "You can't back out of it now, anyhow. You've publicly announced it."

He released her hands and Polly said: "I think we'd better hit the hay. I'm absolutely a wreck. Good night, Larry!"

She was half way to the stairs when Jason Ortola came limping in from the kitchen. His eyes were smoldering fires in their deep sockets. His slash of a mouth was compressed, as if with pain.

"Polly, your father is very ill. A complete nervous breakdown. After the experiment, he went into the basement and smashed his alcohol still into bits. Muller has been with him since. He has been only partly conscious for the last two hours. I sent him to Hartford in an ambulance. Muller went with him."

"I'll start at once," Polly said.

The chemist compressed his thin lips and shook his head.

"There's nothing you can do. Muller will attend to everything. Your father simply needs a long rest, away from all excitement. That means a sanatorium for, I should say, several months. I think his alcoholism is largely responsible. It is a great pity. He has an iron constitution, and will, without question, pull through. But he must be managed more carefully after this."

"I should never have left here," Polly, said in a woeful voice.

"You could have done nothing with him. It was the excitement. Now, thank God, it's over. The future will certainly be easier. What are your plans, Polly?"

"I haven't any."

Ortola said: "I am going to Hartford to see your father has every possible attention. I must be in New York by to-morrow noon. Do you think you can handle the situation alone, Galloway?"

"I'll do my best," Larry answered. "It's a job. I think the farm should be better policed."

The chemist said that he would attend to that. "I'll see the Governor in Hartford and ask for more troops, and I'll send up another hundred guards from New York. Washington, I hear, has retired. How long did he talk on the radio?"

"Almost two hours."

"I suppose you've made no plans."

"None," said Larry. "I'll talk to him in the morning."

"The whole thing has come off splendidly. If you need me, I can be reached at my Newark plant to-morrow afternoon. Good night, Galloway."

"Good night."

The chemist gazed curiously at Polly.

"Good night, Polly."

She said softly: "Good night, Jason."

When he had gone, she yawned and said: "Aren't you going to bed, Larry?"

"I've got to work."

"You poor kid! Can I make you some coffee?"

Larry seated himself at a typewriter, inserted a sheet of paper and looked up. Polly was staring at him with round, troubled eyes.

"I'm full of enough stimulus to run me for a year," he said and tried to laugh, but it was hardly more than a groan.

Tears filled her eyes again. She turned abruptly and went up the stairs. His eyes remained upon her.

At the top of the stairs she stopped and looked back.

"Good night, Old Dignity!"

He briefly waved his hand.

"Good night, Gloria Swanson!"

Polly disappeared.

For a moment he considered the keyboard. Then he tapped out in capitals at the top of the sheet:

MY IMPRESSIONS OF GEORGE WASHINGTON

By Lawrence Galloway

George Washington, reborn to-night in the laboratory of Professor Morgan, requires the support of no heroic legends.

With his own nobility of character, his own courtly poise, his own alert, forceful mind, he begs nothing of glamorous tradition.

Larry's prodding fingers stopped. He read the two sentences, frowning. He removed and crumpled the sheet, inserted a new one and began again:

The man who once made history will make history again. My two hour talk with him, which was broadcast to millions of radio listeners, clearly established that he will bring to this present stormy era a fresh and resolute viewpoint; will with honesty and frankness analyze this new America in which he finds himself; will unhesitatingly reprove the citizens of this nation which he fathered for the faults and weaknesses he finds; will, in short, prepare us for and guide us to a finer and richer civilization.

Larry stopped and read it over.

A mocking voice said: "Stupid, dull, pompous things."

"No," he declared vehemently to himself. "Truthful things!"

The voice derided: "Washington must be made deadly and dull."

He groaned—and tore the sheet from the typewriter, to try once more.

I have looked for two hours into the steady, piercing blue eyes of George Washington. I have studied him. I have weighed his every word as he uttered it. I have come surely to the conclusion that his nobility of character, his courtly poise, his swift and forceful processes of thought will... truth, truth, truth, truth, the truth.

"I! I! I! I!" chanted the gay, disembodied spirit of Mrs. Horace Glen Islington.

"But," he argued, "I tried to keep it dignified!"

"You and your hellish dignity! Gallop out of the lime-light! Giddyap! Giddyap!"

"I'm a sap."

"You're jealous of Polly."

Larry shook his head. All these derisive voices. He must concentrate. In an effort to do so, he pressed his palms against his temples.

He lighted a cigarette. He looked disgustedly at the keyboard.

Dawn was creeping in at the windows by the time his impressions of the new George Washington had been reduced to a form that satisfied him.

25

A HUMAN BEING

A BLANKET OF hot golden sunlight upon his face aroused the earnest managing editor of *The Daily It* at three o'clock in the afternoon. He looked at his wrist-watch. The time was, actually, three-fifteen. He had been asleep eleven hours.

It seemed to him that every joint in his body was sore. He felt absolutely limp, burned out. His eyes ached.

By pushing himself up on his elbow he could look out a window and across a bright green field. He saw the leaves of an elm tree rustling in a vagrant breeze. He heard the murmuring of the brook. A warm current of air, sweet with the odor of some flower, crept in at the window. He sniffed approvingly.

Larry seated himself on the edge of the bed and reached for a cigarette and matches as the white porcelain door-knob stealthily revolved and the door opened sufficiently to admit the anxious face of McWhorter.

The reporter's expression was gladdened by a smile.

"Goshamighty, boss, I was beginning to think we'd have to put you in that white cylinder to bring you back to life!"

Larry asked him what was new. "How's Washington?"

"He's fine. The morning and noon papers just came up by plane. I'll go get 'em."

He left and Larry went to the window. A group of perhaps twenty men were in the front yard, talking. He saw other men lounging about the small tent city which had been erected to accommodate newspaper men, telegraph operators, news reel photographers, radio crews. Smoke was rising from a stove near the community mess tent.

Larry saw no signs of mobs, but he heard, in the distance, a muffled roaring. Later he would learn that the country for miles about was swarming with countless thousands of people; that all roads leading to this section were hopelessly jammed with traffic; that enterprising men with telescopes on distant hilltops were charging, for one peep at the Morgan house, one dollar, two dollars, even five.

The whirring of an airplane drew his eyes toward the bright sky. A biplane was banking, preparing to alight in the flat meadow behind the laboratory.

He saw it come to earth; saw it immediately surrounded by men in blue uniforms; saw it at once take to the air again. He grinned. Detective Sergeant Walker evidently had the situation well in hand!

Connecticut troops, he would later learn, surrounded the Morgan farm in shoulder-to-shoulder formation, a human picket fence of bayonets.

McWhorter returned with a heavy bundle of morning and afternoon newspapers. Flashlight photographs of Washington, dazed and staring, occupied every front page. He glanced at the headlines. Unanimously they screamed that Washington lived again. The feeling of last night's mob panic was in them all.

When he had glanced over the front pages, after briefly scanning his two prominent stories in *The It*, he looked into the inner pages. Congress, he learned, had approved an appropriation of fifty million dollars with which to pay for the resurrection of the fifty greatest dead Americans.

Congress was frantically determined to dictate George Washington's program.

Professor Morgan, in a serious but not critical condition, had had opiates administered in a Hartford hospital and, at last report, was still sleeping.

George Washington, in the Morgan farmhouse, had arisen at 8 a.m., breakfasted upon oatmeal, ham and eggs, coffee and toast, and had consented to be interviewed.

Larry eagerly read the questions and answers.

"What was your first thought upon returning to life?"

"I was bewildered."

"Did you think you were in hell?"

"I believe I did."

"What do you think of modern America?"

"It is too soon to express an opinion."

"What do you think of the radio?"

"I do not understand it."

"What are your plans, colonel?"

"I cannot answer that until I have consulted with Mr. Galloway."

"Ah!" breathed Larry.

"Listen, boss," the faithful McWhorter interrupted him, "let me skip down and cook you up a mess of eggs and fix you some coffee."

"Go to it," said Larry, and read on.

"Were you in love with Martha Custis or Sally Fairfax when you can last remember anything?"

"I refuse to answer any questions of that nature."

"What do you think of modern women?"

"The few I have seen are charming."

"What do you think of the short skirts the girls of to-day are wearing?"

"I won't answer such questions!"

"Good boy!" murmured Larry.

"Are you glad to be alive?"

"No normal man wishes to be dead."

"You said last night over the radio: 'Why was I brought to this?'"

"That was last night. I was bewildered. To-day, I am beginning to find myself."

"Would you rather be alive in this age or in the eighteenth century?"

"I would rather not answer that kind of question."

"Is your memory a perfect blank, colonel, after that day in July, near Fort Duquesne, in seventeen fifty-five?"

"It is."

"You haven't the slightest recollection of being the first American President or leading the Colonial forces against the British?"

"None."

"Have you any recollection of any kind of your existence since then?"

"None."

"But you must have been existing somewhere, colonel. Do you think you have been in heaven or hell or where?"

"I have no means of knowing where I have been. My

memory, all consciousness of my existence, ceased one hundred and seventy years ago."

"Would you accept the Presidency of the United States if it were offered to you?"

"I will not answer that question."

"They can't rattle him," Larry approved. "And they won't rattle him."

"What do you think of modern men's clothes?"

"I thought at first that they were effeminate. I think now that they are sensible. They are comfortable."

"Would you prefer wearing the costume of your own time?"

"No."

"Does it surprise you to know that you have been, since your death, the idol of all Americans—that upward of one hundred and thirty millions venerate your name; that your birthday is a national holiday?"

"It does, naturally."

"Do you know that the principles of American democracy you laid down have, in many cases, been violated?"

Washington did not consider that an answer was necessary.

"Do you know that your last speech to the American people is chiefly remembered because you said that America must enter into no entangling alliances?"

Washington seemed greatly interested by this question.

"Did I say that?" he answered.

"What do you think of it now?"

"If I said it," was his grave answer, "I must have meant it."

"What do you think of the prohibition amendment?"

"What is the prohibition amendment?"

"A law that prohibits any one in the United States and its possessions from drinking, buying or selling any beverage containing more than one half of one per cent of alcohol by volume."

"What do the American people think of it?" Washington countered.

"Some of them are for it and some of them are against it."

"Is the law being obeyed?"

He was puzzled by the outburst of laughter that answered him.

"It is being violated," he was told, "in every city, town, village, hamlet in the nation. What is your opinion of that?"

He answered slowly: "I have not been in this new America long enough to form opinions on such difficult problems."

"Do you realize that people for miles around here are crazy for a glimpse of you?"

"I have been told so."

"When will you let the American people see you?"

"I said before that I wish to consult with Mr. Galloway before I make any announcement of my plans."

"What is the one thing, or the one place, you want to see most?"

"My home at Mount Vernon."

"What next?"

"The site of Fort Duquesne."

"And then what, colonel?"

"All America."

"What do you think of modern firearms?"

The glow that came promptly to Washington's eyes showed how thoroughly his interest had been captured.

"I have not seen modern firearms. I should like to."

One of "Professor Morgan's Constabulary," who was in the crowd about Washington, removed a Colt's automatic pistol from his holster.

Colonel Washington, as he had elected to be styled, examined the weapon with the greatest interest.

"I'd like to fire this," he said.

He was conducted to an open field beside the house. He pulled the trigger, aiming the pistol at the ground.

Some one urged him to pull it again.

Washington did so. For the first time since he was restored to life, he was seen to smile. It was a quick, grim smile.

He continued to pull the trigger until the magazine was empty. He gazed from the pistol to the holes in the turf with awe and amazement.

"Nine shots from one pistol!" he marveled. "With a company of a dozen men armed with these, I would have engaged every Indian and every Frenchman in America!"

"You hated the Indians, colonel?"

"Most heartily. Where are the Indians now? I have not seen one."

"Almost gone, colonel. They have died off. The few remaining ones live off by themselves on reservations. Many of them drank themselves to death; many starved to death; a few of those who remain have become millionaires because of the oil under their lands."

"Oil?" Washington repeated.

"Petroleum."

"Petro—" he began. "I do not understand."

An attempt was made to explain petroleum to him, and gasoline.

"I am sorry any Indians are rich," he presently interrupted. "Do they still scalp their enemies?"

He was told the Indians are now a subdued race, and was reminded that he had expressed a wish to use automatic pistols against the French.

"Indeed I would!" he exclaimed.

"Do you hate the French?"

"With every drop of blood in my veins!" he exclaimed.

"But, colonel, you later became very friendly with the French. One Frenchman, a man named Lafayette, became one of your bosom friends. You had a bedroom at Mount Vernon specially set aside for him."

"I did?" He seemed amazed.

"The French," he was told, "joined with you in the war against England which freed the American Colonies."

His amazement increased. "What treachery did they have in mind?"

"None, colonel. And since that time the French and the American people have been on terms of loving friendship."

"Times have changed," he murmured.

An attempt was made to draw forth from Colonel Washington an even more violent expression of opinion against the French, but he seemed to realize that he was on dangerous ground, and refused to commit himself.

Larry was frowning as he reflected: "I'll have to warn him. They trapped him that time."

The interview proceeded. Washington was asked what

he thought of the airplanes which were continually flying
over the Morgan farmhouse with loads of sightseers.

"They are outside my imagination."

"Would you like to fly in one?"

Washington hesitated before answering, his eyes following a small monoplane that was skirting about high above.

"I would; yes."

A reporter told Colonel Washington that an American
author had recently written a book about him which had
caused a furor because in it he had stated that Washington
was a drinking man.

Washington asked: "Why was there a furor?"

"Because," he was told, "the American public has been
taught to look up to you as a man who had no vices. The
book was called 'George Washington, the Human Being
and the Hero.' The claim was made that the author
besmirched your image."

"I have no quarrel with him," said Washington. "I was
and am a human being. I am not aware of being vicious. I
will read the book. Perhaps, in later life, I cultivated vices.
I did not intend to."

He was asked: "Do you realize that, to us, your accent is
strongly English?"

He answered: "Yours is very strange to me. And many
of the words you use are unknown to me."

The questioning shifted back to American inventions.
He was asked his opinion of electricity, the electric light.

"It is magical," he said.

"If Professor Morgan would consent to perform the
experiment, which of your contemporaries, man or woman,
would you select to bring back to life?"

(Continued on Page Ten.)
Larry turned to page ten, but he did not read page ten. His attention was captured by what he saw on page eleven.

It was a full page advertisement of the Kolledge Kut Klothing Manufacturing Company. Block type roared:

GEORGE WASHINGTON FAVORS

KOLLEDGE KUT KLOTHES!

Our Summer Model 49-C in Gray Tweed

Fits Him Perfectly!

From measurements obtained from old records, a Ready-to-Fit suit of Kolledge Kut Klothes was selected yesterday by Mr. Lawrence Galloway in the Ready-to-Fit Department of Cromach Bros., and taken to the Morgan Laboratory by airplane.

President Washington has expressed his delight at the coolness, the smartness, the general all-around comfort of this popular model.

Such Approval Must Be Merited!

The 49-C Model; four pieces: coat, vest, trousers, and plus-fours, gray or brown—

WHILE THEY LAST—$49.75!

"What Is Good Enough for the Father of Our Country Is Good Enough for You!"

(Copyright application of this slogan has been filed.)

KOLLEDGE KUT KLOTHING MFG. CO.

New York, Chicago, Boston, San Francisco, Dallas, Detroit, Cleveland, Philadelphia, Pittsburgh, Denver, Duluth, Jacksonville, Miami, Tampa

Larry, with strange sounds in his throat, turned the page and encountered another one:

WASHINGTON'S FEET FIND COMFORT IN
SNUG-ARCH OXFORDS!
Our Beloved First President Heads the List of Successful,
Well-Dressed Patriots Who Will Accept No Substitute for
America's Smartest, Most Comfortable, Longest-Wearing
Shoe—the SNUG-ARCH!
STEP INTO LINE IN THE SNUG-ARCH!
Priced from $16.95

Larry glanced with growing indignation through other newspapers. He learned that George Washington was keeping cool in Cool-Cut Athletic Underwear; that he was honoring a Neckford Shirt, and a Mallory Foulard Cravat of a dark-blue shade, which the manufacturers stated would hereafter be known as "Washington Blue."

One full page was entirely white except for a little square of type in the center.

WELCOME TO LIFE-GEORGE WASHINGTON!
PEAVER'S PRODUCTS PLEASE THE PALATE!
For His First Breakfast in 170 Years Our Celebrated Visi-
tor From the Past Enjoyed a Slice of Delicious broiled
PEAVER'S HAM!
WHY WAS HE GIVEN PEAVER'S HAM?
Your Palate Knows!

Where, he wondered, had they obtained that information? Advertisers, he sourly reflected, were far more resourceful and enterprising than newspaper reporters.

There were other beneficiaries of Washington's miraculous return to life. Prominent among them was Polly Morgan. She had been caught simultaneously, it would seem, by at least twenty cameras in the act of kissing Washington. One of the tabloids carried a photograph of a Miss Rebecca Levine, of the Bronx, seated on her apartment doorstep, revealing delightful legs, weeping because she could not similarly greet the Father of her Country.

Advertisements of the Classic Features Corporation, containing photographs of Polly Morgan and her camera smile, boasted of her speech over the radio; quoted it all in full. Her first film under Classic Features auspices would be entitled "Polly of Lake Shallon," and would thrill the nation with its authentic glimpse of her life and the heroic part she played in the miracle of Washington's resurrection.

Larry gave his attention to the editorial pages and read vigorous criticisms.

"What a pity," bemoaned the *New York Times*, "that the dignity of the conference between George Washington and Mr. Galloway should have, at the end, been cheapened by Miss Morgan's efforts to gain notoriety for herself and a film company. Her behavior is an irritating commentary upon the femininity of the America in which Washington finds himself. Accustomed as he was to the womanly virtues of reticence and modesty, he must surely have been rudely shocked.

"The episode is to be regretted."

The Sun said:

The action of Miss Polly Morgan, in seizing the microphone at the termination of the Galloway-Washington conference, was mischievous and unfortunate. It came in the nature of a jarring discord after Mr. Galloway's commendable effort to present Washington to all-listening America as the intelligent, straightforward young man he appears to be. In our opinion, this young woman has been grasping opportunity indiscreetly. We are reminded, to our sorrow, that the secondary function of the old-fashioned hairbrush has been permitted to languish.

"Can nothing be done," bitterly inquired the *Evening Post*, "to prevent notoriety hunters from exploiting America's latest and greatest hero? Will no one intervene to spare him the ignominy of exploitation by ambitious cinema amateurs and tactless advertisers? Has our noblest American been returned to us for the purpose of testifying to the sterling qualities of popular pickles, pastries and pork? It has come to our attention that an offer of one hundred thousand dollars is to be made to him for his written approval of a certain cigarette.

"Is George Washington to be ashamed of the great nation that he founded? Let us unite to quash all attempts at tampering with the dignity of our beloved hero!"

Larry frowningly examined the editorial page of *The It*. Printed in red and blue, it rang with a rhapsodic acclaim of the hero's return to his people.

McWhorter presently entered with Larry's breakfast.

"The colonel went out horseback riding with Polly before I could nail him, boss. He left word he'd be back in an hour and wanted to see you. I've got to do a story on you now. Is there anything in particular except that for eleven hours you gave a fine imitation of a buzz-saw messing around with knots and heartily breakfasted on Peaver's Palate Pleasing ham and four cups of Oh-So-Good Coffee?"

"I want you to wire, Morrisy," Larry grimly answered, "to have a red-hot editorial written, if he hasn't already done so, condemning all these advertisers who are exploiting Washington. It's disgraceful. Did you see the other editorial pages?"

"No, boss; I've been too busy sorting out telegrams. There are three bushel baskets of them out in my tent for you. Most of them are from nuts. There are twenty operators taking messages for the colonel. Everybody wants to know what the colonel is going to do. Where's he going from here, and when does he start?"

Larry said: "I don't know. I'll have a talk with him."

"It would be a shame if Washington hogged him the way they did Lindbergh. At least forty Congressmen have wired saying he's got to make his first appearance in Washington. Can't you fix it for him to see New York first?"

"I haven't anything to do with it."

"Everybody thinks you have. Every other thing he says is 'I'll have to consult Mr. Galloway.' At first, he wasn't going to say a peep to that gang until he had you with him. They finally wore him down. I think he'll do whatever you tell him to. He's sold solid on the idea that you're safeguarding his interests. You ought to play it for all it's worth, boss."

A firm rapping came on the door.

The reporter opened it.

George Washington, in riding clothes, strode in. His

face was flushed. His eyes were sapphire-blue. He was not smiling.

He bowed gravely to the man in pink pyjamas and said: "Good afternoon, Mr. Galloway. I trust you are refreshed."

26

THE INTERESTS OF
MR. WASHINGTON

LARRY REMOVED THE breakfast tray from his knees to the foot of the bed, pushed newspapers out of his way and stood. He was rosy with embarrassment.

Colonel Washington, occupying a chair, said heartily: "I hope I did not disturb you. It was important for me to have a talk with you, Mr. Galloway."

Larry made confused murmurs.

"You must have been exhausted," the poised young man in riding clothes said kindly. "I have been talking to men from newspapers—reporters, they call themselves—since breakfast time. I am beginning to understand a great many things. May I ask—is our conversation being listened to by millions?"

Larry assured him that it was not.

Washington went on gravely: "Miss Morgan and I had a splendid ride. Of all the novelties I have been introduced to, I am sure that the young lady of to-day will puzzle me the longest. Miss Morgan's aunt is amazing—and delightful, too."

One of his rare smiles illuminated Washington's firm, long mouth.

"I wonder if I may sample these curious white tubes that you call cigarettes? Everybody seems to smoke them. I have declined them all day long. I have been curious to try one, but I wanted to make the experiment in private."

Larry unsealed and gave him a fresh package of Golden Glows.

Washington's expression became clouded.

"I am constantly disconcerted by these reporters. They are like a pack of eager hounds. They bark questions faster than I can answer them. When I manifest surprise at something new, they laugh. I saw one of them make fire for a pipe with small splinters which he struck against a black substance on the box. They laughed when I attempted to make fire with the splinters by striking them elsewhere than on the side of the box.

"I wish now that I had refused to talk to them until you had wakened. Their questions puzzled me. Their persistence in referring to the prohibition question irritated me. They drew certain statements from me concerning the French that, I realize now, were in poor taste."

Washington had removed a cigarette from the package and placed it gingerly between his lips. He watched the spitting blaze of a safety match, fascinated.

He tasted the smoke, exhaled and puffed again.

"The flavor," he pronounced "is not that of tobacco, but I rather like it. I understand that Americans smoke cigarettes at the rate of billions a year. It seems incredible. Mrs. Islington smoked several after breakfast. She drew the smoke into her lungs and exhaled it through her nostrils. It was amazing. She insisted that I try one, but I declined."

Washington continued to puff at the cigarette. Once he

coughed and tears came into his eyes; but Larry did not smile.

"I am anxious to see America, as you say, 'from coast to coast.' But I hate to leave here for the excitement that that will probably mean. And so many strangers! It is hard for me to believe that the only people I know in the world are the ones I have met since last night. Every one has been very kind. Mr. Muller gave me a long talk this noon at luncheon on modern inventions. I wonder, when I leave to see America, if some of these good people cannot accompany me."

"Such decisions," Larry assured him, "are entirely yours and will be acted upon."

Washington smiled briefly. "When I leave here, why won't it be possible for these people who have been so kind to come with me? Then I do not feel that I am among total strangers."

"It can easily be arranged," Larry told him. "Whom do you wish in the party?"

Washington answered promptly: "Mr. Muller, Miss Morgan, and Mrs. Islington. All of them, by the way, assure me that I could make no wiser choice of an adviser than you. I want your counsel on all matters. My most trivial utterance is being seized and capitalized by these reporters. Miss Morgan told me that I had made a great mistake in referring to the French and the Indians as I did. I must be more guarded in what I say.

"I conclude that everything I say must be of tremendous interest to America. It is hard for me to see why America should be so interested. And I am amazed by the swiftness with which my words find their way into print. Comments

I made this morning I read in the New York newspapers this afternoon; yet New York is more than one hundred miles away.

"My first opinion of this dazzling modern age is that you have conquered time and space. Time, with the telegraph, the telephone, and the radio. Space, with the airplane, the automobile, the railroad and the steamship. I have so far seen all but the railroad and the steamship. What, Mr. Galloway, will America expect of me?"

Larry answered: "What would you really like to do, colonel?"

"I would like to enjoy America. I would like to see these great cities, ride on railroads; have all the modern wonders shown and explained to me. But what will America expect of me?"

"For the present," Larry answered, "America will be content to worship you. Your presence will be demanded in a thousand places at once. I should say that the two birds could be killed with one stone. I mean, America can see you while you are seeing America.

"The cities are already quarreling over you. New York and Washington each insist that you go there first. So does Hartford. Boston wants you. Chicago is determined that you go first to Chicago. New York and Washington quarreled once before when a popular hero returned to America."

"Who was he?" Washington asked.

"Charles Lindbergh."

"What did he do?"

"Lindbergh was the first man to fly an airplane from New York to Paris without stopping."

"Which city received him first?"

"Washington! And New York was furious."

Washington shook his head and murmured: "What a puzzling place this new America is! I do not understand why New York was furious. Washington is the national capital. Why should not returning heroes visit Washington first?"

"Because, long ago, the precedent was established of receiving returning heroes in New York first; largely because New York is the port at which all the great steamships from Europe call. New York, in the past twenty years, has been making more and more of an occasion of a hero's return. Some people think that this holiday spirit is a sign that America is learning to take herself less seriously."

"Your return, from what I've gathered from a glance through to-day's papers, is being celebrated all over the country. Schools, factories, shops, and offices are closed. Every man, woman and child will want to see you. Your opinion will be demanded on every conceivable subject. The most persistent questions will deal with prohibition, tall buildings, and short skirts. America, at least in the East, is more agitated over those three than any others. Your opinion will be wanted on American government and all American institutions."

"But I know nothing of statecraft. I have learned that I only became interested in that after seventeen fifty-five. It seems to me that people are interested only in what happened to me after then. I am—I mean, I was—a farmer, a surveyor, and a soldier."

"People will, none the less, expect and value your opinions."

Washington gave vent to a sigh of exasperation.

"Mr. Galloway, I am not interested in any of these ponderous questions. I am excited by airplanes and electricity and steam engines. I want to see them all. I want to see everything. I don't want to be asked to decide national problems. Let somebody else decide them.

"Mr. Galloway," the young man earnestly continued, "I came up here to tell you that I want to place myself in your hands. I need your advice on hundreds of things, and I trust you. I want you to be near me wherever I go."

Larry murmured that he would be delighted to place himself at his disposal indefinitely.

"I would like to have you decide all these serious, ponderous questions for me."

"I would prefer," was Larry's answer, "to have you decide them for yourself. I will give you my honest opinions on all subjects that puzzle you. My most important duty, as I see it, as your adviser, is to safeguard your tremendous popularity from mistakes, and to see that it is used for some constructive purpose.

"Beyond giving the American people the opportunity for the greatest display of good will and good feeling that has ever come to them," Larry earnestly went on, "it seems to me that you have two serious responsibilities. There are dozens of constructive things you might do; I have boiled down the list to what I honestly believe are the two most important."

"I'll do just what you tell me, Mr. Galloway," Washington said promptly; and Larry found himself wishing that this young man would not take his responsibilities so lightly.

"Have you," he asked, "seen a modern map of the United States?"

He saw that Washington's waning interest had been thoroughly recaptured.

"I was thunderstruck!" he exclaimed. "Miss Morgan showed me the United States in an atlas. I could not believe that the country has become so thickly populated, and that so many large cities have sprung up."

"In spite of all these modern inventions," Larry continued, "the States are still loosely held together. The New England States are still hated by the Southern States; the East has problems which do not affect the West, and vice versa. It is in your power to knit all sections more closely; to give every part of the country an understanding of the hopes and problems of every other part."

Washington's eyes had become vague again.

"That is, as I see it, your first duty," Larry added.

"And what is my other duty?"

"To overhaul the machinery of government!"

"I do not understand."

Larry explained: "The American people are too busy, too much interested in other things, to care how the country is run. They hire politicians to run it for them. They think they do! As a matter of fact, the politicians decide themselves who will or won't occupy an office. They arrange it all to suit themselves. When election time comes, the people elect the man the politicians want them to elect."

George Washington was beginning to fidget again. He set fire to eight or ten matches in an attempt, eventually successful, to light another Golden Glow. His wandering eyes returned to Larry's face. There was a look of heaviness in them.

Larry briskly continued: "Men who have had no training and no experience to fit them for the jobs become Congressmen, Governors, mayors, judges, ambassadors, even Presidents. Often a candidate's only qualification for office is that he is too lazy or incompetent to do anything else. The people don't care; they aren't interested. They are furious when a crooked office holder is found out. But they soon forget.

"We have even seen the spectacle, colonel, of a man's reelection when he has been proved, on prima facie evidence, guilty of theft, graft, misconduct.

"The people are not sufficiently interested in city, State, Federal government to do anything about it. As a consequence, more and more power has been grasped by the politicians, many of whom are rogues, concerned only with their own schemes."

Colonel Washington concealed a yawn behind his cigarette hand. And Larry tried not to lose his patience. He proceeded:

"The general result is that the people no longer have the power to decide issues vital to them. Politicians make their decisions for them. Or the newspapers behind the politicians distort the truth until the people are convinced that black is white.

"What the country needs," Larry energetically went on, "is a rough shaking up. It must be made aware of these conditions. It must take an active interest in the running of the government; it must face and decide important issues.

"Prohibition must be settled one way or the other. The

law must be repealed or enforced. Its greatest effect has been corruption in all branches of government. A disrespect for all law is growing. Your real responsibility to the American people is to awaken them. Once they are awakened—"

"Do you know," Washington murmured, "I believe I am going to like cigarettes."

Larry, to conceal his exasperation, lighted one for himself.

"Well, colonel, what is your opinion?"

"I am tremendously interested in all these problems of State and so on," was the young man's reply. "And I am sure that I could not have selected a more able man to advise and guide me, Mr. Galloway. We must discuss all this later. When will we start on my tour of America, and where shall we go first?"

"The decision on both questions is yours, colonel," Larry said somewhat stiffly.

"Shall we start to-morrow morning, immediately after breakfast?"

"If you wish."

"And where shall we go first? I suppose it would be better, more tactful, to visit Washington first. After all, it was named after me, was it not? Yes," he answered his question. "Washington was named after me, and we ought to go to Washington first. Besides, I am anxious to see Mount Vernon; the changes. But I am even more anxious to see these tall buildings in New York. Miss Morgan has been telling me about them. I cannot imagine buildings so tall. By all means, let us go to New York first."

"Very well, colonel."

"And let us go in an airplane. I understand there are airplanes large enough to carry a dozen people. Can one of them be sent here to carry us?"

"It can be arranged simply. I will notify the newspapers that we will fly to New York immediately after breakfast tomorrow morning. To-night, I would suggest that you talk on the radio again.

"Newspapers all over America are urging you to do that, not only for the tremendous interest every one has, but to keep people all over the country from gathering in such mobs in the streets. Last night the crowds were out of control in almost every city in the country."

George Washington did not look happy.

"I will talk on the radio if you insist," he said. "You are my adviser, and you know what is best, and I will do just what you want me to do. But Miss Morgan suggested that we spend the evening dancing to the music from that strange cabinet which amazingly reproduces the strains of an orchestra. To me, that cabinet is even more marvelous than the radio, which I do not grasp at all.

"Miss Morgan has most generously offered to teach me the modern dance steps, but, of course—"

He stopped. His gaze had wandered to the window. He was looking out, absorbed by that which he saw on the ground below.

Larry, following his gaze, saw a knot of photographers posing Polly and her aunt. Mrs. Islington was chattering to the photographers; gesticulating with both hands, and the photographers were laughing.

The crowd of men suddenly moved back to their cameras. Mrs. Islington, with her voice and both hands, was urging Polly to do something. Polly, in every line of her body, was resisting the argument.

George Washington was now standing and bending over to look out the window.

Larry, behind him, saw a camera man begin to crank; saw Mrs. Islington fall back a few steps from Polly and then, to his amazement, saw Polly pull down the hem of her pale green afternoon dress; gaze brightly about her; and turn two perfect cartwheels.

The cameramen yelled and cranked. Aunt Sally laughed, Larry, retaining an image of flying beautiful legs, of fluttering pink silk, quickly glanced at George Washington's profile.

He did not in the least approve of the look he saw on the young man's face.

Another cheer went up. The crowd below had seen Washington at the window. He waved to them, but did not smile.

When the cheering stopped, Aunt Sally called up:

"Come on down, George! The movie man is here with the films he made of us last night. He's going to run them in the library."

George Washington hastened to the door. With hand on knob, he bowed hastily to Larry.

"It is a great relief to know that you are to be my adviser," he got out in one breath. "Until later, Mr. Galloway."

27

WHEN WOMEN FIGURE IN

THE CRUSADER SADLY contemplated the closed door. Somehow, he had reached the conclusion that George Washington was not the serious young man history portrayed him to be.

Reviewing that conversation, it struck Larry that Colonel Washington had, at every step, taken pains to avoid responsibility. Had refused to take his mission seriously. Had, without actually saying so, refused to accept any obligation to the nation he had founded.

Larry found himself regretting that George Washington had not returned to life at the age, say, of forty-five; at the age when he had put frivolity behind him, had settled down to the serious business of organizing and directing a nation.

"What more," he ruefully asked himself, "can I expect of twenty-three?"

He sighed. He himself hadn't been frivolous at twenty-three; hadn't, in fact, been frivolous at any age. Washington was behaving as any normal man of twenty-three would behave. Considering his youth, he had conducted himself, so far, amazingly.

Larry growled: "It's that damned woman!" And he

thought: "She will ruin him, if she gets the chance, just as she's ruining Polly!"

He consulted a notebook in which, in the course of his research reading, he had jotted down many notes. And read:

"Super horseman. Jefferson said he was best of his age—magnificent on horseback. Manner always grave. Fastidiously clean. Big barber and laundry bills. At, dinner always drank a pint of Madeira besides rum punch and beer. Very fond of fish. Fish and honey favorite dishes. Went to theater often and to the circus. Rode to hounds. Fond of duck shooting and horse racing. Played cards almost daily. Read only books on agriculture in early manhood. Later, political science, history, and statesmanship. Loved dancing. Once danced for three hours without stopping. Danced High Betty Martin and Leather the Strap. Something of a dandy. Liked fine clothes. Not amusing, but liked amusement."

Larry tossed the notebook aside and entered a tub of cold water. There, his grouch was dissipated. It occurred to him forcibly that Washington, if he remained pliable, would be merely an instrument upon which he would play; a mouthpiece.

Through this light-minded young man, he would awaken America!

He thought, rhapsodically: "I will be to modern America what Washington was to young America!"

His ego complained: "But you will receive none of the credit."

His honesty answered: "But you will be freeing America from corruption, lawlessness, and ignorance!"

In a glowing mood, Larry went downstairs. With shades drawn, the library was in darkness, except for a flickering on a sheet that had been pinned up across the shelves at one end.

A motion picture projector was whirring at the far end. The room was crowded and noisy.

Larry paused in the doorway behind the projector. He saw himself, alone on the veranda, his hair disheveled, his expression wild as, up the steps, came Washington and Ortola.

Now, Polly, her tattered condition magnified by the lens, determinedly advancing, seizing Washington's hands, kissing him.

The spectators in the library broke into a louder babbling.

Silence again, except for the whirring of the machine.

Then: "Polly, don't you think—"

Voices rose and drowned the rest of it. The voice had been George Washington's. *Polly!*

Larry, his glow somewhat diminished, slipped out of the house and made his way toward the press tents. In one respect, George Washington was as modern as a university undergraduate. It struck Larry that the colonel and Polly Morgan must have covered an amazing amount of ground on that horseback ride.

Reporters quickly surrounded him. Brown, at one elbow, growled:

"You haven't been letting much grass grow under your feet, have you, Galloway?"

Larry said: "I don't get you."

"You've got things pretty well sewed up, haven't you?"

Larry, beginning to protest innocence, was interrupted

by a snarling snort of "Oh, hell; every damned question we've asked him since he came down from your room he's referred to you. 'Ask Mr. Galloway!' Great guns, how sick I'm getting of asking Mr. Galloway. Well, what's the lowdown—or is it exclusive to *The It?*"

"Colonel Washington," Larry answered, "has asked me to be his adviser. Hereafter, most statements from him will come through me. You might as well get used to it."

"Are you going with him on his tour?"

"I am."

"What did you talk about up there?"

"A great many things. You fellows may as well know he is sore at the way you laugh at his mistakes and the way you try to bully him into making injurious statements."

"All we get from now on, I suppose, is pap."

"You'll get straight truth, but you won't be given the chance to quote him injuriously. Paste that in your hats."

"All right," growled Riley of the *News*. "We're going to be so good we'll each earn a little gold cross. Will you spill something? What happened up in that room?"

Larry smiled grimly. "The colonel came to me for straight facts about America. He was tremendously interested."

"What did he say about prohibition?"

"He asked dozens of questions about it, but he isn't going to say a word until he's looked things over. That's flat. He asked dozens more questions about city, State, and Federal government. He is, of course, very much interested in politics."

"He wasn't when he talked to us!"

"Well, he was when he talked to me. He is going to make

a thorough study of all branches of government from one end of the country to the other. American progress and American politics are the two subjects which interest him most."

"When does he leave?"

"To-morrow morning, immediately after breakfast."

"The hell he does! Why didn't you say so?"

"Why didn't you ask me? I'm being interviewed," Larry answered and laughed. He heard a half dozen men curse him.

"Where does he go?"

"New York."

"Wow! Not Washington?"

"He wanted to see New York first; Washington next. He'll go by plane. I'm going to order it now."

"Who'll make up the party?"

"Miss Morgan, Mrs. Islington—"

"Say! Where does that dame get off to go horning in as if—"

"Shut up!" snapped a dozen voices.

"—and Paul Muller."

"And yourself."

"That's all."

"It's one too many, if you ask me!" said a young news-getter.

"Why the mob?" asked Brown.

"The colonel's wishes. In his own words: 'I am alone in this new world among strangers. My only friends are the ones I have made since last night. I want them to go wherever I go!'"

"Will he drag that mob with him everywhere?"

"He will."

"Hot dog, what a joy ride!"

Larry attempted to restore the craft of dignity to an even keel.

"Paul Muller used to be a university instructor," he said. "The colonel likes the simple, understandable way he explains things. Miss Morgan is going as her father's representative—"

"And to cop off a million dollars' worth of publicity!"

This Larry ignored. "Mrs. Islington is going as Miss Morgan's chaperon."

A man broke in with: "Who is this mysterious Gore woman?"

"I don't know anything about her except that she is the wife of a vivisectionist who assisted Professor Morgan."

"Where is Gore?"

"I don't know."

"Where's he from?"

"I don't know anything about him. I never met him. His work in connection with Professor Morgan's experiments was kept secret from every one. He cleared out when the experiment was finished."

"Washington has a crush on the Morgan girl, hasn't he?"

"Certainly not!" Larry snapped.

"Aw, how do you get that way? You've got one on her yourself!"

Larry retorted angrily: "You've got a big story, haven't you? Why not leave silliness out for a change?"

"I've been reading up on Washington as a young man," a reporter said. "He's fallen for this Morgan wren like the proverbial ton of bricks. It may be silly, but it's news."

Larry insisted: "If he falls in love with Miss Morgan, I'll know all about it; I'll tell you."

A chorus of jeers apprized him that the reporters' opinion of him was unchanged. They would probably remain suspicious, skeptical, and sore until the bitter end.

"The Islington dame is making a harder play for him than the Morgan girl," said one of them. "She razzes him and he eats it up."

"Washington never understood women," a reporter from the *Chicago Tribune* put in seriously. "He was turned down by one of them after another. His technique must have been awful. If he doesn't watch his step, Sally Islington or Polly Morgan will make a sap out of him. I agree with Galloway on that angle. If we play up this girl stuff he's going to get sore. You saw how riled he got this morning when we began whipsawing him on prohibition. My dope is to lay off the girl stuff."

Larry quickly added:

"That is sound dope, Washington will begin paying attention to the papers pretty soon, and if you make a fool of him, he'll close down on all of you."

The reporters drifted off to file their stories, and Larry made his way to the telephone tent, where booths had been installed. The switchboard operator informed him that, of the hundreds of calls that had been coming in for him since early morning, at least every third one had originated in the office of Groton Wafer, chairman of the New York reception committee.

28

CITY OF HEROES

IN THE RECEPTION it extended to George Washington, the City of New York, so well schooled in the profession of welcoming returning heroes, overreached every former mark; nobly outdid itself.

The largest crowd that had ever assembled to watch a parade saw the George Washington parade. Approximately ten million men, women and children packed the sidewalks and hung out of windows along the line of march.

More policemen than had ever been assigned to handle a crowd were on duty, their ranks augmented by policemen from Long Island, New Jersey, and Westchester towns, generously loaned for the occasion.

Groton Wafer, the able chairman of the reception committee, as soon as he learned when George Washington would reach New York, informed the newspapers where the line of march would be.

By seven o'clock that evening, with the parade still fifteen hours away, people had begun to gather along the route. With bed pillows, with boxes and packages of lunch, with sleeping and crying babies, they occupied the curbstones.

All night long the city was in a ferment, as special trains from all points brought in load after load.

Several newspapers announced that the day would be a holiday. These announcements were superfluous. The millions of New York's office, factory and sweat-shop workers simply took the day off.

The day dawned clear and comfortably cool. It was a forerunner of weather that would come to be known as "typical Washington weather."

The amphibian plane which carried the Washington party from Lake Shallon to New York was escorted, it was estimated, by upward of five hundred aircraft of all ages, shapes and sizes.

Twelve aërial casualties occurred before the great silver amphibian, after circling about the Woolworth Building, volplaned down to the bay. Of these, six planes, a pair at a time, met fatally in collisions. One plane out of control, crashed in Central Park. Another came down in flames in Sheepshead Bay.

New York, meanwhile, went mad. Every whistle in the city was blowing when the amphibian passed over.

Washington's journey up the bay to the Battery—in the Macom—his first ride in a steam propelled vessel—was declared by every one who saw it to be the most impressive spectacle of its kind that had ever taken place.

The boat, followed by a flying squadron of small craft, made its way through a lane of battleships, the big guns of which were belching in the salute given only to visiting kings and other rulers.

With Groton Wafer on one side of him and the mayor of New York on the other, Washington stepped ashore at the Battery. Motion picture cameras continued to grind.

It was estimated that the record of Washington's activ-

ities on that one day consumed more than one thousand miles of cinema film.

Record after record was being broken. It was as if the return of previous heroes had been merely for the purpose of educating New York for the return of the greatest of them all.

Profiting by experience, Groton Wafer had caused to be constructed during the night a float upon which George Washington and the mayor would ride. No one else would occupy the float. It had been built on the chassis of a speed truck and was simply and appropriately covered with red, white, and blue bunting.

In the center of it was a seat large enough to accommodate two people. Groton Wafer had decided upon this float because, in the past, when great crowds assembled to watch a celebrity pass, short people in the rear had hardly glimpsed the hero. This time every one of those ten millions would see him and not a neck would be craned.

Groton Wafer had, in fact, thought of everything and of everybody.

The parade started promptly. It made its way up Broadway, through a blizzard of confetti, ticker tape, and macerated telephone books, to City Hall. Here it paused, while George Washington was given the key to the city.

Again New York outdid itself. The key presented to Colonel Washington resembled only in shape the keys which had been given to previous heroes.

The mayor, in presenting it, said: "With this key, colonel, we are setting a mark for other cities to shoot at."

The key was of solid gold, two feet in length and heavily encrusted with precious stones. It weighed eighty-five pounds.

A quartet of famous opera singers sang "My Country, 'Tis of Thee" after the presentation.

Washington was then asked to say a few words to the millions who had been unable to attend.

"I can say nothing," the young man spoke into the microphone. "I am so overwhelmed that I cannot speak."

The mayor said: "What do you think of our tall buildings?"

Washington answered: "I don't see what prevents them from toppling over."

The mayor asked: "Do they scare you, colonel?"

He answered: "Yes, I think they do."

"Do you know, colonel, that we have taller ones and more of them than any city in the world?"

"What happens to these towering buildings in a windstorm?"

"Nothing, colonel."

"Don't they sway?"

"The highest of them may sway a fraction of an inch, but

no more than that, They are built of steel and stone and concrete upon solid rock, to last forever!"

"It is incredible," was Washington's comment.

They returned presently to the float and the parade continued. It made its way through madly cheering throngs up Broadway to Fifth, up Fifth to One Hundred and Tenth Street, across to Broadway and, so, downtown again to Forty-Second Street, and across town to the Commodore Hotel, where two thousand covers were laid for luncheon.

Here, surrounded by the flower of New York's social, business, and political life, the colonel was asked those questions which were to become so familiar. His answers were deliberate and careful; he did not grow angry at their silliness or impertinence.

"Colonel, what do you think of modern America?"

"It is too wonderful for me to grasp."

"Has it developed as you wished to see it developed?"

"I am sure it has."

"Which would you rather live in, this age or the one you used to live in?"

"This age, unquestionably."

"What is the most wonderful thing you have seen?"

"It is hard to answer that, because I have seen so many wonderful things."

"What was your first impression when you came to life in Professor Morgan's laboratory?"

"I really couldn't describe it. It took me hours to get over my bewilderment. I am still bewildered. This morning, before we reached New York, I was sure I wouldn't be bewildered any more. Then, when I came up Broadway and saw those tall buildings that seemed to be leaning over upon me, I was more bewildered than ever."

"How does the automobile compare with the stage coach?"

"I do not understand what makes the automobile go; or the airplane. They are both mysteries that Mr. Muller is trying to make me understand. My brain aches from trying to understand. There is so much to grasp."

"Back in your days, when you gave thought to it, what did you think America would be like about now?"

"I don't know. Certainly, I didn't picture what America has become. No one could. Everything is so tremendous: the size of the cities, the size of the war vessels, the size of the crowds. I am told that ten million people watched the parade. I am sure there weren't ten million people in America and England together in seventeen fifty-five."

"What, in this modern age, impresses you most?"

"That is hard to answer. First, I think it is an electrical age, then I think it is an age of steel, next I am sure it is an age of transportation and communication. I suppose it is all of those things. But what a wonderful age it is to be living in!"

"What impressed you most with your reception this morning?"

"I think, at first, the war vessels did. But since then, it seems to me I have been most impressed by the orderliness with which it all happened. Ten million is such an appalling number! I understand that Mr. Groton Wafer deserves the credit. I thank him and congratulate him."

"What do you think of modern dress?"

"It seems sensible and comfortable."

"What do you think of modern women?"

"They are beautiful."

"More beautiful than the women of your day?"

"At least as beautiful—and there are so many more of them!"

"How do you like bobbed hair?"

"It startled me at first, but now I like it."

"Are you glad to be alive again, colonel?"

"Indeed I am! Life is so much more exciting than it used to be!"

Such of his utterances as were not heard by radio audiences on the loop which enabled all America to listen in to the New York ceremonies, were faithfully repeated by the press, not only of New York, but of America and, in fact, of the entire world.

Never since the radio, the cable, the telegraph, and the telephone had enmeshed the earth in one vast system of quick intercommunication had one man's remarks been attended with such eagerness.

This reborn Washington was such an enthusiastic, bewildered boy! He was so carried away by these latter-day marvels!

The world took him to its throbbing, capacious bosom; adored him overnight; continued breathlessly to adore him.

That afternoon George Washington traveled on special trains over the New York subway, the New York elevated. He went aloft into the tower of the Woolworth Building; was taken over Brooklyn Bridge; visited the power house of the Brooklyn Edison Company and saw the largest electric generator in the world.

"I do not understand it, but it is wonderful," he said. "It

is hard to believe that this stuff which can neither be seen, smelled, tasted nor heard can, as I am told, turn the wheels and light the homes and streets of this nation."

He was treated to a mild shock from a toy magneto and said, jerking his hands from the electrodes:

"It is witchery!"

He was pale, from the surprise, an hour afterward.

That night a banquet was given in Washington's honor in the Yankee Stadium, with covers for twenty thousand. Every one of the twenty thousand guests was fed. Every one of the twenty thousand guests heard, by means of loud speakers, every word uttered at the speakers' table.

The banquet was Groton Wafer's triumph.

George Washington, speaking into the microphone to the eagerly listening nation, said:

"I am dazed and exhausted by the wonderful things I have seen to-day. I am afraid that people will think I am slow at grasping things. The people of this marvelous nation, I hope, will bear with me. I want to see all of America."

His voice was husky with weariness. His face was drawn with fatigue. But he answered, carefully and courteously, the questions with which he was already so familiar.

"What do you think of New York?"

"It is beyond my powers to grasp."

"Do you still wonder what keeps the tall buildings from falling over?"

"I still do."

"What is the most wonderful thing you have seen to-day?"

"New York."

"What do you think of short skirts?"

"Everything about modern women is charming."

"Did you miss wine with your dinner?"

"No; I was too interested in the things you gentlemen were saying to me."

"Do you think prohibition is right or wrong?"

"I can't answer that—yet."

"Do you realize that upward of fifty million people in America, and a great many more millions in Europe, are listening to what you say?"

"It is bewildering," said Washington.

From the Yankee Stadium he was escorted, amidst tumultuous throngs, down Broadway to the Populo Theater, which seated fifteen thousand people. A special program had been arranged, but it was doubtful if any one but Washington paid any attention to it. Scenes at Mount Vernon, in Washington, in the foremost American cities were flashed on the screen, while a two hundred-piece orchestra and five pipe organs rendered national airs.

Most of the music was unheard. The occupants of the fifteen thousand seats and the other thousands who occupied standing room cheered incessantly.

Three hundred policemen were required to hold the crowd back when he was spirited out of the theater to the automobile waiting to speed him to the Pennsylvania Station.

It was an utterly exhausted young man who sprawled, a little later, in a chair on the special train taking him to the national capital.

Alone with his adviser, the managing editor of *The Daily It*, he said hoarsely:

"When you mentioned responsibilities yesterday, I had no idea what you meant, Mr. Galloway. I am beginning to understand."

He tried to raise a glass of water to his mouth. The glass slipped from his hand and fell to the carpet.

"I can hardly lift my hand. It must have been shaken by five thousand people to-day."

"I will see that handshaking is stopped," Larry promised.

"Will there be this much excitement everywhere I go?"

"I'm afraid there will, colonel."

Washington looked thoughtful. "I like it," he said presently. "But people, I suppose, will expect more and more of me. I have been asked about prohibition at least one hundred times since we reached New York. Did I say the right things?"

"You were splendid."

"What shall I say in Washington? I am so afraid of making mistakes."

"My suggestion," Larry answered, "is that you simply continue to enjoy yourself. Don't worry about your responsibilities yet awhile. I understand that you will be asked to make some kind of a speech to Congress."

"What shall I say?"

"I would be noncommittal. If they ask questions that embarrass you, tell them you will return later to answer them. I should like very much to have you return, after your trip over America, to Congress. That is the logical place to deliver any message you may have for the American people."

"I want the American people to like me," Washington

said in his husky, tired voice. "Will you write the speech for me?"

Larry left him, went on past the two guards at the door into the press car, where he was promptly surrounded.

"The colonel has just retired," he told the reporters. "You can say that he is exhausted, but delighted with the reception New York gave him."

"What did he say about his first railroad ride?"

"It is too much for him to grasp. The speed and the smoothness amaze him. He wants to ride in an engine some time. I don't know how he's going to keep up this pace. While I was talking with him, he tried to lift a glass of water to his mouth, but it slipped out of his hand. He can hardly lift that hand. I've decided there's to be no more handshaking. He said that upward of five thousand people shook his hand to-day."

"Are you sure it was a glass of water?" asked one of the reporters.

29

THE GILT ON THE IDOL

WITH UPROARIOUS ENTHUSIASM, Colonel Washington was welcomed by the city which had, more than a century and a quarter earlier, given itself his name. Airplanes dropped roses on him and millions cheered as the triumphant procession wound through the streets.

The outstanding feature of his visit to Washington was the short speech he made to Congress.

Standing beside the Vice President, more than a little self-conscious, pale, and so serious that his words commanded breathless attention, he said:

"You, gentlemen, have honored me by asking my opinion of modern America. I have been in modern America, as you know, only a few days. It is too soon for me to express an intelligent opinion. Some time later I earnestly hope that I may be permitted to do so.

"All my comment so far has been, I realize, exclamatory. I am amazed by America's progress, her size, her importance among nations. I will, I know, continue to be amazed. But I am as certain that the time will come when my eighteenth century point of view can be turned to some constructive value.

"I mean that a man from another century may be able to

judge modernity with a mind so open that it is unique. His prejudices will be clouded, but they will be less clouded, I believe, than modern prejudices."

He hesitated. The Vice President said:

"When you have finished your inspection of America, we will be honored to have you return and give us your opinions."

Washington made the courtly bow of which the newspapers had already said so much.

"I will do so gladly. I am anxious to see everything in America, particularly her great industries. As you know, there was, in my time, no such thing as a factory. Scattered here and there, to be sure, were small mills; but the factory, as such, I learn, did not come into being until after the first quarter of the nineteenth century.

"In my time, each home was a producing and consuming unit. Meat, vegetables, and fruit were preserved in one way and another and stored through the winter. Sheep were sheared and the wool was carded, spun, and woven. It was the same with other things. Each home was a self-contained, self-sustaining entity. Life was simpler and harder then than it is now.

"The most important development since my time has been, I believe, organized industry. My mind is groping for causes and effects. I am beginning to realize that modern inventions—electricity in its many uses, the railroad, the steamship, the telephone, telegraph and so on are results of this modern condition, rather than causes of it.

"In any event, America has leaped so far that I doubt if I ever will be able to catch up. I have been asked time after time if I prefer this new America to the old America. I can only say again that I do, most heartily!"

The press of America applauded Washington's address to Congress; spoke glowingly of this thoughtful side of his nature that had been revealed and continued to record in minute detail the comments and activities of "America's most glorious hero."

Congress unanimously passed a resolution to advance his rank from colonel to that of brigadier general; approved simultaneously an appropriation of one million dollars to defray the cost of a special sightseeing train, and entered upon a bitter quarrel over the selection of a Congressional delegation to accompany him.

A Senator from the Middle West introduced a resolution in which George Washington was made dictator of the United States and all possessions. It was greeted with wild enthusiasm, but died a mysterious death overnight.

The quarrel in Congress continued. George Washington, through his spokesman, Lawrence Galloway, issued a statement which settled the matter.

"I should like very much to have every member of Congress accompany me on this trip. Inasmuch as this project is impracticable, perhaps it would be wise not to inject politics into my journey."

The statement was issued from his old plantation at Mount Vernon during his two-day sojourn there. And Congress accepted it as an ultimatum—without a murmur.

It was hard to believe that the popularity of America's distinguished guest from the past could increase; yet it did. He was so earnest, so interested, so courteous in the face of the most foolish, most impertinent questions.

His courtly bow was soon adopted by all men who made any pretense of being gentlemen. His slow English speech threatened to alter the accent of the nation.

All other events were forgotten. The radio stations of the country, after a few sporadic attempts to continue with programs, gave over their circuits to him. His voice was clear, rich, sometimes ringing—it transmitted perfectly.

From Mount Vernon he went to Pittsburgh. His bewilderment when shown the blast furnaces now standing on the site of Fort Duquesne was so pathetic that women, all over America, wept.

Leaving Pittsburgh, the special train went to Columbus, Cleveland, Buffalo, Detroit. He was taken through factories, universities, power plants. Word by word his comments were reported to the nation.

America learned how electricity and aluminium were made by water power; how an automobile was put together; how steel was made and rolled. It underwent, in short, a swift and tremendous education as Washington sped from city to city, from factory to factory.

And the conscientious spokesman of the popular young man saw to it that America learned a few of her shortcomings. Washington's comments were becoming shrewder.

In Detroit, he said:

"The speed with which automobiles are made and assembled is amazing. I am bewildered again and again by machines which seem invested with human intelligence. What a tumultuous age it is! I am beginning to grasp the meaning of standardization. And I am beginning to perceive its faults. I think Americans must guard against standardized minds."

In Chicago:

"I am overwhelmed by the majesty of Chicago. It is hard for me to realize that when I was on earth before, nothing existed here but a crude fort and a handful of little houses.

"The efficiency of your stockyard methods is amazing. So is the speed and efficiency with which you load and unload these great lake steamers. Efficiency, I think, is the god of this modern age. Every man, every machine, is judged by efficiency standards.

"I cannot accustom myself to the efficient work that you crowd into one of your modern days. But when do Americans have time to live, to think? When do Americans find time to deal, for example, with their system of government?

"I have been asked repeatedly to-day to make some comment on Chicago's crime epidemic. Why should this epidemic exist in this city in this age? I understand that, yesterday alone, one bank was robbed, one mail truck was held up, four people were murdered and a half-dozen others were, at the point of guns, relieved of their valuables.

"I am puzzled. Why does this condition exist?"

In Los Angeles, after a flying trip through motion picture studios and the homes of some celebrated actors and actresses:

"I am, once again, bewildered. When I think that I have grasped the meaning of this new age I find that I have to begin at the bottom and learn all over again. I have thought, at various times, that this is the age of transportation and communication, of electricity, of factory efficiency; but now I am ready to believe that it is the age of luxury. Never, I am sure, has the world known such luxury.

"This afternoon I have seen millions of dollars being

spent in the production of these pictures that flicker on a curtain. I have met at least a dozen men and women whose monthly salaries were greater than the yearly income of the President. I have been shown bathrooms of lapis lazuli and ivory and solid silver and gold.

"I am convinced that this age is one of luxury and haste. Everywhere I hear the word 'Hurry!' I am convinced that Americans work too violently and play too hard. What is your goal? Is no price put on leisure?

"To me, looking back upon the old days, leisure was valuable. What a gulf stretches between our old customs and yours! In the old days, a guest would come to a house, occupy the room set aside for him, often not see his host for days. No demands were made upon him, and he made no demands upon his host. He rode, he hunted, he fished, he read—enjoyed himself as he saw fit. He came and went as he pleased.

"It must be as difficult for you modern Americans to picture that as it is for me to grasp the American situation to-day. I think America could profitably cultivate leisure."

George Washington's spokesman was typing the final sentence of this statement in the drawing-room set aside as his office when Mrs. Horace Glen Islington appeared in the doorway in the gown she had worn at the evening reception.

He glanced up from the keyboard and said wearily: "Hello, Sally. Isn't it past your bedtime?"

She steadied herself against the lurching of the train and answered:

"Larry, I want to have a talk with you. What are you writing?"

"The colonel's statement on Hollywood. I'll take it into the press car, so they can file it at Sacramento, and be right back."

"Let me read it."

Larry gave the typed sheet to her and watched her large blue eyes as they darted from line to line. Finishing it, she placed it on his desk and seated herself on the couch.

"Close that door, Larry. I don't want us to be disturbed."

Larry, mystified, closed the door.

"Sit down here beside me."

He obeyed.

"Are you aware," she began, "that Polly is on this train?"

He answered, somewhat peevishly: "Of course I'm aware of it."

"Do you realize," Aunt Sally persisted, "that she had made all plans to stay in Hollywood and begin work on her first picture?"

"I said days ago," he answered irritably, "that it made no difference to me whether or not she went ahead with that picture."

"I'm not referring to that, Larry. She isn't on this train now because you disapproved of her going into pictures. She's here because the colonel insisted on her staying. You didn't hear, of course, about the row they had this morning?"

The crusader's attention had seemed to be wandering. Now he looked at her steadily.

"Did they have a row?"

"Did they have a row!" Aunt Sally mocked. "You poor dumb lamb, do you realize that this whole beautiful scheme of yours is going to be smashed if you don't do some mighty quick thinking?"

"I don't understand," Larry muttered.

"You are worse than the colonel. 'I don't understand.' 'I am bewildered.' 'I cannot grasp it.' 'It is beyond my comprehension.' Look through that pile of papers. See how many references there are coupling the colonel and Polly! You can't see it because you refuse to see it. You are the blindest man I ever knew. He is simply mad about her—and you refuse to see it!"

"I refuse to believe it," Larry said stubbornly.

Aunt Sally sighed.

"And you refuse to consider me as anything but a flighty, shallow minded woman. You won't believe me when I tell you that night after night I've cried myself to sleep— worrying about you. You're so pitiably pathetic! You're so determined to put great lofty sentiments into that dummy's mouth! I said dummy!" she growled.

He started to speak, but she rushed on:

"You know as well as I do that he's a dummy. The only props under him are Muller and yourself. Pull you away— and he'd come down like Humpty Dumpty!"

"Oh, Sally—"

"Doesn't everybody know it?" she cried. "Haven't you heard Muller night after night trying to drive things into his head?"

"He is simply dazed!"

"My dear, he is simply dumb. Perhaps the excitement has been too much for him. Perhaps he can't and never will make an adjustment to this modern age. Perhaps it's because he's so infatuated with Polly. Perhaps the brain of seventeen fifty-five wasn't on a par with the brain of to-day. Justify it any way you wish, but the fact remains that he is nothing but a dummy.

"Muller and Polly and I know that these grand and glorious sentiments he utters are yours; that you've written every speech he's ever made, given him every thought he's ever used."

Larry objected: "His New Orleans speech was perfect!"

"Do you know whose it was?"

"It was his."

"My dear, it was Muller's!"

She considered him anxiously.

"I want to help you. That's why I'm here now. Your mind is on nothing but this beautiful opportunity to uplift America. You haven't time for anything else. And you are doing it beautifully. You're so darned earnest, you're so courageous, you're trying so hard— Honestly, Larry, I do cry myself to sleep—often! And when I think of those reporters out there, waiting for your first false move, to pounce on you and rend you limb from limb—Larry, you have got to do something about this love affair."

"I refuse to consider it a love affair."

"Yes; and you refuse to believe that Polly adores the ground you walk on. The poor kid is— Well, if you weren't busy being a crusader twenty-four hours of the day, you'd see it for yourself. He can't keep his eyes off her. She must be with him everywhere he goes. He has every one of the symptoms of puppy love.

"If you are going to continue to uplift America, you have got to do something about it. I admit now that it was poor policy for Polly and me to come on this trip. I thought it would be loads of fun. I thought it would do Polly worlds of good. As late as this afternoon I was hoping that the situation would be saved by her staying in Hollywood.

"Ever since we left Pittsburgh, the papers, especially the sensational ones, have been saying things about Polly and the colonel. They've mentioned the way he constantly stares at her; they've even accused him of holding her hand!

"You can't keep it bottled up much longer. And once it comes out, America's glorious idol is going to crash from his pedestal. And all your beautiful schemes for America are going to crash with him.

"I admit I was wrong in starting Polly as I did—making her go up to him and kiss him—snatching the microphone that night and putting over her publicity stunt. Yes; I admit I was wrong. The public got the wrong idea of her. People think she's a cheap little sensation hunter. I mean, they still think so, in spite of her beautiful conduct since.

"Do you see what I'm coming at, Larry? Thanks entirely to you, Washington has remained on his pedestal. What a crime it was to bring that poor dazed thing into the world! If the world finds out that he has fallen madly in love with Polly—good-by everything!"

Larry groaned: "Suppose you are right, which I don't yet admit, what can I do?"

"Lay down the law to him! Do you know where he is now?"

"In bed," said Larry.

"On the observation platform, sulking, because Polly refuses to pet!"

Larry said: "I'll have to think this over."

"Yes, you'd better think, and think fast," she warned him.

30

COULD THERE BE A
LINK MISSING?

LARRY WENT INTO the press car with Washington's latest statement and answered the usual questions. What time had the colonel retired? How was his health? What did he think of Hollywood?

George Washington's spokesman answered the questions and returned to his own car and knocked on Paul Muller's door. The osteologist opened it and came limping out.

"Where's the colonel?" Larry asked.

"He just turned in."

"Stories have been coming to me," Larry said heavily, "to the effect that he has fallen in love with Polly. What do you know about it?"

"I know all about it," Muller answered. "It's true. He's goofy about her. I've argued with him too, Larry—and he won't listen to a damned word I say. It started the minute he met her, and it's been getting worse ever since. What are we going to do with this fellow?"

Larry gazed at him in silence.

Muller peevishly burst out: "Stop kidding yourself! He

isn't fooling you or me or Sally or Polly. What's going to happen to him?"

Larry said wearily: "I don't know."

"Well, it's something to think about." He looked at Larry queerly. "You know, don't you, that what words you haven't been putting into his mouth, I have? I'm getting tired of it. I want a rest. I'm homesick for the laboratory. I'm fed up with trying to make a dumb kid understand things he isn't even interested in. I'm ready to quit."

"Why don't you?"

"How can I? You can't swing this alone. You're too busy writing his speeches to school him on what to say next day."

"Are you doing that?" Larry gasped.

"I've been doing it ever since this damned tour started! And I'm sick of it and I want to quit and I can't. Both you and I have a bear by the tail and we daren't let go. What a hell of a mess!"

"He's dazed," Larry argued. "He's never got over his original bewilderment."

"He never will!"

"We've never given him a chance. We've tried to make him take the world in one swallow."

"One swallow," muttered the sardonic Muller, "doesn't make an education. What I want to know is, what will happen to him when he's cast loose to shift for himself? He's been in the center of the stage now for nearly three months. It's too long for a hero, even as big as Washington, to hold the stage.

"You're thinking we owe it to the nation, somehow, to keep him up there on the pedestal. Are we going to devote the rest of our lives to making the world think that a—a poor dazed kid is an intellectual giant?

"We didn't create a monster; we created a fine, normal human being. It's since then that you and I between us, aided by the damned gullible public, have created the monster. We've manufactured between us a fictitious ideal hero. If our monster had coöperated, we'd be safe. But he hasn't coöperated. He hasn't got it in him to coöperate. Now what are we going to do with him and ourselves?"

"It makes me feel sick," Larry admitted.

"And we're going to feel a lot sicker before we feel any better. I suppose things could have drifted along as they have if it hadn't been for this infatuation. You can deal with a dazed but willing kid. You can't deal with an infatuated man. I'm in love with Polly myself. I won't stand for his pawing her!"

"Has he been pawing her?"

"He's been trying to."

Larry sighed heavily. "I've been too busy—"

"—writing his speeches—"

"—to pay close attention. I'll talk to Polly. I think this tour had better be stopped short. I want him to speak to Congress before he loses any prestige."

"What are you going to have him say to Congress?"

"That is the one thing that puzzles me," Larry answered. "He insists he has a message for Congress. He's been saying so ever since we left Dallas."

"It's probably a medley of all the things you've been saying for him."

"He won't tell me. What do you hear of Professor Morgan?"

"His condition is practically the same. It's a complete nervous breakdown. He won't leave the sanatorium for months. In his last letter, Ortola said they were giving the old man ten grains of morphine a day. That means he's pretty bad.

"At that, I don't know but what I'd willingly change places with him. But it's a relief to know we're at last headed for Congress. Good night, Larry."

Larry said good night and proceeded through the car and the next one to the observation platform. He found Polly alone under the dim bulb in the enameled dome, huddled down in a chair, staring into the receding night. The lights of a town whisked past.

Larry sagged into the chair beside her.

Polly flung herself about and showed him a white face and a pair of burning brown eyes. Only once had he seen her so angry: the night she and Jason Ortola came to his cabin; when he doubted them.

She demanded, in a wrathful voice:

"How much longer is this going to last?"

He grinned wanly. "This trip?"

"This farce!" she snapped.

"Muller just asked me the same question. Your aunt asked it first, a few minutes earlier. I was asking it of myself when she came in."

"I can't stand it!" Polly exclaimed and banged the chair arm with her fist. "What are we going to do? What's going to happen to us?"

"I don't know."

"I've made a mess of everything!"

"It isn't your fault he's fallen in love with you. He's only one of a large, distinguished company, Polly."

"But he—he's so dumb!"

Larry sighed. "I hate to hear you say that. I didn't suppose anybody realized it but myself."

"Yes," she said in a low voice. "You fooled me for a month. I thought he was saying all these beautiful things. I tried to make him say some of them to me, but all he did was to repeat the old ones. Then I discovered that he is absolutely nothing but a parrot—repeating over and over the bright things you and Paul tell him. He is nothing but a walking phonograph—a human talking machine.

"Larry, I've thought—I've often wondered— Do you suppose, somehow, dad's experiment wasn't *quite* complete? He went to pieces just before it ended. Do you suppose some—some chemical was left out? I've been thinking about that a great deal lately. I was thinking about it one day when—when he tried to kiss me!"

Polly shuddered.

"I've wondered the same things myself," the crusader admitted.

"I hoped he'd get over it. But it only grew worse. To-day was the grand climax. Do you know what happened to-day?"

"Didn't you have a row?"

"I suppose Aunt Sally told you."

"She intimated that he wouldn't let you stay over in Hollywood."

"Larry," the girl said fiercely, "he told me that if I stayed in Hollywood, he'd stay, too. He said, in just those words, he didn't care a damn about the trip or about America.

All he was interested in, he said, was me. I asked him if he didn't feel he owed you something, and he said no. I asked him if he didn't feel he owed any of us anything for having brought him back to life in this exciting age, and he said he had paid all his debts and was going to do just as he pleased.

"What is going to become of him? I can't stand him, Larry. He gives me the creeps. And he swears he's going to tell the reporters he's in love with me and going to marry me. I'm through. How can I slip away without spoiling your plans?"

"A number of people, including myself," Larry answered, "seem to be wondering the same thing—how they can escape without upsetting the boat."

Polly groaned. "I'll stick to the bitter end. But how far away is it?"

"I'm going to tell the reporters now that the junket is over. Our last stop is Seattle, with an hour or two in Portland. From there we're going to Washington."

"He's ready to address Congress," Polly said. "He's told me so; but he's terribly mysterious. He says his message will startle the world. Who wrote it?"

"I don't know. I didn't. Muller didn't."

"Is there anything I can do to help you—just once?"

"You can try to find out what his speech will be about. You can prevent him from making an ass of himself in public. You can try to convince him that he will ruin everything if he announces his—his infatuation."

"I have been doing that. I'll keep on doing it. But can't I do anything for you?"

"You're doing a great deal for me."

She sighed. Her eyes upon his were owlish.

"You're hopeless. One of these days I hope you'll need me. Terribly! I hope I'm handy."

"I hope so, too, Polly." He rose.

"Because," she informed him in a defiant tone, "America, even if it knew, wouldn't appreciate what you're doing. America doesn't want to be awakened or educated or uplifted. All it wants is boosts. Washington's popularity—I mean, his sustained popularity—is due to the fact that he's the biggest, most enthusiastic booster America ever had. Not himself, but boosting has endeared him to the hearts of his countrymen! 'What a wonderful, place America is!'" she mocked. "'What, a glorious country to live in!'"

"He's sincere about that," Larry murmured.

"So is an orthophonic!" she snorted. "All this boosting is nothing but the sugar coating on the pill you're trying to shove down America's throat. Muller is putting on the sugar coating and you're mixing the medicine."

Polly laughed rather wildly.

"I'm nothing but a monkey wrench in the medicine factory! And, Larry, I did try so hard to be the nice kind of person you wanted me to be! I wanted to be fine and helpful. I really thought I could be of some use to you on this trip. And I've done nothing but ball everything up!"

Larry was leaning against the door jamb, looking down at her.

"I wonder if you're right."

"About what?"

"Boosting. I was sure that this shaking up would do the country a lot of good."

Polly shook her head. "America doesn't appreciate it.

Only the few people who know you do. We think it's wonderful, but I, for one, hate to see you burning yourself up. What's your reward going to be?"

Larry opened the screen door and answered: "I don't expect any reward. Good night, Polly."

"Good night, you poor old dear!"

He went in. At Washington's door he stopped and knocked.

George Washington, in pale blue pyjamas, a cigarette dangling from a corner of his mouth, opened the door. He gazed at Larry with cold blue eyes.

"I have been wondering, colonel," Larry began, "if it wouldn't be judicious to cut this trip short and return as soon as possible to Washington for your speech to Congress."

Washington frowned.

"What made you decide that, Larry?"

"I think the time is ripe."

"What makes you think it's ripe? I haven't seen nearly all of America."

"There are several reasons, colonel. You have been occupying the center of the stage for almost three months. No matter how popular a hero is, the people sooner or later grow tired of him. I'm not saying that your popularity is waning, but it might. I don't think we should run any risk.

"Every one is tremendously interested in what you're going to say to Congress. We've been building that interest up very carefully. We've wanted the nation to be on tiptoe for that speech. It is. You told me you'd seen enough of the country to prepare yourself for your speech."

"But I want to see more of America. I'm having a

wonderful time. I don't want it to stop. No, Larry; I'm not ready to make my speech to Congress. We'll wait another month."

"We're too tired to go on another month," Larry said. "I mean, Paul, Polly, Sally, and myself."

"You don't have to go on," argued the stubborn young man. "I can go on by myself."

"Who will write your speeches?"

"I will! I'm tired of these heavy things you and Paul are having me say, anyway."

Larry groaned. He had seen this difficult young man in these moods before.

"Who will write your speech for Congress?"

"I will!"

"What are you going to say?"

"I won't tell you, Larry. I won't tell anybody. It's my speech, and I'm going to make it."

"Won't you tell me what it's about?"

"I won't tell anybody what it's about. It will startle America."

"Will it have anything to do with the subjects we've been hammering on—the need for America's awakening to the problems of government, the necessity of one part of the country understanding the other parts?"

"It may. I've decided, as a matter of fact, that I heartily disapprove of America!"

"You aren't going to say that!" Larry exclaimed.

"I don't intend to say just that, but I do intend to say some things that will startle the country."

Larry shook his head hopelessly. "Do you realize that every word you say before Congress will be listened to by practically every one in the United States, South America, and Europe?"

"I do."

"Don't you think you should consult Paul or me before you make that speech?"

"I do not! I don't need anybody's help."

"It's painful to remind you, colonel, that Paul Muller and I have made every effort to guard your popularity."

Washington snorted. "All Paul has done is to make me say a lot of high sounding things, and all you've done is to quote me as saying more of them. People aren't interested in such stuff."

"Perhaps not."

"I know they're not! They like to be told how wonderful they are, not what their faults are."

"You mean, colonel, you don't think you owe anything to America?"

"I made America a free country, didn't I, when I was here before? I'm giving America a mighty fine time looking at me now."

Larry said deliberately: "Another reason I've decided to cut this trip short is your attitude to Polly."

Washington's lips met in a hard line. "I won't have you meddling in my private affairs."

"Your private affairs are national affairs."

"I don't care. I'm human," the young man answered sullenly. "And it's none of your business."

Larry, bristling, came back with: "If you say one word to any reporters about this infatuation of yours, as you've threatened to do, Polly Morgan will leave this train at the first opportunity and you won't see her again!"

"I wish you'd mind your own business!" Washington burst out, peevishly.

"I'm going to the press car now," Larry told him, "and issue a statement to the effect that you have decided to go directly from Seattle to Washington."

George Washington, his voice high and thin with wrath, cried:

"You can go to the devil!"

The door was slammed in Larry's white face.

He went on to the press car and announced to the reporters:

"Colonel Washington has just decided that he will go directly to Washington from Seattle."

Forty reporters burst into questions. Larry silenced them and said:

"He has seen America from one coast to the other and from one border to the other. After almost three months of first-hand study, he feels that he is prepared to express his opinions of America before Congress."

One reporter said: "There's been a row, hasn't there, Mr. Galloway?"

"Certainly not! The colonel needs a rest."

"Is he sick?"

"No. Simply tired. We will be in Sacramento in a few minutes. I'll instruct the conductor to hold the train until you've filed your stories."

"What will he say in his speech to Congress?"

"No one knows but himself," Larry gravely answered. "He has intimated to me that it will be startling, but he has taken no one into his confidence."

When he had spoken to the conductor, Larry returned to

the observation platform, hoping to find Polly. He wanted to talk to her; wanted to argue with her about America, perhaps for no other reason than to upset her arguments, to strengthen his wavering convictions.

The platform was empty.

He settled down in a chair and lighted a cigarette.

Reviewing this evening's revelations, it seemed incredible to him that the newspapers of the nation could be blind to the tragedy; that all America could continue to adore this hollow shell of a personality, this papier-mâché hero.

Weeks ago, he had begun to wonder if, perhaps, something had gone wrong at the last moment in the laboratory; if those numerous delicate chemical balances had not been upset by Professor Morgan's attack upon the apparatus; by the explosion, some seconds before the twelve minutes had elapsed, of the retort.

He reflected: "It is wrong to experiment with life and death. Washington should never have been brought back to life. Even if he has a normal brain, he can never adjust himself to this bewildering age."

He wondered what thoughts were formulating in the back of that groping, dazed mind to be expressed before the members of Congress, to be broadcast to the eagerly attentive world.

Wondering, a chill perspiration formed on the crusader's forehead. What would that poor, incomplete human machine say to the world?

"It will startle America! I heartily disapprove of America!"

Larry dropped his sweating face into his hands and groaned.

31

WASHINGTON'S CONGRESSIONAL ADDRESS

THE RETURN OF George Washington to the national capital was the return of a triumphant hero. He had, in his three months' tour, conquered America. This mighty nation which he had, nearly eight score years ago, guided through wars and dissension to independence, now thrilled to his lightest utterance, greeted with mad enthusiasm his opinions, his comments, his criticisms.

He had, in spite of police and military protection, been mobbed by hysterical patriots in a dozen different cities. His hand, in spite of the ruling against the practice, had been grasped by countless thousands.

Men, women and children had dropped to their knees at sight of him; had madly cheered and wept and fallen unconscious in their terrible ecstasy.

Now that the American people from the Atlantic to the Pacific, from the South to the North, had glimpsed him, worshiped him, they were prepared to follow where he led, this hero who had been so miraculously returned to them.

Days before the special train reached Washington, the city was clogged with visitors.

Martial law was enforced forty-eight hours before the

special was due. The population of Washington increased tenfold in those two days.

A cordon of soldiers twenty deep was thrown about the Capitol building, and it was closed to all but those who had official business there.

The public, it was announced, would not be permitted in the House for Washington's speech. Accredited representatives of the press would be admitted only upon the presentation of passes countersigned by the Secretary of War.

The special train reached Washington at ten in the morning. All night long, mobs had milled about the Union Station. From midnight until dawn, they cheered.

Wild rumors flew from mouth to mouth. The train had been wrecked. Washington had decided not to come to Washington.

At a few minutes after ten, the train came in. Washington was surrounded by a company of marines and escorted to his limousine. With a flying wedge of motor cycle policemen opening the way, he was driven to the Capitol.

Washington's entrance to the House was greeted by a cheer from the assembled Senators, Representatives and reporters which lasted for forty-two minutes.

Arrangements hours ago had been completed to relay Washington's speech, by radio, to every corner of the civilized world. The fifty highest powered transmitting stations in the United States were connected on one loop.

From the General Electric station at Schenectady, Washington's voice would be carried to England, where it would be picked up and repeated over Europe, and to Rio Janeiro, where it would likewise be relayed over South

America. Australia, New Zealand, and Africa were listening in.

In a double-breasted blue serge suit, brown Oxfords, a white shirt with a soft collar, and a black polka dot bow tie, a pale, distressed young man faced the battery of microphones and listened to the roar of lungs.

He stared uneasily at the microphones, as if trying to grasp the fact that his voice would presently be heard by more people than had ever, since the world began, listened to a human voice.

For forty-two minutes he stood on the platform, with hands hanging beside him, face set in grim lines, waiting for that roaring to come to an end.

Silence eventually came.

He began in a frail, trembling voice:

"Gentlemen of the Congress of the United States—"

His voice stopped. He drew a deep breath, began again, this time under better control:

"Gentlemen of the Congress of the United States: I promised, on my visit here some months ago, to return and talk to you when I had studied conditions throughout the country.

"I have, since then, been living up to the first half of my promise. I have been seeing America. I have visited your leading cities. I have visited your leading factories. I have visited in the homes of your leading citizens.

"I have seen America. I have gone, in turn, from stunned bewilderment to amazement, to wonder, to enthusiastic admiration.

"I have found some faults. I have spoken frankly of

America's lack of interest in her machinery of government. I have mentioned the evils of standardization and of haste.

"Those and other evils which I have come in contact with in this dazzling new America I have, time and again, dwelt upon.

"But I have persistently refrained from dealing with the greatest evil of all—the evil that is turning the United States into a lawless nation, the evil that is corrupting American institutions, the evil that is bringing down upon America the scorn of the world!

"I am referring to prohibition."

A sustained roaring prevented Washington from continuing for twenty minutes. Then, when silence again prevailed, he went on, in the same steady, machinelike voice:

"I had not returned to mortal life a dozen hours before I had been asked again and again my opinion of prohibition. It is the one question that has been put to me, during my trip, oftener than all others.

"I have given the prohibition law my closest attention and my most profound thought. I have studied the effects of the law upon the home, the industrial, the political life of the people. I have learned of the corruption it has caused in the judicial, the legislative, the enforcement branches of city, State, and national government.

"I see the United States, which I helped to found, being destroyed from within by the rampant vice which the prohibition law has loosed. I see it setting up false gods. I see its strength being undermined. I see it prepared to totter and collapse before the first vigorous invasion of our enemies!

"You have asked for my opinion. My opinion, gentlemen of the American Congress, is that the Eighteenth Amendment is the most vicious and most degrading piece of legislation ever enacted in history!

"It has made the vaunted liberty of America a butt for the ridicule of every intelligent nation! It has brought down contempt for all law.

"My message to you, to the American people is: Repeal this pernicious piece of legislation!"

32

A HOUSE OF CARDS

AND WHILE THE most sensational radio address in the history of that modern medium of communication was being hearkened to by the entire civilized world, Lawrence Galloway, crusader, with stunned, reeling mind was groping toward a realization that he, the American people, the civilized world, had been victimized by the most audacious hoax ever perpetrated upon gullible humanity.

He was trying to grasp the incredible fact that this George Washington who stood before Congress, addressing rapt listeners by the hundreds of millions, was a hillbilly named Gore.

A venomously jealous woman was bringing to a rude conclusion the world's most fatuous, most beautiful dream.

They had been seated before the cone-speaker of a radio receiver in the official suite at the New Willard, he and Polly, her aunt and Paul Muller and Jason Ortola, waiting for the roaring in the House of Representatives to cease, waiting for George Washington to begin speaking.

The door had opened and Mrs. Gore had come in: a woman with blazing green eyes and chalk-white skin; creaking in stiff new shoes, rustling in the black water silk of a country woman.

Directly to Polly Morgan she had gone; her voice, menacing as the whir of a rattler, had penetrated the rough roaring which issued from the cone-speaker.

"You let my husband alone or I'll tell every reporter in Washington who he is!"

Polly repeated: "Your husband?"

"This man who's calling himself George Washington!"

Jason Ortola thrust himself between them. He seized Mrs. Gore by the shoulders. And shouted:

"Mrs. Gore, come into this next room and I'll—"

Larry switched off the radio as the first words came booming through: "Gentlemen of the Congress of the United States—"

And in the quick silence he heard the woman saying: "—not browbeat me any more, Jason Ortola!"

Polly had sunk heavily into a chair; was nervously gnawing at her finger nails.

"There are absolutely no grounds—" Ortola began.

"She's been trying from the very beginning," the Gore woman stormed, "to get my husband away from me. I'm not going to let you make a fool out of me any longer."

Aunt Sally was saying, over and over; "Good Lord! Good Lord! Good Lord!" And pacing along a seam of the blue carpet.

"This woman," Ortola shouted, "is stark, raving mad! Call the house detective, Galloway!"

"Mad?" Mrs. Gore cried. "I ought to be mad! Letting myself be made a fool of! Letting myself believe all the nonsense you told me!"

"Galloway, phone for the house detective!"

Paul Muller, sagging wearily on a window sill, snarled:

"Oh, for the Lord's sake, Ortola, stop it. The beans are spilled. Make the best you can of a bad mess."

Larry, trembling so that he could hardly stand, was grasping Ortola by one elbow and Mrs. Gore by another. His eyes flickered wildly from face to face.

He said thickly: "What is this woman trying to say?"

"She is absolutely out of her mind!" Ortola cried.

"Mr. Galloway, I am not out of my mind. I am simply sick and tired of being made a fool of. I knew, from the very start, that nothing good would come of this."

Larry selected the favorite phrase of the fraudulent Washington from a torrent of exclamations: "I don't understand."

Muller snorted: "You'd better begin, Larry. You're in as deep as the rest of us now."

Larry ignored him. Holding tight to Mrs. Gore's elbow, as if for strength, he tried to speak coherently.

"You mean— You mean—"

"I mean that man speaking in Congress this minute is not George Washington! I mean, he's my husband. He's Ernest Gore."

"Ernest Gore!"

"Yes, Ernest Gore."

"That laboratory experiment was faked?"

"It was all faked. Every bit of it was faked!"

Larry reiterated: "I don't understand."

Ortola broke in: "Galloway, I will explain."

And Larry growled: "I don't want to hear from you—yet. I want Mrs. Gore to go on. Go on, Mrs, Gore."

The angry woman broke away from him.

"I won't talk to you or anybody else. I've said what I came

here to say. If that Morgan girl doesn't keep away from my man, I'll tell every reporter in Washington the truth!"

"The truth," Larry repeated. "Why— Why, this means—"

He turned slowly about, his blurred eyes looking for Polly. She had crammed the half of a handkerchief into her mouth; was bending over staring at the blue carpet.

Ortola said, in a calmed voice: "You'd better let me explain, Galloway. As Muller says, you're in this as deep as any of us now. You might as well know everything. The idea was mine. I take, wholly, the blame."

Larry stared at him. He said, stupidly, "I can't grasp it. I can't make myself believe it."

Polly cried suddenly: "Jason, why did you do it?"

He answered: "I'll answer all your questions as fast as I can. Galloway, you'd better have a drink, hadn't you? Muller, get the bottle of Scotch you'll find in my bag."

"I don't want anything to drink," Larry muttered.

"I intend to make an honest, thorough explanation," Ortola went on. "I would have made it earlier, but I was afraid of you. Now, in Muller's words, you're in as deep as the rest of us. I mean, you won't dare expose us."

Larry said nothing. His somnambulistic eyes were fixed upon the chemist's face.

Aunt Sally impatiently interjected: "Stop beating about the bush. I wouldn't blame him, Ortola, if he wrung your filthy neck!"

The chemist snapped: "I will not be called names. The six of us are faced by a tremendous problem. Somehow, we have got to solve it."

"I'm going to Europe on the first steamer," Aunt Sally announced. "That's how I'm going to solve it."

Larry said, in a thick voice: "Ortola, I'm waiting for your explanation."

"And I'm more than willing to give it to you. The scheme, the hoax—call it what you wish—was my own idea. I take that responsibility. I worked it out alone. I have been trying for years to devise an effective scheme that would defeat prohibition. I am, you may as well know, at the head of the Society for the Abolition of Prohibition. We have spent millions so far, and we are willing, if necessary, to spend millions more."

Ortola hesitated.

"I will go so far as to say that I, as the representative of that society, will willingly give each one of you in this room one million dollars—if it is necessary. I say that, not in an attempt to bribe any of you, but to give you some inkling of our determination. We were determined to defeat prohibition, and we have defeated it. I think there is no longer any question of that."

Larry interrupted: "You wrote that speech he is delivering before Congress now?"

"I did."

Aunt Sally exclaimed: "Ortola, you are the most diabolical fiend that ever lived."

Larry said, in a voice that sounded calm and reasonable: "I want you to tell me just how you did it, Ortola. I want you to tell me everything."

"I will, gladly," agreed the chemist. "I want you to understand not only the steps we have taken, but the motive behind them all. The idea originated during a motor trip

I took through the Selkirk Mountains a little more than three years ago.

"I think now, sincerely, that every step I took was guided by fate. I lost my road. I found myself on a lane that wound along the face of a precipice. The first house I came upon, miles off in that wilderness, was the house of Ernest Gore.

"He was whittling on his porch steps. I was dumfounded by his resemblance to portraits of Washington as a young man. I asked him a great many questions. Not until months later did the project which we have seen to-day carried to such a happy conclusion, begin to form in my mind.

"Shortly afterward, I discussed the matter with Professor Morgan. His imagination was captured. He thought it would be a great joke. As you all know, he is so violently opposed to prohibition—"

"That he will be a sick man the rest of his life," Aunt Sally finished for him.

Ortola ignored her interruption.

"Between us, for a period of months, we invented and discarded schemes by which we could use this man who so strikingly resembled George Washington."

Mrs. Gore, standing a few feet away, glaring up at him, cried vindictively:

"If I had used the shotgun on you when you came up that road—"

"This woman," Ortola harshly interrupted her, "has, from the beginning, been the only serious threat to our plans. I hope that I will never again have to deal with an old woman married to a boy. How much money have I given you to keep that clacking tongue of yours still? Well, I am going to give you more—plenty of it!"

The hill woman glared at him.

The chemist stretched out his long white fingers in a gesture of hopelessness.

"You are making me feel like a criminal, all of you. I am not a criminal. I have done a great good for the American people, I am proud of what I have accomplished. It is unfortunate that I could not take you into my confidence earlier."

"Finish your explanation," Larry curtly instructed him.

"The first and only man we took into our confidence," Ortola continued, "was Muller. Muller was at that time engaged upon experiments in animal behaviorism. He, too, is a violent anti-prohibitionist."

"Not any more," growled Muller. "I'm sick of it all. Tell him about the dog, Ortola. Tell him everything."

"You had just become managing editor of *The It* when the idea was taking form," the chemist went on. "You fitted our plans perfectly. You took your summer vacations— alone—not far from Lake Shallon. You, too, were violently anti-prohibition. For awhile we thought of placing our project before you. Then we learned more about you—and changed our minds."

"I insist on telling him about the dog," Muller broke in again. "It will amuse you, Larry—and you look as if you could stand a little amusement. I trained the dog, Larry. A few of the scores of private detectives he hired to find out all about you got me all the information I needed for training a dog. The time I spent at your cabin, Larry! I started that Airedale as a pup, forcing him to adore you.

"He didn't eat—until he'd sniffed some clothes of yours.

The time came when he would yelp with joy when I let him sniff one of your old shoes!

"And meanwhile I was training Ernest Gore, making him believe he was George Washington. His accent—I even taught him that. In time, he lived the part—to the best of his poor ability. This moment, do you suppose he is aware that he is deceiving the world? Larry, he has lived that part so long, I have pounded it into him—or him into it—so thoroughly that he believes he is the man he is pretending to be.

"I honestly think we deserve, not blame, but admiration for the pains we have taken. The laboratory experiments, for example. They were thrilling, weren't they? That blue fog was a thin mixture of tear gas, to make you see triple at the critical moment.

"You may feel like condemning us now, but I think you will, in time, come around to our point of view. We have put across the cleverest, most elaborate hoax the world has ever known."

"And we are faced, as I said before," Ortola put in, "by only one problem; What are we to do with Ernest Gore?"

"Drown him!" bitterly suggested Aunt Sally.

"You can hardly blame him for his inflated ego," the osteologist said, ignoring her. "Never, in the history of the world, has a man received such homage, such flattery. That is unfortunate, but it was inevitable. There isn't a man living who could have stood up against such an ovation without a swelled head. My suggestion is that he be taken to some quiet spot until the excitement dies down. He can't mysteriously disappear and never be heard of again, now, can he?"

"I'd thought of doing something of the kind," Ortola

took him up. "Letting it be known that he had died—drowned."

"You're clever enough to get away with it," Aunt Sally smartly interjected.

"I'd like to hear from you, Galloway," the chemist said. "You've proved, unexpectedly, the most valuable member of the conspiracy. What is your suggestion?"

"I understand," said Larry, addressing neither Ortola nor Muller, but Polly, "that this is as much of a surprise to you as it is to me."

She answered in a small, crushed voice: "Larry, I swear, I'm as dumfounded as you are. I am too sick to think. I can't believe my father would have gone into this so deliberately. How can you let the world know that it has heard nothing but lies for three months?"

Ortola repeated harshly: "We want your suggestions, Galloway."

"One more question: What was the idea of emphasizing that you'd charge a million dollars to resurrect any man?"

"There were all sizes of red herring in our barrel, Larry," Muller answered.

Larry now fixed his eyes steadily on Ortola. His body swayed. His face was gray except for a hectic spot that burned on either cheek bone.

He fumbled for a chair and sank into it. Placing his hands on the arms, he tried to push himself up.

He removed a handkerchief from his hip pocket, slowly unfolded it and passed it in small, quick jerks over his forehead, his cheeks, his mouth.

"You've asked for suggestions," he said in a low, toneless voice. "I'm going to make them. You can act on them, or not, as you see fit. My first suggestion is to you, Ortola. It is that you take the first ship sailing for some foreign country from which you cannot be extradited on a warrant of conspiracy."

"I knew it," Muller groaned.

Ortola was staring glassily at the editor.

"You'd better go with him, Muller," Larry went on in the same lifeless tones. "When the people recover from the shock, I don't think this country will be healthy for either of you."

Ortola gasped: "You wouldn't dare—"

Muller broke in eagerly: "Larry, you can't do it. I know how you feel. You think you've been victimized. This thing, coming as it has, makes you look ridiculous. At least, that's how you're looking at it. It's struck you on your most sensitive spot—this awful seriousness with which you take yourself. What you'll see, after you've given it a little thought, is that, no matter how badly your pride is hurt, no matter how loudly you want to howl about it you can't give us away.

"Look at it this way: In these past few months, the world has come to accept the fact that science has conquered death. The world has seen a living demonstration of the fact. You've seen people all over this country going into hysterical convulsions; fainting in fits of rapture. You've seen the look in the eyes of intelligent people. When you think of all that, you won't dare strike such a blow."

"I have an answer for that," Ortola took up. "The world can continue to believe that science has conquered death. But the secret of the process, the method, is locked up forever in the sick brain of Professor Morgan. Professor Morgan can, conveniently, have some kind of amnesia. Or he can simply announce that, after mature deliberation, he has decided that no mortal should interfere in the business of God."

"You would have an idea like that," Aunt Sally put in viciously.

"Your eagerness to be at the center of all this," Muller continued, addressing Larry anxiously, "has put you in the boat with all the rest of us. If you rock the boat—we'll all drown. Do you think people will believe you weren't a part of this hoax?"

Polly wailed: "Don't you realize, either of you, what you've done to him? You knew his reputation for honesty. What you've done is to turn him into the greatest liar that ever lived!"

"You'd better think of your father," Ortola put in quickly.

"My father deserves to be punished with the rest of you!" Polly angrily answered. "He's accomplished what he set out to do. So have both of you. And you're simply tickled pink with yourselves. You don't care how much you've hurt Larry or me; you aren't sorry for the people you've been cheating. All you want is to keep us shut up until the law is repealed."

"Yes," Muller agreed, "we've made of the most truthful man in America the greatest liar the world has ever known. And, to save his skin, he's going to keep on lying to the bitter end."

Polly blurted out: "You—you've killed his future! You've crushed him!"

Larry said harshly: "Never mind me. You're mistaken, Muller. I'm not going to lie any more. I'm going to give you two twenty-four hours to make yourselves scarce. I'd like to go down into this lobby and tell the reporters now. But I won't. I'll give you twenty-four hours—"

The door opened. Larry, turning, caught a glimpse of olive drab uniforms. They parted to divulge a tall, broad-shouldered figure in blue serge.

Ernest Gore strode into the room and the door closed.

33

HIMSELF, TO THE END

THE MAN WHO had for more than three months lived the part of George Washington looked quickly about the room.

Six pairs of eyes considered him.

His faint smile vanished. Hesitantly, he began: "Well—" And stopped, his still glowing blue eyes fixed on Larry's face.

"Certain things have just been explained," Larry said. "I mean, I know who you are, all about you—Gore. I've just been making some suggestions. I'll repeat them and—go on to you."

"Look here—" the young man indignantly began.

Larry wearily interrupted: "I've just given Muller and Ortola twenty-four hours to make themselves scarce. I'm going to give you the same length of time."

"I have only time to dress for the reception at the White House!"

"You'd better notify the White House that you have suddenly become ill. My suggestion is that you start for the Selkirk Mountains as soon as you can. And my further suggestion is that you remain there—permanently."

"You aren't going to tell!" the man who posed as Washington exclaimed. "You can't do it, Larry! Let me go on! Please let me go on! I—I can't go back there, after what I've been."

"I'm giving Ortola and Muller," the implacable man went on, "twenty-four hours. This news is going to break twenty-four hours from now."

Ernest Gore wheeled on his wife. He lifted his right hand as if he would strike her. She said evenly:

"We're going home to-night. You told me you wouldn't fool with any woman. You made me a promise. You broke it. You've let this Morgan girl lead you on and make a fool of you. I told you I wouldn't stand for any women. We're going home."

Ernest Gore sank into a chair and covered his face with his hands.

Milling thousands in the streets below were roaring for him.

Jason Ortola snatched up the telephone from the desk.

He said: "Notify the newspapermen that Colonel Washington has collapsed from the strain. Will make no more public appearances. Notify the management that no one is to be permitted on this floor; and see to it that no phone calls are put through here. I cannot answer your questions."

He placed the receiver on its hook.

"Galloway, you are not going to spoil my plans. I have given five years to the perfection of this. I will write you my check this moment for one million—"

"Yourself, Ortola, to the bitter end," Aunt Sally interrupted him.

34

"YOU'RE A FAKE, TOO"

WHILE THE WORLD waited in dreadful suspense for bulletins relating to the mysterious disappearance of George Washington; while a Ford closed truck, driven by a green-eyed woman, made its way by a devious route toward the Selkirk Mountains; while Mrs. Horace Glen Islington, using for the last time her privileges as an intimate of the hero, obtained, by a ruthless slashing of red tape, a passport entitling her to enter England, France, and Italy; and while Jason Ortola and Paul Muller, under a glowering sky, sailed in a Fokker cabin plane toward Mexico; the managing editor of *The Daily It* wrote his story of the most elaborate hoax that had ever been perpetrated.

A few minutes before one o'clock in the afternoon, Larry finished the story and pressed the button on his desk which summoned Miss Hanson.

"I want forty carbons of this," he said. "You'd better get help."

"Mr. Galloway," she said in a wail, "won't you tell me where Washington—"

She stopped. Her eyes had fallen to the line of capitals which ran across the first page of the manuscript he was extending to her:

WASHINGTON AN IMPOSTOR!
ANTI-PROHIBITIONIST'S HOAX EXPOSED!

Miss Hanson fainted into her employer's waiting arms. **IT WAS MIDNIGHT** when the weary crusader had satisfied the curiosity of the last clamorous reporter; had heard the last of them utter some variation of the observation that he had got what was coming to him.

He had, at least, convinced them that he was an innocent member of the conspiracy.

EPILOGUE

RAIN, DRIVEN BY a boisterous fall wind, lashed the walls of the cabin, crackled on the window panes, drummed on the roof. In the shortly spaced interludes, Black Bay hissed under the downpour. Branches lashed about in the strong wind; lent their creaking to the tumult.

For two days the gale had been blowing, and the man in the cabin, whose mood it suited perfectly, wished it would blow forever. From time to time he tossed a log upon the fire, then resumed his pacing, while the Airedale on the hearth followed him with alert golden eyes and occasionally whined low in his throat.

It was the crusader's third day of retreat; his third day of tramping through the woods in the rain, of pacing up and down in the cabin until he was too exhausted to stand. Trying to find relief for his torn pride, trying to fashion some structure out of the ruins of his hopes.

Up and down, forth and back, he tramped, with hands knotted behind him, head sunk low on chest.

"I have a message," he said aloud. "I have a message for the American people. Listen to me, America!"

His voice stopped upon a thick, rather terrible laugh.

Above the wind he had heard a whine, unlike the whining of the wind in the chimney, the whine of the wind at cracks.

"Indians!" he said very low, to the dog. The Airedale whined mournfully, began to thump the flagging of the hearth with his stump of a tail.

"Sic 'em—Paddy!"

The dog came, with low growls, to his feet, his eyes alertly on his master.

"Charge, Paddy!"

The Airedale sank back upon the hearth with ears sharply forward.

"You're a fake, too," the man told him. "Everything's a fake."

He heard a sound at the door; turned about as it was opened.

He remained motionless as Polly Morgan, in a glistening black raincoat, came in and shut the door.

She said: "I thought I'd find you here."

Polly came toward him and looked with frightened eyes into his face. It was the color of clay and expressionless. His eyes were black holes under his forehead.

He said nothing.

The girl removed her hat and raincoat; tossed them on a chair. She went to the fire and held out her hands to its heat.

"I thought you might need me. You never have, but—I thought you might. Now."

He still said nothing. He had not changed his posture. With hands behind him, head jutting forward and down, he considered her.

Polly nipped her lip and seated herself on the edge of a

chair. She sat far out on the edge, as if she were prepared for flight.

She was blinking moisture out of her eyes.

He said harshly: "Well, America is waked up. I'm the most hated man in the world, but from now on I'll be—"

His voice broke. He swayed. She thought he was going to fall.

He tried to go on, but his voice was a strangled sob in his throat.

He pitched toward her. He fell on his knees, groping for her. Then he found her. His head sagged into her lap while incoherent sounds came from him.

She lifted his head and held it close to her breast.

"You poor darling!"

He seemed to relax, as if a strain, a great weight, had been lifted. She sighed:

"All I'm good for is this. It's all I'm good for."

The crusader lifted his head.

www.ingramcontent.com/pod-product-compliance
Lightning Source LLC
Chambersburg PA
CBHW020640030726
47498CB00002B/304